VAMPIRE NATION

Novels by Thomas M. Sipos

Manhattan Sharks

Hollywood Witches

Vampire Nation

VAMPIRE NATION

Thomas M. Sipos

Copyright © 1998, 2000 by Thomas M. Sipos.

Library of Congress Number:		99-91622
ISBN #:	Hardcover	0-7388-1140-8
	Softcover	0-7388-1141-6

All rights reserved. No part of this book may be reproduced or transmitted in any form or by any means, electronic or mechanical, including photocopying, recording, or by any information storage and retrieval system, without permission in writing from the copyright owner.

This is a work of fiction. Names, characters, places and incidents either are the product of the author's imagination or are used fictitiously, and any resemblance to any actual persons, living or dead, events, or locales is entirely coincidental.

This book was printed in the United States of America.

To order additional copies of this book, contact:
Xlibris Corporation
1-888-7-XLIBRIS
www.Xlibris.com
Orders@Xlibris.com

CONTENTS

ACKNOWLEDGEMENTS 9
AUTHOR'S NOTE 11
PROLOGUE 13

ONE 17
TWO 25
THREE 36
FOUR 45
FIVE 56
SIX 65
SEVEN 76
EIGHT 87
NINE 95
TEN 105
ELEVEN 110
TWELVE 120
THIRTEEN 126
FOURTEEN 136
FIFTEEN 151
SIXTEEN 161
SEVENTEEN 175
EIGHTEEN 181
NINETEEN 190
TWENTY 201
TWENTY-ONE 207
TWENTY-TWO 214
TWENTY-THREE 221
TWENTY-FOUR 228

TWENTY-FIVE 236
TWENTY-SIX 249

AFTERWORD 255

TO MY PARENTS,
FOR COMING TO THIS SHINING CITY ON A HILL.

ACKNOWLEDGEMENTS

This is a work of satire inspired by history. Descriptions of some historic persons and places have been altered for dramatic purposes.

Especially helpful for its eyewitness recounting of historic figures' behaviors, mannerisms, unctuous fawnings, and obscene diatribes was *Red Horizons: The True Story of Nicolae & Elena Ceausescus' Crimes, Lifestyle, and Corruption,* by Lt. Gen. Ion Mihai Pacepa, Former Head of Romanian Intelligence.

Also helpful for background research were *Ceausescu and the Securitate: Coercion and Dissent in Romania, 1965-1989,* by Dennis Deletant; *Pinstripes and Reds: An American Ambassador Caught Between the State Department and the Romanian Communists, 1981-1985,* by David B. Funderburk; *Journey To Freedom,* by Nicholas Dima; *In Search Of Dracula: The History of Dracula and Vampires,* by Raymond T. McNally & Radu Florescu; *The Black Book of Communism: Crimes, Terror, Repression,* by Stéphane Courtois, Nicolas Werth, Jean-Louis Panné, Andrzej Paczkowski, Karel Bartosek, and Jean-Louis Margolin; *Victory: The Reagan Administration's Secret Strategy That Hastened the Collapse of the Soviet Union,* by Peter Schweizer; and *Stalin's Secret War: A Startling Exposé of His Crimes Against the Russian People,* by Nikolai Tolstoy.

— Thomas M. Sipos

AUTHOR'S NOTE

I have over the years seen the nation of Rumania spelled variously as Rumania, Romania, and Roumania. When I was growing up in the 1970s the preferred spelling was Rumania, and my word processor and electronic dictionary, both creatures of the 1990s, still think so. The spell checker on my WordStar 7.0d for DOS (1992) insists on Rumania, and my American Heritage Dictionary for DOS (1991, 1992) also redirects me from the other spellings to Rumania. Yet it seems today most American books spell it as Romania, my dictionary notwithstanding. As for Roumania, I suspect that was always chiefly a British spelling.

I have opted to side with my childhood, my WordStar, and my American Heritage Dictionary. The spelling used in this work of satire is Rumania.

PROLOGUE

"You accept that your . . . *ancestral castle,* is now property of the people of Rumania?"

"With your doctors' kindness, I understand . . . " What was this century's proper honorific? "*Comrade* Colonel."

Colonel Popiescu snorted, skimmed the report. "Farkas. You are Hungarian?"

"My ancestors . . . " Count Farkas waved the subject aside with the delicate hand of an aristocrat, pulled his hand away from the pale sunlight spilling through the grimy window, illuminating air heavy with dust. He stared at the dour, sluggish soldier. Peasant. In spite of the bright red stars piercing his drab brown uniform, Colonel Popiescu was still just a slothful, anemic peasant. Weak blood nourished on potatoes and vodka.

"You also understand, Transylvania has been liberated by the Rumanian People's Army from Hungarian fascist occupation?"

Count Farkas smiled with thin red lips. "I am happy to hear it." The dusty calendar on the wall read 1977. Until he awoke a month ago, it had been a hundred and twenty years since he walked the earth. Luckily, he knew Rumanian, now apparently the dominant language in this portion of the old Hapsburg Empire.

Colonel Popiescu set the report aside, pressed a button. "Of course, the Constitution of the Socialist Republic of Rumania guarantees equal treatment to every citizen, regardless of ethnicity. Did you not find this to be true at our state psychiatric hospital?"

Count Farkas eyed the Colonel's medical certificates hanging beside portraits of pasty-faced bureaucrats. An office without vitality, aside from that blood red flag. A nation of cattle, patiently awaiting slaughter. As soon as Farkas established himself... "The doctors are very... agreeable."

Popiescu nodded, pressed the button. "The people considered prosecuting you for criminal assault, but the people's psychiatrists diagnosed you mentally ill." Popiescu pressed the button, slammed it, bellowed toward his door, "Nurse! Water!" He turned to Farkas. "The report states, *Count,* you no longer believe your delusion of aristocracy."

The Count winced on cue. "Please, Comrade Colonel, refer to me only as Comrade Farkas."

Popiescu grunted, satisfied.

A fat woman with thick ankles shuffled into the office carrying an aluminum tray, glasses, bottles of mineral water. She set the tray atop Popiescu's papers, wiped her sweaty brow with her stained apron. She found a bottle opener, wiped a glass with the apron, opened a bottle, poured its water into the spotted glass.

Count Farkas narrowed his red eyes, snatched a bottle, saw a dead fly and bits of insect debris floating atop the water.

The woman took the bottle from him, glanced at it, saw the fly. Expressionless, she opened the bottle, poured the fly and debris onto Popiescu's floor, poured the remaining water into another spotted glass, handed it to Farkas.

Popiescu watched this incident with glazed eyes, limply held his own glass in a dirty hand.

The woman shuffled out of the room, gray hair spilling from her babushka. Farkas espied one of her hairs stuck to his glass.

Popiescu drank before continuing, dribbling onto his soiled tunic. "It is good, Comrade Farkas, you no longer suffer from these delusions. The people require clear-headed workers, uncontaminated by ancient superstitions."

Farkas leered. This was the best news upon awakening. "The doctors cured me of all such superstitions. I no more believe in aristocracy than in Christ, heaven, or... vampires."

Popiescu nodded sleepily. "Comrade General Secretary Ceausescu is correct in stating that once atheism is firmly anchored in the class consciousness of the proletariat, then revolutionary Marxism-Leninism shall enter a new stage of dialectic materialism in which scientific socialism . . ."

Count Farkas let the Colonel drone on. This was better than *Monsieur* Voltaire's influence in France. If the vampire's strength is that no one believes in him, what more could he ask than to awaken in a nation of atheists?

Farkas exited his apartment, shuffled along Brasov's broken sidewalks, seeking quarry. He squinted against an overcast sky. Still enough sun to burn him. Shrugging, he scratched a lesion, wiped the pus against his trousers.

Peasants and laborers, faces blackened by nearby refineries, slumped against empty store windows, clutching liquor bottles. A soft breeze stank of benzene. A slovenly group of soldiers, red patches upon shabby uniforms, bantered beneath a large bleacher, one of them urinating in public.

Farkas squinted at the bleacher, empty and dilapidated. Its sole vitality derived from massive blood red banners, hung beside colossal portraits of bureaucrats. Everywhere, scarlet banners draped buildings, lampposts, monuments, bleeding the nation.

Comrade Farkas browsed for prey. Everyone was too distant, or too unruly, or too much trouble. Shrugging, he shambled back to his state-owned apartment.

ONE

Henry Willoughby craned his neck across the aisle. He liked aisle seats on an airplane, found them less constricting. And he was hungry. As he assumed were most of the other passengers.

TAROM flight 31 from Amsterdam to Bucharest had been delayed for five hours. It arrived late, then sat in Amsterdam for three hours. No explanation was offered, no estimate on when it might begin boarding passengers. Might be any minute. Or not. Henry decided to wait, forgoing a meal at the airport, expecting one a short time later aboard the plane.

Gray clouds streaked the morning sky when Henry began his vigil. Winter sunlight gleamed off the Boeings taxiing along the tarmac. Henry waited, drank coffee, and watched a procession of tall blond stewardesses giggling and pulling luggage carts. The KLM flight from New York had teemed with such stewardesses, each sporting supermodel looks. Not the kind seen on American planes, not anymore, the unions and lawyers saw to that.

Each hour intensified Henry's determination not to spoil his appetite, his TAROM meal already paid for. When time came for boarding, his stomach was afire, his head pounding. And he was exhausted despite being buzzed from all the coffee.

Henry found his aisle seat and waited for a Rumanian stewardess. They weren't too shabby, although their burgundy uniforms were more modest than the KLM girls' powder blue outfits, their skirts a bit longer. All had dark hair, either cut short or pulled back under garrison caps.

Henry watched these tall burgundy brunettes glide noiselessly along the aisle, high-heels silent upon the red carpet, muffled within the aircraft din. He wanted to confide in them, tell them his secret, impress them with the same secret he had wanted to tell the KLM supermodels in Amsterdam. That he was a man on the move, on his way to fame and fortune. A month ago he was a cipher in a cubicle in Manhattan, but now he was a movie mogul on his way to do lunch in Transylvania.

"I have an appointment with Greg Goff."

Henry relished the sound of that phrase. He had an appointment. Not some wannabe trying to crash Lion's Den Productions. His presence was requested. He was a man with an appointment.

The receptionist asked him to be seated, then ignored him.

Henry had expected her to be more impressed. Well what did she know? It was 1986 and here she was, sporting red and green spiked hair. How *passé*.

With exaggerated nonchalance, Henry eased into a red leather sofa, selected a copy of *Billboard* from amongst the trades on the end table, scanned its video rental chart for horror. Might find some fresh ammunition to assure Goff that he was making the right move, optioning Henry's witch script. Indicators forecast an end to the early 1980s horror boom, but Henry believed that only applied to slasher films. The market was ready for fresh horrors, as witness last year's *Re-Animator*.

Greg Goff erupted into the anteroom like a cannonball. "Mr. Willoughby! Quick, what does NASA stand for? Don't look at Miriam. She's heard this one."

Henry saw the receptionist grimace. He didn't blame her, he'd heard it too. But he knew better than to upstage Goff, a short energetic man with a black beard and dark Mediterranean features.

Goff grinned. "Need another seven astronauts. Get it?"

Henry forced a smile. Of all the *Challenger* jokes, this one had the most resiliency. A month after the incident it was still making the rounds, no matter that everyone had heard it.

Henry followed Goff into his cluttered office, dirty windows overlooking Broadway, Columbus Circle a few blocks north. A late afternoon sun cast deepening winter shadows.

Henry tried to sound casual. "So when do we start principal photography?" Payment was due upon start of principal photography.

"Miriam get you coffee?" asked Goff.

"No, I'm fine."

Goff phoned Miriam for coffee.

Henry pressed his point. "It's getting late if you're still planning a Halloween release date."

Goff leaned back into his chair, punctuating the empty space with his fingers. "How would you like to shoot your film . . . in Transylvania?"

"I thought we were gonna shoot in New England. Or somewhere in North Carolina, made to look like New England."

"How would you like to shoot your film . . . in Transylvania?"

Sounded like another excuse for delay.

"Transylvania sounds great," said Henry. "But my script's about a witch, not a vampire. Witches come from Salem. I think that maybe, aesthetically—"

"How would you like to shoot your film . . . in Transylvania?"

Henry sighed. "Well if you want to shoot in Transylvania, yeah, that sounds great."

"Hear me out, hear me out. We've been given an opportunity, you have been given an opportunity, to shoot your horror film, in Transylvania."

Forcing a smile, Henry resisted correcting Goff that it was the director, and not Henry, who would shoot the film. Assuming there would even be a film.

"Do you know where Transylvania is?" asked Goff.

"In Rumania."

Goff grabbed his phone. "Miriam. Cigar for Mr. Willoughby." He turned to Henry. "Picture it. Horror fans are fascinated by Transylvania. But no horror film has ever been shot there."

Henry shrugged, doubting it was true.

"And Eastern Europe is very topical right now. Everyone wants to know about it."

"You mean, because of Gorbachev?"

"On the nose! We shoot in Transylvania, we kill two birds. Horror fans will flock to it and there'll be crossover mainstream appeal."

"Isn't it tough shooting behind the Iron Curtain?"

"No, no, no. It's a plus. They want us there. They love American dollars. Unbelievable what the dollar buys." Goff gave Henry a folder. "Your itinerary and Rumanian contacts."

"My contacts?"

"Stefan Andrei is their money man. He's greasing the wheels in Bucharest, assisting our business affairs people in arranging a co-production/co-financing deal with their government. You may or may not meet him."

Henry found Andrei's name in the folder. His full title was Central Committee Secretary for Economic Affairs.

"Ion Stanescu will schlep you around," Goff continued. "He's their official tour guide. He'll show you Dracula's castle."

Henry noted that Stanescu's title was Minister Of Tourism and Sport. Something more than a tour guide.

"Why would a witch go to Dracula's castle?" asked Henry.

"I don't know. It's your rewrite."

"My rewrite?"

"The castle exists you know."

"I know," said Henry. "Vlad Tepes."

"Who?"

"Vlad the Impaler. The real life Dracula. Basis for Stoker's Dracula."

"I told Miriam you were our man."

Henry doubted that. "You want me to go to Rumania?"

"Only if you want your rewrite to accurately reflect the new locations."

Henry hated travel. "I don't have a passport."

"We can arrange that. We already have your visa."

This was happening too fast. "My screenplay envisions a New England location."

"Up to you. I have the highest awe and respect for writers. I remain incredibly excited by your script, as you know. Only problem is that co-financing is contingent upon our shooting in Rumania. Dollar buys a lot there. Now that doesn't mean we won't shoot your script. Just means that our finances currently necessitate that our next film be in Rumania. But if you want to hold onto your script, maybe come back to us at a later date, that's up to you."

Miriam entered with black coffee in two paper cups.

Henry knew that a later date may never come. He was twenty-four and had never left US soil. Didn't want to now. But he was vegetating at TVR, getting nowhere, just getting older. For the past three years his brain had atrophied, number crunching TV ratings. Input them into a computer every sweeps period, delete them five sweeps later. It was dead end. Time to take a risk. He had always imagined his first risk would be a move to Hollywood, but a man can't always choose his breaks.

Miriam's coffee tasted as strong as her enthusiasm.

Henry set down his coffee and picked up his folder. His was a mission to Bucharest. Behind the Iron Curtain. He felt like James Bond.

"May I offer you a glass wine, sir?"

"Just coffee."

"I am sorry. We have no coffee. We have wine."

Henry lowered his dinner tray. The stewardess set down a cloth napkin and a glass of red wine. After she departed, Henry noticed the man across the aisle from him was eating Swiss cheese on rye. He also had an apple on his tray. No wine.

Henry waited for his sandwich. Nothing arrived. He looked

about, saw that all the passengers across the aisle were eating sandwiches and apples. He saw no stewardess pushing a sandwich cart. Henry sipped his wine and waited, the alcohol fueling his headache.

Dusk was descending outside. The plane's interior was dimly lit, shadows blurring its red decor, shades of maroon and burgundy and scarlet trimmed in pale gold. Henry sought a button to hail a stewardess, but found none. Turbulence jostled the plane. Henry called down the aisle, but he hated to shout and his speaking voice was muffled by aircraft noise, by wind and jet engines and a pressurized cabin.

Henry swirled the wine in his glass, more crimson than red, a dark purplish hue within the dim plane, its eddies reflecting the tiny yellow lights that dotted the ceiling. He hated alcohol but he was starving, head pounding, so he drained the glass. The wine burned his empty stomach.

Henry fumbled with his tray, stumbled out of his seat. The plane dipped and bounced. He grabbed the back of his seat for support, struggling down the narrow aisle toward the kitchen.

A group of stewardesses were gathered together, huddled over some item of business, their backs to Henry.

Henry tapped a stewardess on the back. She ignored him. He held her shoulder and gently nudged. She straightened up, turned about, stared at him with vacant eyes, smiling but disinterested. Stray black hair fell loose from under her cap, dark rouge smudged her mouth.

Some other stewardesses glanced at Henry, still intent on mixing drinks for themselves, unconcerned that Henry saw.

Henry addressed the one with the smudged mouth. "Excuse me. I haven't been served dinner yet."

"Yes. We served everyone."

"No, not me. I only got wine."

"Yes. We served you wine." She spoke with a deep Rumanian accent. "Feteasca. It is very good. Only for tourists."

"Yeah, but I didn't get dinner."

"You get wine."

"Yeah, but no dinner. All the other passengers got sandwiches and apples."

"No, not all passengers. Passengers on left side of plane get sandwich. Passengers on right side get wine."

Henry turned around, noticing now that all the passengers on his side of the plane only had empty glasses. No empty plates.

Henry raised his voice. "Why didn't I get a sandwich?"

The stewardess glanced at her compatriots, anxious to rejoin their drinking binge. "You get wine. Wine is very good. I like wine very much."

"But I wanted dinner."

"Wine is dinner. I always have wine for dinner."

"But why can't I have a sandwich?"

"There is not enough sandwiches for all passengers. We only bring sandwiches for half of plane."

"Why?"

"If we bring sandwiches for entire plane, and plane is not full, then sandwiches go to waste. If we bring sandwiches for half of plane, sandwiches almost never go to waste. Enough for everyone."

"No, not enough for everyone! I didn't get one."

"You get wine."

"I wanted dinner. Why couldn't the other side of the plane get the wine?"

"There is not enough wine for all passengers. We only bring wine for half of plane."

"And for yourselves," Henry grumbled.

The stewardess ignored his remark. Her dark eyes gazed past him, glazed and bored.

Henry felt the plane swoon beneath his feet, wind and engine noise muffled by his plugged ears, clogged sinuses stabbing his throbbing head. "Why couldn't I have an apple and wine? That makes more sense. At least that approximates a dinner."

"There is not enough apples for all passengers. We only bring apples for half of plane."

"You miss the point." Henry looked past her into the kitchen seeking food, saw only wine, saw something he'd seen all along but never noticed until now. The stewardesses in the kitchen saw him and ignored him. The one he'd been talking to returned her attention to the others.

Henry returned to his seat, sank into its red cushions, fumbled for his seat belt, remembered there was no seat belt. He searched for his wine glass, saw it was still in his hand. Dark red hues stained its surface. Henry sniffed, smelled alcohol, its aroma blurring his consciousness.

Henry dropped the glass onto the empty seat beside him. He was hungry and tired. He was in pain. He was tipsy. He thought back to what he saw, yet knew he could not have seen.

A dreary young stewardess had slumped against the wall, her dark eyes disinterestedly staring at a hypodermic needle stuck in her pale arm, a tube dribbling her blood into a dirty pan. Pans were collected and emptied into dirty wine bottles, blood diluting the wine, water, and whatnot other liquids. Stew? An older stewardess drank blood from the younger one's other arm, from just above her wrist. Occasionally, the younger one sucked her own arm, or so Henry now thought he remembered her doing. Another stewardess had cuts on her hand and under an ear. A third had a crude scar under her chin, near a fresh cut.

Dulled and dirty steak knives and forks lay scattered across the countertop and floor in pools of blood. Stewardesses cut and drank in casual, haphazard fashion. No passion was evident. No anger, no lust, no love. Henry may watch them or not, it made no difference. They saw and ignored him.

Henry felt his empty stomach swoon with the plane's descent, his sinuses explode. Reviewing what he'd seen, it was that last part that convinced him he'd been drunk or dreaming. Nothing so bizarre and barbarous could be accepted with such casual indifference.

TWO

Henry had expected to deplane through a jetway, as at Amsterdam. Instead he stepped onto airstairs and entered a 1940s black and white film. Approaching twilight cast Otopeni International Airport into shades of gray, colorized by a blood red sun sinking behind distant trees, their barren branches exposing antiaircraft cannons.

Otopeni was dead. No airplanes taxied along its tarmac, no arrivals, no departures. A second TAROM jet idled in the distance, no other commercial planes in sight. Military aircraft sat beside troop transport trucks. Two soldiers eyed the departing passengers, a porcine officer smiling vacuously and a grim private with a machine gun slung across his shoulder.

Cold air snapped Henry alert. He descended the airstairs. A stewardess muttered *bon voyage*. Henry thanked her, but although she looked at him, she never saw him. Another stewardess herded the passengers into a squat steel and glass building. Dim fluorescent tubes cast its interior in pale gray hues. A long line led toward the sole passports & visa official. Other officials and soldiers loitered about. Henry wondered if the soldiers carried live ammunition.

An hour later it was Henry's turn with the young man behind the counter. The man picked his nose, then scratched a lesion on his pale cheek. Heavy green and gold epaulets sagged from his dirty white shirt. Henry gave the man his passport.

The man pursed his lips and frowned. "Amerikanski?"

"Yeah. American."

"You are here for business or pleasure?"

Henry forced a smile. "Maybe a bit of both."

The man's frown deepened. "You do not know why you are here?"

Henry dropped his smile. "Business. I'm here for . . . I have an appointment with your government . . . " He searched his pocket, found Stanescu's letter of introduction, and gave it to the passport official.

The official studied the letter, raised his finger for Henry to wait. He called over a soldier. They conversed in Rumanian. Henry strained to hear a familiar word or phrase. The official entered a nearby office, leaving the door open. Henry heard him make a phone call. The soldier scrutinized Henry with suspicious eyes. Henry smiled. The soldier narrowed his eyes.

The official returned with Stanescu's letter, newly stamped and signed. He also stamped Henry's passport several times. He handed back both documents with a sour smile.

"Enjoy our beautiful country."

"Thank you," Henry barely croaked.

The wait for customs was longer. Henry wondered who all the other tourists were. None spoke English. He heard what sounded like German, what might have been Hungarian. They looked like well-fed Westerners, visiting relatives left behind. Henry wondered if the airport had a restaurant, or at least some vending machines. He saw nothing. Perhaps after customs . . . ?

Two officials searched Henry's sole baggage, a carryon. A shapeless woman in a brown uniform emptied Henry's suitcase, felt for hidden items, rifled through his paperbacks, stuck pins into his toothpaste tube. A tall gaunt man squinted at Henry's passport. The woman seemed determined to find something wrong. She settled on a horror film magazine, *Fangoria*. She showed its gory photos to her partner. The man squinted suspiciously at Henry.

Henry showed the man his Stanescu letter. The two officials called over a soldier. The man made a phone call. Afterwards the woman stuffed Henry's items back into his suitcase, sans *Fangoria*. The man stamped and signed Henry's passport.

"Enjoy our beautiful country, Mr. Willoughby."

He pronounced the "g" but Henry made no complaint.

Before Henry could search for a restaurant, he was required to exchange money at another booth. He gave $100 in travelers cheques to a shriveled official. He received some paper *lei* with pictures of bureaucrats, some *lei* coins with pictures of tractors or smokestacks, and some tin *bani* coins. A total of 1500 *lei*.

Finally, with a pocketful of *lei,* Henry searched for a restaurant. He found nothing. The building's interior was spacious but barren, with only enough illumination to reveal its void. It held people but no life. Soldiers outnumbered passengers and both were listless and surly. Henry's flight seemed to be the only order of business that day and nobody seemed especially pleased about it. Flights were an unwelcome intrusion for this airport.

Henry spotted a TV set held by a ceiling brace. TV was a familiar, welcome sight. He sat on the vinyl bench facing it. The program appeared to be a black and white documentary on agriculture. Endless wheat fields, tractors, orchids, and smiling collective farm workers in peasant costume laboring under heavy baskets of copious food. Henry finally dared to think what had been building in his mind for hours.

What have I done?

He had made a Big Mistake. He had been safe and secure and comfy in America but that hadn't been enough. He had to travel. He had to listen to all those idiots who said travel broadened the mind and was a great adventure. He had to listen to Goff's bilge about overseas business opportunities and now here he was, trapped in some foreign sinkhole.

What was I thinking?

A small man with a sweep of gray-white hair appeared on TV, addressing an assembly of pasty bureaucrats while cutting the air with his hand. The bureaucrats applauded, chanting in unison for unceasing minutes. Inlaid in the small man's podium was a hammer and sickle, framed by wheat and topped by: PCR.

If Henry could have boarded a plane back to the States he would have done so immediately. But there were no escape flights from Otopeni, not today, perhaps not for a week. He was stuck. Nothing to do but go forward.

Which was where?

Henry had thought Stanescu was to meet him at the airport. Maybe not. Henry never really understood anything Goff said, and he suspected Goff intended it that way. Goff initially claimed he had all financing in place for Henry's script. Only gradually did Henry realize that this was likely untrue. Henry hoped the promised Rumanian contacts were more solid, that he wasn't to be stranded here. In which case, where was Stanescu?

Henry searched for a pay phone under the watchful eyes of . . . everyone. Uniformed officials of various sorts eyed him from all directions. All other passengers had departed. His presence was beginning to look suspicious.

Henry found what looked to be a pay phone, a bizarre behemoth of a steel box with slots and dials and buttons and instructions in several languages, including Russian Cyrillic. But not English.

Henry pulled some papers from his pocket, found a scrawled string of numbers he thought was Stanescu's office. He generously shoved several *lei* into several slots, dialed the rotary, heard clicks and rings, then a Rumanian voice.

Was it Stanescu, his ministry, an operator?

Henry replied in English.

The voice became hostile, screaming furiously.

Henry hung up.

He saw several soldiers staring at him. Some wore brown uniforms with red epaulets and stars. Two wore blue uniforms with a sharper police cut. Or maybe it was gray. Difficult to tell in this pale fluorescent light. All were heavily armed.

Henry snatched his suitcase and ran casually from the building.

Outside was nothing. A deserted concrete vista ringed by a horizon of distant trees, empty branches stark against the purple sky. Dark silhouettes huddled in heavy overcoats, unhappy shapes lurking and watching. Petroleum fumes saturated the frigid night air. A solitary unmarked car idled a block away, engine rattling. Its dim interior light revealed a driver, waiting.

Henry trudged toward the car, his breath visible in the cold moonlight. Hoping the car was a taxi, he was about to knock when the driver threw open the passenger side door.

Henry hesitated but got in.

The driver wore a black cap and belted black leather jacket, collar pulled high. He looked fiftyish, but might have been in his late thirties. His hair was black and white and gray, with oily streaks of glistening green. Hair the color of a bug.

The driver shot away from the curb, careening along sharp and narrow paths, away from the airport and toward a highway.

Henry figured he should provide a destination.

"Hotel Intercontinental," said Henry. He knew that much. Goff claimed to have made reservations for him.

The driver grunted.

"In Bucharest," Henry added, unsure of the driver's ability or intent. He sought its address on his scraps of paper, but couldn't see anything in the dark. "Hotel Intercontinental in Bucharest."

"I know. I take you there. You pay me in dollar."

"I have *lei.*"

The car skidded to a stop, throwing Henry forward, then back again as it accelerated. The driver glared at Henry as he drove, black bloodshot eyes set in yellow. He bared dull yellow teeth, snarling, "You are Amerikanski?"

"No—"

"You have dollar?"

"No, I mean, yes. I have dollar. I'll pay you in dollar."

The driver grunted and faced the road again.

The tin box of a car careened at every rapid turn. Already bruised, Henry sought a seat belt but found only part of a buckle dangling above his window.

They sped over a moonlit gravel road, concrete walls on either side. Then wooden fences and mud drainage ditches fronting peasant shacks. Then gaping holes where shacks had been. Uprooted trees, barren soil, deep ditches, rubble.

"See you got some project in the works," said Henry.

The driver grunted.

"Putting up some new buildings? Should be nice." Then Henry realized the road was dark. Too dark. "I'm just curious. Can I ask a question?"

The driver grunted again.

"I don't think your headlights are on."

"No headlights."

"Wouldn't it be safer to drive with headlights?"

"No. Engine don't work if I turn on headlights."

Henry nodded as though he understood. "Why not?"

"Headlights turn off ignition."

"I see."

The car struggled up a steep hill until the driver turned on the wiper blades. This seemed to shift the car into gear.

Henry asked, "What kind of car is this?"

"This is Rumanian car."

"No, I mean, what's it called?"

"This car is Dacia."

Henry nodded, as though impressed. "Just curious again. What made you choose a Dacia?"

"Every car in Rumania is Dacia."

"So. It's a popular brand."

Eventually the shacks gave way to a darkened city with empty streets. Cars were few, and all sat parked on sidewalks, and all were Dacias. Street lamps were silhouetted in the moonlight, but none were lit. Henry thought he occasionally saw a dark overcoat lurking in a doorway, or a bent shape scurrying in alleyways, but the car was going too fast for Henry to be certain.

A dim yellow glow lit the sky ahead, brightening as they neared it. Soon they passed lit street lamps and new buildings. To Henry's relief, the driver followed the lighted lamps, finally stopping before a modern triangular building bathe in dazzling light.

Henry paid the driver in dollars, then followed a bellhop to the front desk of the hotel. Henry pulled out a wad of *lei*.

The bellhop hissed. His lips were curled tightly shut, yet he hissed.

Henry gave the bellhop a dollar.

The bellhop dropped Henry's carryon and departed.

Henry perused the lobby as he waited for a desk clerk. After ten minutes another bellhop came for Henry's carryon. A fortyish man with dark matted hair and a dirty maroon uniform.

"Your room is?"

"I don't have a room number," Henry apologized.

"You are a guest?"

"I have a reservation."

"Room number?"

"They didn't give me one yet."

The bellhop glared.

"It's not my fault," said Henry.

After another ten minutes a balding desk clerk arrived. Henry explained his reservation. The clerk shoved a registry toward him. Grateful that all was in order, Henry gave the clerk a dollar.

The clerk pocketed it without glancing at Henry. "Enjoy our beautiful country."

The bellhop was still waiting. Henry followed him up a flight of fire stairs. Seeing his room key was 1431, Henry said, "If you want to take the elevator, that's okay with me."

"Elevator is not working."

"Okay. I hope you have a restaurant in this hotel?"

"Yes, there is restaurant. Hotel Intercontinental is finest hotel in all of Rumania. Most luxurious. Hilton himself come to Rumania to copy Hotel Intercontinental. All the finest hotels in West are modeled on Hotel Intercontinental."

"Is the restaurant open?" asked Henry.

"No. Restaurant closes at ten."

"I think it's just past seven."

"Oh. Then maybe it is open. I thought I saw it was closed."

On the 14th floor landing, the bellhop struggled to open the fire door leading into the hallway. He shouldered it, kicked it, finally broke it open with a metal groan.

The 14th floor smelled like an old damp carpet. The bellhop threw Henry's carryon into Room 1431. Henry thanked him and gave him a dollar.

Shutting the door behind him, Henry sighed relief. The room looked modern, but dimly lit. He sat on the bed, heard it creak. Its rose-colored comforter smelled of ammonia. Its mattress felt uneven. Henry lay down, resting his face on his arm rather than on the comforter, and considered his next move.

Nobody knew who he was or why he was here. And he was running low on dollar bills. He must contact Stanescu as soon as possible. He needed a guide. Call Stanescu, then eat.

A heavy black phone sat on an end table. No rotary dial, no buttons. Henry lifted the receiver, heard a succession of clicks and beeps, then a surly woman asked, "You are wanting whom?"

She spoke English. Right off the bat. Henry gave her Stanescu's office number.

"The Ministry is closed now," she said.

Henry never mentioned any Ministry. "When will it be open?"

"Comrade Minister Stanescu will be contacting with you tomorrow."

"Do you know Stanescu?"

A pause. Then she answered in Rumanian.

"Do you know who I am?" asked Henry.

"I know nothing." English again.

"Do you know if the hotel restaurant is open?"

She hung up.

Henry pulled out Goff's map of Bucharest. A few spots were marked. The Hotel Intercontinental, some ministry buildings, the American Embassy. No restaurants. He hoped he would not need to know that, hoped the hotel restaurant was still open.

Hungry as he was, he felt too filthy to eat. He entered the bathroom to wash up. He considered a shower, but saw hair in the drain, cobwebs in a corner, a tiny spider lurking within. He'd tackle the shower after dinner.

The toilet was dry, until he pulled its chain. He washed his hands but found no soap, only a frayed and soiled towel. He opened the medicine cabinet.

A giant spider web faced him.

Giant spider web, spread across the cabinet's interior.

Henry froze.

A big spider sat motionless in the middle of the web. A big black spider with red and yellow stripes.

The spider shifted.

Henry slammed the cabinet shut, its door bounced open, he thought he saw the spider fall out . . .

He ran, crashed into the bathroom door, grabbed it, screaming, threw the door against the wall, ran from the bathroom and escaped into the bedroom.

Henry leaped onto the bed, sweeping his arms down his body, jumping and brushing any spiders off himself, jumping up and down and around until he stepped into empty space and tumbled off the bed, grabbing a lamp fixture, yanking it from the wall as he fell to the floor.

The threadbare carpet cushioned his fall. Barely.

Henry lay on the floor, assessing his aches. He noticed the lamp fixture in his hand, black cables extending from its base to a gaping hole in the wall. He wondered if they executed foreigners for breaking state property. Maybe he should contact the American embassy. According to Goff's map, it was a few blocks away.

Then he noticed a thin wire exposed in the broken ceramic lamp, attached to a microphone. It looked like a microphone, except that its diaphragm was encircled by tiny metallic serrations, like a toothy worm.

Henry had cut his finger. A single blood droplet ran down his finger, toward his knuckle, then veered a course for the microphone's mouth . . .

He hurled the lamp fixture against the wall.

Henry exited Room 1431 determined to eat. He'd set the lamp back into the wall, careful not to get blood on it, where it now hung in pieces. Maybe he'd tell Stanescu about the accident. Goff said Stanescu would cut red tape for Henry. Or maybe he could convince the maid that the lamp was already broken. Perhaps even aid her memory with a dollar.

Henry pulled at the fire door, yanking and tugging until it finally cracked open. He squeezed through into the stairwell and descended to the lobby.

He found the entrance to the hotel restaurant. A menu in four languages—English, German, French, Italian—was displayed beside its glass double doors. The doors were shut. A sign in four languages explained: Restaurant Closed Due To Repairs.

Maybe the desk clerk knew of an open restaurant?

Henry returned to the front desk. It was unattended. He searched a display rack but found no restaurant brochures. He called for assistance. No one responded.

Then he heard grunts and groans and foreign exclamations from the room behind the front desk.

Whatever it was, better not interrupt.

He leaned over the counter, espying some maps on a desk. Hotel clerks were often asked about local restaurants, and marked them on tourist maps.

Henry scanned the lobby. No one in sight. He stepped behind the counter and sifted through the maps. His head throbbing from hunger, he selected a map and saw its colors shift. First it was a plain road map of Rumania, then a pattern of red stars materialized across it. Some stars were set above test tubes or atoms, some above machinery or missiles, some wreath in barbed wire.

Henry raised the map and the stars were gone.

He blinked, uncertain. Map looked okay now. Must be his headache. And his hunger. He remembered why he was there.

Henry set the road map aside and found a local map. A black and white street map of Bucharest. He leaned in and saw a web of red lines crisscrossing it, like a New York subway map. But when he shifted his body, the lines disappeared.

A woman screamed.

Henry spun around.

A woman hollered from the room behind him, the groans increasing, then lessening. Henry crept to the door, already ajar, edged it open, peeked inside.

The desk clerk sat hunched before a switchboard, headphones covering his bald scalp. He looked like a switchboard operator, except for the bank of reel-to-reel tape recorders whirling behind him. He calibrated dials on an electronic panel. The woman's voice yelled and grunted from his headphones.

Blood trickled from his ear, down his neck, into his shirt.

He turned to flick some switches. He saw Henry.

Henry backed away from the doorway, went around to the front of the counter.

The clerk exited the room.

Henry's head swooned. "I'm looking for a place to eat."

The clerk glanced at the maps on his desk.

Henry cleared his throat. "I was wondering if you could recommend . . . ?"

The clerk glared at Henry.

Henry continued backing out of the lobby. The clerk shouted to someone. Henry exited the hotel. A surly bellhop watched him walk into the night.

Henry only looked back once, when he had reached the end of the block. Several dark silhouettes, one with a peaked military cap, stood before the hotel. All were staring in his direction. And although none followed him, Henry knew they all saw him.

THREE

Henry tried not to run, the brightly lit streets now several blocks away. As near as he could tell he was not being followed. He was alone. No cars to be seen aside from the occasional Dacia parked on the sidewalk. And no pedestrians. Just empty windows and darkened doorways. No way to tell if they led to shops or offices or apartments. Nothing here looked like back home.

One storefront looked as though it might be a grocery store. But no food was displayed in its window, only pictures of food. Another window displayed pictures of bread and pastry. Still another displayed pictures of meat. The faded pictures almost looked appetizing. But he was close to forgetting his hunger. Bucharest smelled like a petrochemical waste dump.

Henry crossed an empty street, seeing the red light too late. He wondered if he might be arrested for that. He still wasn't sure if he'd done anything wrong back at the hotel. They had stared at him, but did not pursue.

He saw movement in the shadows behind him, froze and waited. A sharp wind tossed dust against concrete buildings and bent barren green saplings set at distant intervals. Shivering, he pocketed his hands. His safari jacket seemed appropriate for a movie mogul, but its cotton khaki provided little warmth. Cold air crept under his thin cotton pants.

Shadows shifted about Henry but nothing approached from the darkness. Everywhere, dark shades of gray, aside from the bright green saplings . . .

Barren *green* branches?

Henry approached a sapling, the small tree rooted in a dirt

patch surrounded by sidewalk. He stroked a branch, then scratched it with his thumb. Bright green paint flaked off.

Great. He'd just committed another act of vandalism.

Henry pressed the paint flakes back on as best he could, then continued wandering in circles, as he had for the past hour. He didn't want to lose sight of the hotel's bright lights; it was his point of reference. Judging by Goff's map, as he remembered it, the American embassy was two blocks behind the hotel, then a block or two to the side. Sort of. Blocks were irregularly shaped, as in New York's Greenwich Village, so the number of streets you must cross varied depending upon where you stood.

Turning a corner, Henry saw a solitary street lamp in the distance. Its cold glare illuminated a gate set within a wrought iron fence. Behind the fence stood an elegant Victorian building with a gabled roof, topped by a stone railing that might be functional or decorative. Warm yellow light shone from tall windows. A small yard fronted the house, and a flagpole. A spotlight at the base of the pole lit the flag on top.

An American flag.

Henry quickened his pace toward the embassy, toward the pool of cold light in front of the gate.

Shadows disassociated from the surrounding darkness, hulking shadows entered the light, a tall silhouette blocked the gate. A voice barked a command. A hand grabbed Henry.

Henry saw a pale face in a dark blue uniform, red patches on his collars, red star on his peaked cap, thin red lips spitting foreign words.

Henry explained he was American, repeating it as if it were a magic phrase, a license to go free. This seemed to calm the official. He held out his gloved hand, and barked more words at Henry. Henry understood "passport."

Henry hadn't been to Mass in a decade, yet he thanked God he had thought to bring his passport.

The official took the passport and the letter from Stanescu. Henry frantically began conceiving excuses as to why he might want to visit the embassy on his first night in Bucharest.

It proved unnecessary.

The official returned the passport and letter, then barked a command. The tall silhouette blocking the gate moved aside, his greatcoat and rifle butt disappearing into darkness.

The other shadows disappeared as well. So too the official.

Henry stood alone in the pool of light.

A metallic Great Seal Of The United States gleamed upon the iron fence. The gate itself was barred by an electronic lock.

Henry pressed the buzzer beside the lock. An American voice answered from the intercom.

"Hello?"

"Ah, hi," Henry shouted. "I'm American."

"Yes?"

"Yeah, ah, I'm American, and I'd like to come in."

"Do you have an appointment?"

"No, but I'm an American." Henry gripped the doorknob. He saw his breath in the cold air.

"Is this an emergency?"

Henry envisioned shadows lurking and listening nearby. "No, but, I'm an American. I want to see my Ambassador."

"Sir, you'll have to make an appointment during regular office hours. Unless this is an emergency—"

"Yeah, it's an emergency. I need dollars. Need to wire in some dollars. People around here don't accept their own money."

A pause. Then the gate buzzed.

Henry rushed up the stone pathway. The embassy's front door buzzed open quickly. Henry soon stood in an elegant foyer, warmly lit, blue carpeting trimmed with gold. A Marine guard in dress uniform sat behind a desk.

"Ran out of greenbacks?" the Marine grinned. He gave Henry a blank form. "In case you'd like to convert some *lei*."

"Great." Henry sat down on a velvet upholstered chair, uncertain where to begin. He began by filling out the currency exchange form. "No point in holding money you can't spend."

"That's the truth."

"I can't believe . . . " Henry shook his head. "You should see my hotel. It ain't the Holiday Inn."

"First time out of the States?"

"Yeah. Strange country."

The Marine shrugged. "No more than most."

"You think so?"

"Seems strange at first. You get used to it."

"I think I'm being followed."

The Marine grinned. "You probably are. They do that here."

"You don't mind?"

"We're Americans. They watch us, but they don't bite."

"I'm not so sure." Henry wondered how to explain the maps. "My hotel phone is bugged."

"Really?"

"And the light fixtures. They're bugged too."

"That is rough."

Henry decided to go for broke. "And they drink blood."

"Your light fixtures drink blood?"

"No. The microphones in the light fixtures."

"Oh, they're the worst." The Marine restrained a smile. "I try to avoid those."

Henry continued completing the form. The Marine returned to his paperwork. Henry knew he must see someone else. Someone higher up the ladder. If not the Ambassador, then maybe his assistant. Guy must have an assistant.

Then Henry noticed the woman.

She stood outside a doorway, pulling on gloves. Perhaps she had just exited. She glanced at him, then saw past him. Yet she wasn't like those TAROM stewardesses with dead dark eyes who saw without seeing. Her sharp gray-green eyes seemed aware of everything around her. She just hadn't found Henry very interesting.

She appeared a young twentysomething, yet seemed far more mature. She stood and moved with the poise of a runway model, and bore the same haughty disdain. Tall in her suede burgundy boots, maybe no more than 5'7" barefoot. As with her age, her demeanor added to her height. She wore a gray layered attire: ankle length skirt, greatcoat, cape. Shimmering golden brown hair fell from under her fur hat. A white silk scarf protected her long neck.

The Marine grinned at Henry. "See anything you like?"

Henry shrugged.

The Marine whispered, "That's the Countess."

"Out of my league."

"For all us guys. But a man can dream."

Henry perused the Countess, trying not to ogle. She avoided eye contact. He finally gave up and faced the Marine.

"I have another situation," said Henry. "Maybe a problem, maybe not. I accidentally saw two maps at the hotel. One, a map of Bucharest. But it wasn't accurate. I don't think it was accurate. Maybe it was, I don't know. It had red lines crisscrossing city blocks, like a subway."

The Countess strode past carrying a violin case.

The Marine frowned. "No subway in Bucharest."

Henry watched the Countess exit into the night. She didn't seem afraid to go out there. Made him feel cowardly. Maybe his imagination was overworked. Still, better safe than sorry.

"Is there an official I can talk to?" asked Henry.

"I can get you a map." The Marine began searching his desk.

"No, it's more complicated than that. I really need to talk to a high level embassy representative."

The Marine scowled. But he finally picked up the phone.

Henry soon sat in the trade attaché's spacious office. Presumably, Robert Auster was the only embassy official available on short notice at this time of night. Despite his pinstriped power suit, Auster smiled easily, appearing congenial and spruce. His face was unlined. His sandy hair sported a touch of gray. Eschewing his large desk, Auster sat across from Henry in the living area, a marble coffee table separating them.

Henry detailed his travails, from the shoddy flight to the shabby hotel. He described the stewardesses and microphone, but omitted their blood thirst. He described the maps.

"One moment, the red markings were there," said Henry. "The next minute they're gone."

"Oh my." Auster frowned and furrowed his brows.

"It's like, I just shifted and they disappeared."

"My my."

Henry leaned forward. "There's more."

"Is there?"

"I look into this other room. I see this guy listening to a headphone, and all these tape recorders behind him. Obviously he was listening to my room."

"To your room?"

"To all the rooms."

"Oh dear." Auster leafed through Henry's passport. "That's quite a chore. Quite some rooms at the Intercontinental."

"So then he looks up. He sees me. He knows I know."

"My my. It's certainly appropriate you should bring this to our attention."

"Also, I think I'm being followed."

"Surely not."

"They were staring at me. Like I'd seen something I wasn't supposed to see."

"They?"

"These soldiers come of nowhere."

Auster set Henry's passport on the coffee table. "You don't travel a great deal, do you, Mr. Willoughby?"

"I travel more than I want."

"Perhaps that's the problem."

"Look mister, I'm being chased by Commies. I know too much. Now, it's your job to protect me from Commies."

Auster winced. "Mr. Willoughby, we don't use such terminology in this office. We strive to build bridges of understanding, not foster and exacerbate international tension."

"Okay, you don't understand the magnitude of my situation. Let me explain it better. I got *Communists* out to get me. Now, the President put guys like you in charge of protecting guys like me. I need protecting. Such as how? I think Reagan expects you to do more than build a damn bridge."

Auster appeared physically ill. "Yes, well, we at State are perhaps more sophisticated. We don't believe in evil empires."

"There's a fucking microphone in my bedroom!"

Auster folded his long fingers. "Are you sure it wasn't the light fixture's wiring that you saw?"

"I saw *blood* oozing out at the other end, pouring out of the guy's headphone!"

"Excuse me?"

Henry realized he may have said too much. Too late now. "I saw blood coming from the guy's . . . ear. Really disgusting."

Glancing away from Henry, Auster heaved a sigh that conveyed the enormous burden and personal sacrifice of having to deal with such dolts. "Granted, Rumanian health care is not what it should be, but do you see what your problem is, Mr. Willoughby? You've come to this nation with an ethno-centric myopia. A close-minded antipathy which the locals can no doubt sense in you. What you interpret as their hostility is more likely a reflection of your own attitude toward them."

"You mean it's my fault?"

Smiling as though to a child, Auster leaned back and gazed down his long nose at Henry. "You must understand, Mr. Willoughby, health care systems differ from nation to nation, culture to culture. Values differ. So too laws, economic systems, systems of government. Social customs. That's why I queried you on your novice traveler status. What you may perceive as a hostile stare from a hotel clerk may be no more than his understandable dismay at your intrusion into his private work area." Auster raised an eyebrow. "You did invade his privacy, trespassing behind his desk, you will agree?"

Henry glowered at the empty coffee table. Least his embassy

could do was put coffee on the damn coffee table. And maybe some cookies. And sandwiches.

But Auster could be right. All Henry saw for sure were angry stares, and he *had* messed about the guy's desk. The soldier outside the hotel didn't follow him, and the guards outside the embassy let him pass. Rumania was a dump, infested with soldiers, spies, creeps. But they were Commie foreigners, what did he expect? Could be the blood droplet on his hand had taken a random path. And the desk clerk had a bad inner ear infection. And the red markings on the map were a delusion, a trick of the light. And the stewardesses were a dream. Auster lived in this Commie hellhole and he seemed unafraid, as had the Marine, fellow Americans both. The Countess had shown no fear, whatever her nationality, and she was a lone woman.

In any event, Henry knew he could expect no great help from Auster, so he turned to more prosaic concerns.

"I haven't eaten since morning," Henry grumbled. "No food on the plane, no food at the airport, none in the hotel."

Grinning, Auster nodded his understanding. "Bucharest shuts down early on a Saturday night."

"No kidding."

"Please allow your embassy to be of assistance. I know of a café." Auster returned Stanescu's letter to Henry. "Allow me to arrange transport."

Henry folded the smudged, smeared, and stamped document back into his pocket, along with his passport.

Auster approached the phone on his desk. "By the by, do call us for assistance should other such problems or misunderstandings arise in future. The Rumanians are eager for joint business ventures with the West and so you can imagine how terribly anxious we at State are to assist."

"Is that so?"

"Trade fuels the engines of international cooperation and is a foundation of global economic interdependence."

"Yeah. Whatever."

Auster began dialing. "Our State Department is doing all it can to preserve Rumania's Most Favored Nation trading status back in Congress. Your film project facilitates that goal."

Then Auster began conversing on the phone in what sounded like fluent Rumanian.

FOUR

Henry left the American embassy in the back seat of a black Dacia. The driver wore a belted black leather jacket and ignored Henry. Henry assumed the driver spoke no English and that Auster had explained the destination.

The car sped along empty streets. Concrete apartment blocks slid past outside. Drab and featureless, like a New York housing project. Bucharest appeared under a blackout. Not one window was lit.

Henry glanced backward and saw a pair of yellow headlights in the distance. The only other car on the road. Henry's Dacia turned a corner and lost the headlights. A few blocks later Henry saw the headlights turn the same corner and was again behind them. Tall rectangular headlights. Not square Dacia headlights. Mercedes headlights.

Henry's driver turned another corner and the headlights were gone again. A block farther the Dacia pulled up to what must be the café. No windows in its concrete facade, but yellow light spilled from an open doorway. The driver sat silent and immobile. Henry offered him a dollar but he did not turn around to see it. So Henry pocketed his dollar and exited the car.

The Dacia sped off.

Henry vaguely wondered how he was supposed to return to the hotel, but at least dinner seemed near. The café was open and he had plenty of dollars.

Henry had first thought the café door was ajar, but now he saw that it was missing. No door, just empty hinges. Seedy soldiers slumped about the doorway, clutching liquor bottles and hollering what sounded like slurred curses. Raucous shouts from inside the café merged with gypsy string music.

Henry saw the Mercedes headlights turn the corner at the end of the block. Not wanting to be spotted, for no reason he could discern, he attempted to ease past the soldiers without disturbing them.

They stopped shouting.

Henry beamed a smile and nodded a hello. They glowered at him with languid eyes, like sick sharks, too ill to attack. One soldier snarled, displaying broken rows of rotted teeth. Squeezing by, Henry apologized for being in the way. Another soldier spat near Henry's foot. Henry again apologized.

Inside, the café's harsh lighting was muted by a smoky haze. Cigarette butts littered the black and white tiled floor. Cigarettes were as ubiquitous as liquor, though a few aged men smoked long stem pipes. Tiny tables were covered with ashtrays and shot glasses, crowded with unruly drunks in rumpled uniforms, or cheap business suits, or worn leather jackets. Gypsy musicians in folk costume, puffed shirts and embroidered vests, played string instruments on a small platform.

Henry sought an empty table but found none. A stout young waitress saw him standing by the wall. Henry waved tentatively.

Scowling, she spun upon the men at one table, shouting agitatedly while indicating Henry. Seemed she was trying to get them to beat him up. Henry considered running, but the exit was still blocked by the soldiers, who seemed not to want to be disturbed.

Fortunately, instead of beating up Henry, a man at the table grabbed the waitress's corset. Cursing, she pounded him with her tray, dragging and pulling herself away. Still clutching her corset, the man tumbled to the floor. His friends laughed at his plight.

Henry wondered if he would *ever* eat again.

Someone grabbed his arm.

"Mr. Henry Willoughby?"

Jolted alert, Henry spun to see a tall stocky man standing beside him. Dark-haired, middle-aged, in a fine charcoal suit.

"I am Ion Stanescu," the man explained. "Please, let us sit down."

Stanescu directed Henry to a table occupied by three women, crudely sexy, faces brightly painted in the manner of low priced hookers everywhere. Their red mouths nudged against the necks and shoulders of two porcine men, one in a rumpled business suit, the other in a brown uniform heavy with red and gold medals.

Stanescu barked a command.

A hooker snarled, exposing sharply broken teeth, but quickly quieted when she saw Stanescu. Her gums appeared to be bleeding. The men only gaped stupidly at Stanescu, unmoved and unimpressed. Stanescu snapped impatiently, and the women dragged the men from their chairs.

Stanescu smiled warmly at Henry. "Please be comfortable."

"Thanks." Henry sat down. Numerous red and brown droplets stained the dirty white linen tablecloth. Some appeared fresh, some ancient. A waiter arrived to clear the shot glasses, but he left the tablecloth untouched.

Stanescu sat across from Henry. "I am glad we finally meet, Mr. Willoughby."

"Yeah, me too. Nice car."

"Excuse me?"

"Your Mercedes. Very nice."

Stanescu smiled. "Please, I am a patriot. I drive a Dacia. A good Rumanian car."

"Okay. My mistake. Can we get a menu?"

"Please to allow me." Stanescu barked at the waiter. After the waiter departed, Stanescu leaned toward Henry, leaning so low across the tiny table that he was almost bowing, his mouth scant inches above the table itself. "It is my wish, and the wishes of the most esteemed son and daughter of the Rumanian people, President Nicolae Ccausescu, and the beloved Comrade Elena Ceausescu, that you should enjoy our beautiful country."

"Thanks a lot."

Stanescu straightened up. "You are liking the Hotel Intercontinental?"

"It's very nice."

"And your bed? It is comfortable?"

"It's very soft. Very warm. Thanks a lot."

"And for your reading? There is plenty of light?"

Henry froze. He thought he'd fixed the light fixture pretty good, stuffed the wires back into the wall, set the fixture so it wouldn't slip out unless touched. Maybe someone touched it after he'd left the room.

Stanescu was still smiling, his puffy face flushed pink, his droopy eyes seemingly innocent of ulterior motives.

Henry's mouth felt dry, his voice cracked, "Haven't had time to read since my flight landed." He forced a chuckle. "Mainly, I've been looking for food. All the plane gave me was wine."

Stanescu twitched. "You were served . . . *wine?*"

"Yeah. I wanted a sandwich, but I got wine."

"Please, do you know which brand of wine?"

"Stewardess told me, but I forget."

"Red or white? The wine?"

Henry didn't like the sudden interrogation. "Red."

"Cabernet? Cadarca?" Stanescu paused. "Feteasca?"

Within the café's cacophony, it was easy to feign not having heard. Henry ignored Stanescu's question, and instead shouted so that his own voice merged into the surrounding raucous. "Then I find the damn hotel restaurant is closed for repairs." He forced another laugh. "I'm thinking, what kind of dump is this? Who's the clown in charge, you know?"

Although poised with another question, Stanescu cut himself off as he instead hunched over the table. "The Hotel Intercontinental is the envy of Paris. It is the only six star hotel in all of Europe."

Henry strained a laugh. "You'd know. You're head of Tourism, right?"

Stanescu bowed still lower. "I am State Minister of Tourism and Sport, but I cannot take credit for the Hotel Intercontinental. All credit truly belongs to the most esteemed General Secretary, Nicolae Ceausescu, who has imprinted his own visionary genius, his farsighted mind, his bold imagination, and his daring spirit, on all public works projects in modern Rumania."

"Sounds like quite a guy. You're lucky to have him."

"Thank you. We knew you would agree. We know that our most beloved President, Nicolae Ceausescu, and the most esteemed and internationally respected scientist, Elena Ceausescu, are most highly admired and esteemed throughout America and the world."

Stanescu stared up at Henry, inches from the table.

Henry asked, "There something wrong with your back?"

"My back? No." Stanescu straightened up. "Once your plane landed at Otopeni, you were easily able to find Bucharest?"

"No problem. I found a cab."

"Very good. And when you arrive? You were not easily lost in our beautiful city?"

"No."

"So you have seen maps of Bucharest?"

Henry was set to panic.

They were interrupted by an angry command, spat in a foreign language. It didn't sound like the Rumanian Henry had heard till then. It sounded Russian.

The Countess slammed a riding crop onto the table.

Stanescu's pink face drained of blood.

The Countess spat out what sounded like a string of Russian invectives, causing Stanescu to slink off like a beaten dog. She then unclasped her gray cashmere cape and draped it over the back of his chair. She put down her violin case and sat across from Henry. She set a finger to her lips for silence, which was good since Henry had no idea what to say.

Returning with two spotted glasses of muddy brown water, the waiter jerked to a halt upon seeing the Countess, spilling water onto the bloodied tablecloth. He twitched his head about, apparently seeking Stanescu.

The Countess snapped a command in Russian.

The waiter shuddered, his tiny red eyes twitching fearfully. He respectfully set down the glasses, then hurried off to return with a pitcher of cloudy water. When he was gone once more, the Countess plopped the table's ashtray into the pitcher.

"We can talk now." Her voice was deep and silken, but coldly edged with a Russian accent.

Henry hadn't like Stanescu's interrogation, now here was his boss. She must be his boss. He ran when she barked. Made sense. Eastern Europe took its orders from Russia. Stanescu wasn't getting any info about the maps, Henry was too sharp for him, so his Russian puppet master steps forth and takes charge. A Russian from the US embassy. Even the US embassy was riddled with Reds.

Henry stared at the cigarette butts and tobacco bits floating inside the pitcher, desperately conceiving potential excuses for her potential accusations.

"Bucharest tap water." The Countess removed a silver cigarette case from her dark overcoat. "It also kills microphones."

"Also?"

"All ceramic ashtrays have them." She slid a cigarette into a long silver holder. "And ceramic vases. And ceramic lamps."

"Lamps?"

She scrutinized him with large clear eyes, unblinking as she lit her cigarette. Her silver lighter was emblazoned with a coat of arms, its blazon incorporating a double headed eagle and Russian Orthodox cross.

Henry knew that she knew. "I didn't mean to break it."

She suppressed a smile. "What did you break?"

"You know."

"Do not be shy. Tell me."

Henry suddenly wondered why she had busted a Commie mike. A trick? Sure. No need for mikes when she was here in person. "I broke a light fixture by accident."

"At the Intercontinental?"

"That's right. It was an accident."

"Did you see the microphone?"

"Yes. But by accident."

She blew smoke past full, smiling lips. "Then it shall remain our secret."

"Sounds good." Henry wondered if she knew that he already told Auster about the lamp. "I had a meeting with Stanescu."

"Yes. I canceled it."

"That's cool. I guess you're his boss?"

She laughed. "I threatened to report him to Chebrikov."

"Your boss?"

"Viktor Chebrikov is Director of KGB."

Henry felt faint. He gripped his glass of brown water. It felt warm. "When do you think the waiter will bring our food?"

"Do not be impatient. The house speciality is chicken feet and stale bread." Tilting back her head to exhale gray tobacco clouds, she glanced askance at Stanescu, him and their waiter now blocking the kitchen doorway. She smiled wryly. "I spoke Russian, so naturally the idiot assumed I was KGB."

Henry tried to sound casual. "You mean you're not?"

"What do you suppose he expected me to report to Chebrikov?"

Stanescu was shouting at the waiter, then began slapping him silly. Dropping his tray, the waiter cowered against a wall, his shrieks piercing the café's smoky din. Stanescu bent down, slapping and beating him about the face.

Henry turned away. "Guy seems pretty upset."

The Countess tapped her silver cigarette holder against the rim of the pitcher, sprinkling ashes over the submerged ashtray. "Securitate now has tape of me addressing him in Russian. All Russian speakers are suspected to be KGB spies."

"But Russia is Rumania's friend."

"Not Russia. Soviet Union."

"Okay. Sorry. The Soviet Union is Rumania's friend."

"Parasites have no friends, only allies they fear and hate."

Henry wondered who she was, and on which side. "Sounds like you don't even like the KGB?"

She scanned the café amidst languid puffs of smoke. Despite her casual poise, she was alert and ready to pounce. "Ceausescu fears another Prague Spring. Stanescu will likely be reassigned to a non-ministerial post, then disappear in the next purge."

"Not if they thought he was KGB. Rumanians would never hit the KGB."

She smiled again. "How would you know?"

"Wouldn't the Soviets object?"

"And admit to turning an ally?" She settled her roving gaze on Stanescu. "Ceausescu routinely rotates his ministers. It prevents them from establishing independent power bases. Stanescu will disappear in the next reshuffle."

Stanescu gripped the waiter's soiled white jacket and slammed him against the wall several times, slapped him some more, shoved him to the ground and began kicking him. The Minister's face was livid, his mouth foaming, his eyes bulging.

The Countess smiled at the show. "Stanescu once chaired the Ministry of Interior's State Security Council. It is now Department of State Security. DSS. But DSS is often simply referred to as Securitate. Stanescu may still be in Securitate, although Securitate is now led by Tudor Postelnicu. These Marxist pigs devour their own."

Henry wanted to trust her. He needed a friend. But her story had holes. "If the KGB is Rumania's enemy, why didn't Stanescu have you arrested? Or just tell you to go to hell?"

"KGB is not an enemy, but an ally they fear. I put Stanescu between a rock and a hard place. Refuse me, offend KGB. Assist me, offend DSS."

Her story sorta made sense. But she was Russian. And Henry still had questions. "I saw you at the US embassy."

"And I you. You mentioned a map of Bucharest."

"So, you're an embassy employee?"

"They provide me with instructions."

"The American embassy does?"

"Yes. The American embassy."

Henry considered it. "You sound Russian."

Beaming pride, she jut out her chin and exclaimed, "I am the

Countess Anya Amasovich. A very old Russian family. Now, we are losing time. Please describe this map of Bucharest."

Henry still wasn't sure. "Your bosses at the embassy told me the map was no big deal."

"Who told you this? Auster? He is a fool. And he is not my boss. Now please, describe the map to me."

Henry considered it some more. "Why should I?"

"You need us."

"Who's us?"

"CIA."

Henry's mind reeled. Being CIA might explain her presence at the embassy. And surely the embassy knew she was Russian, so she couldn't very well be spying against them. Still, it could be a trick. Stanescu both feared and obeyed her.

Better stall while he decided his next move.

Henry asked, "What makes you think I need the CIA?"

A sharp scream pierced the café's cacophony.

Stanescu was gnawing on the waiter's scrawny throat, tearing off sloppy chunks of raw flesh. Blood sprayed against Stanescu's savage face, splattering his fine suit, the waiter's white jacket, the floor's black and white tiles. Other waiters gingerly stepped over them. Tables shouted for service. Stanescu arose with meat dripping bloodily from his mouth. The waiter thrashed upon the bloodied floor, crying and howling like a wounded beast.

The stout young waitress ignored the tables shouting for her attention. She instead sat slumped in a chair, gazing disinterestedly at the shrieking waiter.

Henry looked away, trembling, wanting to shut his ears to the waiter's animal cries.

"You need the CIA," Anya stated, "because you are surrounded by vampires."

Henry slammed the tiny table. "I never wanted to come here! I *hate* Goff for sending me! I hate this whole country! I never wanted to see any maps!"

"What did you see?" asked Anya.

"Two maps. Map of Rumania. Map of Bucharest."

"You mentioned red lines, like subway tunnels."

"That's what they looked like."

"Do you remember them? In detail?"

Henry thought back. "No. Just black city streets and red subway tunnels. But I only saw the red stuff for an instant."

"Before you saw this, did you drink any blood?"

"What?"

"Did you drink any blood?"

"Only thing I drank all day was coffee and wine." Then he reconsidered it. "I saw these stewardesses do some fucked up things to a bottle of wine . . . "

Glancing about, Anya indicated the waitress. "The bitch is a Securitate informer. Do you see that?"

Henry considered the waitress. A big-boned girl, dark hair, ruddy complexion. "Not too shabby-looking. Not for this place."

"Your wine was strong. But not strong enough."

Anya took a dull knife from the table and strode over to the thrashing waiter. Small hungry groups shifted about him, a pool of blood expanding beside his torn neck. Shoving past the group, Anya collected blood onto the knife. Returning, she dunked the knife into Henry's brown water and stirred. The water reddened.

"Definitely Securitate," said Anya. "Let us hope he is at least a major, though more likely a lieutenant."

She shoved the glass toward him.

Henry took the glass. "What do I do with this?"

She gripped his hand. "I assume no one drank your blood?"

"Of course not." Henry recalled the microphone with serrated edges, like tiny shark's teeth. "They tried to. But I didn't let them."

She released him. "Do not breathe and you will not taste it."

"You expect me to drink it?"

"Do not worry. One cannot steal from a socialist. Their blood is already stolen."

"Oh, good. But, why should I drink it?"

"Because I am your only friend and I told you to."

Henry wanted to believe he had a friend in this hellhole society, and so, holding his breath, he swallowed the rust red water. It felt warm and oily, tracking a filmy layer down his esophagus.

He slammed down his empty glass. His mouth and throat felt grimy, stomach burning, eyes stinging, vision sparkling.

Anya indicated the waitress. "You see the informer?"

Henry looked at the waitress. Her face was undulating, skin shifting to accentuate her skull, red and blue and purple mottles shimmering in changing kaleidoscope patterns, black lips snarling to expose yellow and brown blood-stained fangs, sunken yellow eyeballs glowering like a sickened beast at the café crowd.

The entire room was shifting and shimmering, red and blue and purple patterns polluting the faces and flesh of numerous café vampires, their mottled skin smoldering with dark energy, emitting a smoking black aura, choking the room with its sour blood stench.

Henry shut his eyes.

Anya was unperturbed. "Now you see the informer. Even her flesh strains to inform on her bones."

Henry opened his eyes.

Anya's complexion remained pristine and unblemished. "Concentrate, and you will recall the map. Their blood will aid your memory."

"I don't know about that."

"I do. And if not, you shall drink again. Richer blood. From a vampire of higher rank." Arising, Anya grabbed her cape and violin case. "Come. Let us see where your maps take us."

FIVE

Hurrying along the unlit street, Henry saw monotonous rows of apartment buildings on either side, sightless windows revealing nothing. Anya was a dark form save for the moonlight glinting on her neck and hand, enlivening the silver clasp fastening her cape, the silver cigarette holder within her glove.

They turned a corner and the café's distant light was gone. At the far end of the street, a dark silhouette in a greatcoat lurked beside a black Mercedes. Henry clearly saw the black car against the black of night, the waiter's blood sharpening his night vision.

Henry felt Anya grip his wrist, as though he might otherwise bolt, her fingers long and strong. She strode toward the silhouette at a steady pace, her boots echoing within the concrete canyon of buildings. Henry wondered why the CIA couldn't give their agents sneakers, such as he wore. He was actually better prepared than this supposed pro. If the silhouette hadn't yet seen them, then surely it heard them.

Anya approached the Mercedes without hesitation.

The silhouette advanced. Red patches and gold braids on its steel blue greatcoat, red star and gold laurels on its peaked cap. Its leathery bluish-red face scowled, eyes drooping, purple lips frowning. It touched a black glove to its visor. "Long life to the General Secretary, comrade."

Anya scowled at the creature. "What do you want, Captain?"

"I was not aware the Prime Minister's office had business in my district tonight. I thought I might offer assistance."

"Not required." Anya sounded different.

Then Henry realized that Anya was not speaking English, but Rumanian. And yet he understood both her and the Captain.

The Captain's black tongue licked dried dark blood from his cracked lips. "The comrade will forgive me, but it is my duty to report all activity in my district. You will please provide me with your authorization papers."

Anya raised a hand to her lapel, as if to retrieve them.

Too late, the Captain saw the cigarette holder.

Anya swept his face, flashing silver.

Screaming, clutching his smoking eyes, the Captain collapsed to the pavement, convulsing, boots kicking empty air.

Henry was barely aware of Anya pushing him into the Mercedes. By the time Henry realized he was in the car, Anya was beside him, calmly driving at breakneck speed.

"Do you remember the map?" she asked.

Henry felt something in his lap. Her violin case. He set it between his legs. "You're speaking English."

"As before."

"Before you were speaking Rumanian."

Anya smiled, perfect teeth flashing white. "You drank blood from a vampire. What he understood, you understand. As he saw, you see. Do not worry. It will wear off."

"The Captain. He said you were with the Prime Minister?"

"Highest-ranking *nomenclatura* drive black cars. Only the Prime Minister and his Deputies drive black Mercedes." She smiled again. "And us."

Henry wondered if the CIA couldn't be a bit more inconspicuous. "Is that your cover? Working for the Prime Minister?"

"We are entering old Bucharest. Its historic Rahova, Antim, Uranus districts. Do you recognize the buildings?"

Henry noted that she ignored his question, as before. Seems the CIA knew how to keep secrets. Good. He looked outside. No more monotonous apartment blocks. These buildings were sturdier, with ornate window ledges and doorways.

A full moon shone through the windows. Henry wondered how that could be.

"I don't recognize anything in this city," he said.

"Concentrate. Do any of these structures coincide with your memory of the map? A building in which a red line terminates?"

Henry concentrated, surprised when he recalled a vague image of the map, like a word that had hovered on the tip of his tongue all along, briefly forgotten, now found. Black polygons with red lines crisscrossing through them. But the polygons were outlines of blocks, not pictures of buildings.

"I remember the map, but I can't match it up with anything."

Anya nodded. "Think again. Find a long broad street, fronted by a huge building. That shall be our reference point."

Henry watched the moon glide from window to window, shining from inside every house, a bright silver tenant rushing from room to room. Then Anya turned a corner and Henry saw there were no houses, just empty lots strewn with rubble and demolition machinery. They had been driving past the facades of former buildings. Behind the facades, a coldly lit moonscape stretched for several miles in all directions. Remnant walls stood scattered among the craters and debris, awaiting their turn with the wrecking ball.

A dark horizon of buildings lay ahead, red and white candy cane lights spilling over their rooftops. One massive building towered over the rest, a tiered white wedding cake of a building, dazzlingly lit and visible for miles. Scaffolding and construction cranes surrounded it, yet despite its incomplete state, its brightly lit windows indicated that it was open for business. Perhaps because it was so gargantuan, portions of it were made operational before completion.

A mile of empty lots still separated them from the buildings when Anya pointed. "Militia."

A black Dacia was driving parallel to their Mercedes, a few empty lots to the right. Anya sped up. The Dacia followed suit, but made no attempt to overtake them.

"We are confusing them," she said.

Henry watched the speeding Dacia. "Oh good."

"We are in a high security zone, without authorization. Yet this is a *nomenclatura* car. They do not know what to make of us."

"There's another one." Henry pointed to a Dacia ahead and a block to the left.

"That makes three, counting the one behind us."

Henry turned and saw the Dacia trailing them, headlights dimmed. "Amazing they can see in the dark."

"As do we. Concentrate on the map. Find the largest block fronting the widest street."

"I think I remember it. Lots of red lines connected to it, like Penn Station."

"The House of the Republic. Initially called The House of the People, but Ceausescu cannot make up his mind. Not about its size, nor its name. Really, it is his Presidential Palace. You see?" Anya pointed to the wedding cake building, fast approaching. "Do you recall a broad street terminating at the Palace?"

"Yeah. I think so."

"The Boulevard of the Victory of Socialism." Anya indicated the candy cane lights. Almost as an afterthought, she added, "We are too close for comfort. They are closing in."

The Dacia to their right had moved a block closer. The one behind them also narrowed the gap.

Anya increased speed but remained calm. "The red lines from the Palace. Where do they terminate?"

Henry concentrated on the map, his memory distinct enough to see red lines terminating inside many buildings along the Boulevard. He said as much.

"On the Boulevard is a last resort. Any termination points near the Palace, but off the Boulevard?"

"Several." Henry felt the Mercedes rattling over a rough dirt road, any concrete or asphalt long since torn up for redevelopment. He described several termination points as best he could.

Anya nodded. "The Grigore Alexandrescu Children's Hospital. I suspected that. You will show me the tunnel entry when we get there. But first, pass the benzene."

"The what?"

"Behind you."

Henry turned and saw four metal cans on the back seat floor. He grappled one forward as the car lurched about. By the time he had a can up front, a frosty wind was blasting his face. Anya had opened his side power window.

"Open the can," she shouted. "Get it low to the ground then pour."

Henry's cold fingers grasped the cap and turned and struggled and turned.

"Tell me when you are ready," said Anya.

"Yeah, okay. I got it."

"Then what are you waiting for?"

Henry leaned out the window, gripping the heavy can, freezing wind whipping hands and face, bleary eyes watching the fuel splash against the rapidly departing dirt road. Their car shifted left and right, spreading a wide swath of benzene.

"Can you hear me?" Anya shouted.

"Yes!" Henry screamed into the wind.

"When the car stops, drop the can, open the door, run to the side of the road. Understand?"

"Yes!"

Henry fell against the door frame as the Mercedes screeched to a spinning halt, tossing up dust clouds. The car stopped with his door facing the oncoming Dacia.

Anya threw open her door. "Run!"

Henry dropped the can, opened his door and staggered into the road. The oncoming Dacia bore down on him. Although he was still swooning, he stumbled toward an empty lot, stepping over holes, struggling over rubble.

Glancing back, he saw Anya by the car, dark cape billowing in the wind. Fire flashed in her hand. A flaming silver arc struck the ground. She was already leaping over rubble when fire erupted beside the Mercedes, flames racing along the benzene trail into the oncoming Dacia.

Anya grabbed his arm and pulled him down.

The Dacia was weaving through fire and dust, Militia vampires scrambling within, still fumbling when their Dacia slammed into the Mercedes, both cars disintegrating in a golden fireball. Hot air blasted Henry's face.

Anya dragged Henry away from the burning wreckage, away from the road, into the interior of the moonscape. Another Dacia sped from two blocks away, toward the pileup.

Anya led Henry behind a partial wall, over a pile of rubble, then down into a ditch, past a muddied bulldozer, around a corner, under a steel crane, then up an incline. Glowering fire from the wreckage cast twisted shadows of shorn walls, exposed steel rods, derelict machinery. As they progressed, the dancing fire patterns on the cold moonscape faded.

Having traversed one ravaged city block, they paused to view the pileup. Crouched behind concrete blocks, Henry saw that both remaining Dacias were parked near the fire. Militia vampires stood and stared at the flames, stupefied and aimless.

Henry's hands were trembling. From shock or cold, he wasn't sure. He stuffed them into his pockets, but the thin khaki gave little warmth.

"So what do we do now?" asked Henry.

Anya indicated the horizon of dark buildings. "The demolition site ends there. I can find the hospital. You will direct me to the tunnel's entrance."

"What tunnel?"

"The red lines. They are Securitate tunnels. Somewhere along your journey, before you saw the maps, you drank Securitate blood. Now you see their secrets."

Henry shivered in the cold night air. "That's a big breach of security on their part."

"But not unlikely. Most vampires are stupid, lazy, incompetent. Parasites who feed on others. They are never invisible to those who care to see. I have long seen socialism, and now you do too. The vampire's strength is not that no one believes in him, but that many *choose* not to believe."

Henry recalled the oily blood coating his throat. "I drank stewardess blood. Not Securitate."

"Every Rumanian flight carries Securitate. Everywhere there are tourists. Somehow their blood got into you." Anya picked up her violin case, indicating it was time to move on.

Henry followed her across the moonscape, then up a flight of stairs to a stone floor imbedded with bolts where pews might have been.

"I think this was once a church," he said.

Anya perused a floor strewn with dirt and rat turd. "The Old Spirea Church. Yes, I told you, we are in a historic district." She pointed along the barren horizon. "There was the Cotroceni Monastery. The Vacaresti Monastery. The Spanish Synagogue. Brancovenesc Hospital. Do you admire the architecture? It extends back into the Renaissance and earlier."

Wherever she pointed, Henry saw only rubble. And one broken onion dome topped with the stem of a cross. A pale mist floated at the base of the dome, faintly glowing.

"This whole neighborhood," he asked, "it's being demolished just to destroy a few old churches?"

"To make room for Ceausescu's new administrative complex, of which The House of the Republic and The Boulevard of the Victory of Socialism are the centerpiece. The ruin of the churches is for Ceausescu a bonus." Anya strode across the stone floor and hopped back onto soil, continuing on her way. "Ceausescu is a true revolutionary, sweeping aside old bourgeois history and institutions to make room for New Communist Man."

Henry tore his gaze away from the luminous mist and hurried after her. "Does New Communist Man ever eat?" he asked.

Anya smiled wryly. "Ceausescu has issued ration books for a 'scientific diet.' He says Rumanians are too fat."

They came to a stretch of dirt lined with empty graves.

"Old church cemetery," Anya explained. "The corpses have been disinterred for reburial."

Eating sounds emanated from their left. Crunching, chewing,

slurping. Several pale bloated forms huddled near an open grave, clothed in rags, their blackened fingers pawing a corpse.

"Or perhaps not," said Anya.

The creatures glared at Henry with red rat eyes. Ravenous, mindless, seething indiscriminate hate. They shoveled putrefied corpse meat into their mouths lest Henry snatch it from them.

Henry backed away. "They don't look like vampires."

Anya sneered. "Ghouls. Vampires drain the healthy. Ghouls devour carrion. A nation of vampires creates so much carrion, in time only ghouls may survive. Ghouls ravaged the Ukraine in the 1930s. Under Stalin, ghouls even ate other ghouls."

Three ghouls squabbled over a decomposed breast, shoving one another aside, snatching at it, grunting, drooling. Rats scurried from the grave. Ghouls grasped after them, slobbering. One rat bit a ghoul's scabby ankle.

Anya was already moving on.

Henry followed her across a paved road, leaving the rubble behind. Once again, they trod barren sidewalks amidst concrete uniformity.

"These Securitate tunnels," Henry began, "are they an escape route?"

"Not for us."

"So what do we want with them?"

Anya made no reply.

"We are looking to escape, right? I'm an American citizen. You're CIA. It's your job to get me out of here."

Anya didn't bother to look at him. "I never read that in any job description."

Henry sighed. "We will escape eventually, right?"

"Yes. Eventually. Hopefully."

"So what about these tunnels?"

Anya was picking up speed. "If you are correct, there is an entry in the Alexandrescu Hospital. It is not far."

"Look, if the CIA wants my help with these maps, you better tell me what we're doing."

"Or you will do what? You will go where?"

"Yeah, I was wrong to doubt you," Henry groaned. "Seems you do work for our embassy. You're about as helpful."

"A little more, I think," Anya grinned. "The tunnels will take us to Ceausescu."

"Their President? What does the CIA want with him?"

Anya stopped to scrutinize him, assessing his trustworthiness. Her eyes glittered crystalline green, flashing catlike. Henry wondered about her night vision, about how much vampire blood it took to get eyes like that. Did CIA operatives normally guzzle on the stuff when stationed behind the Curtain, getting drunk daily on vampire blood? And if so, how long before it transformed them into . . . what?

Anya finally replied, casually, "Tonight we shall locate Ceausescu, you and I. And then, I will kill him."

SIX

The lights along The Boulevard of the Victory of Socialism lit the night sky pinkish white. Several blocks away, Henry followed Anya down shadowy side streets, not a car or pedestrian in sight. Sleek aluminum street lamps stood tall and unlit.

"Okay, I can understand them shutting the lights," said Henry. "Vampires see in the dark, so it gives them an edge. What I don't get is, since they run this country, why build so many lamps in the first place?"

Anya glanced back without breaking her clip. "You are half correct. Vampires do see in the dark, but this city is not dark by intent but from indifference. A lack of priority. The state shuts off gas and electricity every night to conserve fuel."

"Tough break, running out of oil in the winter."

"Oh, they have oil. Oil fields from the Wallachian plains to the Black Sea. Can you not smell it?"

He did. Ever since landing at Otopeni, everywhere he'd been, Rumania smelled like a gas station.

"Good thing I'm starving," said Henry.

"Why good thing?"

"Already got a headache from not eating. Don't have to worry about getting one from breathing."

Chuckling, Anya squeezed his arm. Seeing her smile almost made tonight's agony worthwhile.

Since she said nothing, Henry asked, "If they got so much oil, how come they're conserving it?"

"Because of fuel shortages."

"You just said they had plenty of oil."

"And the Ukraine is the breadbasket of the East, yet Soviet

vampires still require US wheat," said Anya. "Vampires perform their own miracles. They steal a hundred fresh loaves and fishes, then redistribute a few moldy slices and rotten heads."

"You mean, corruption? Skimming from the top?"

"No. Some skimming, yes, and a black market. But not so much as to explain the continuing shortages. Their miracle of scarcity is genuine."

Henry remembered the store windows displaying only pictures of food. "Miracle?"

"Or mystery. You see, the vampires themselves have no idea how they achieve this miracle. It baffles them. It angers them. It outrages them. Yet it does not discourage them."

"You're describing fanatics."

"Others call them idealists. And vampires can afford their ideals. They have no need for bread or fish or light. They subsist on others' blood. They can function in cold and darkness. Only their subjects suffer, broken and reduced to ghouldom." Anya turned a corner, scanning every darkened doorway and window for Militia. "Vampirism's fatal flaw is that less blood trickles up every year. In time the slave vampires also hunger. But never the masters."

"Slave vampires?"

Anya shrugged. "Perhaps a misnomer. All vampires are slaves to those above, masters over those below. Naturally, the vampires lowest on the food chain, the ones most dependent on ghoul blood, suffer first. Of course, ghouls too drink blood. In time, the entire nation is comprised solely of bloodsuckers, of one variety or other. That is why the socialist nations are so dependent upon fresh transfusions from the West."

Anya stopped before an old stone building. "The hospital. You recall its outlay on the map?"

"Its outlay?"

"The red line's point of entry."

Henry concentrated and envisioned the Bucharest map. The hospital was several blocks from The Boulevard of the Victory of Socialism. A red Securitate tunnel entered the hospital's corner.

Henry told as much to Anya, adding, "I don't know what floor the tunnel enters."

"The basement, of course. It is a tunnel."

Henry nodded. "Seems you paid attention in CIA school."

Anya scanned the large hospital, tall windows blackened with dust and soot. "We can likely break in with ease. But it may be simpler to enter openly. We are passing through. We will not be long. And it is not a high security area."

Henry shivered, but not from cold. They were gonna do it. Up till now they'd been running. But now they were attacking, turning around and engaging the enemy. It was real now. This lady was gonna do some wet work for the Company and he was along for the ride, like it or not. He felt both afraid and excited. Scared, yet pumped and ready for action. Must be how every soldier felt just before battle.

"I was gonna join the CIA," Henry added. "If I do good on this job, you might wanna put in a word for me."

"Certainly," Anya muttered without looking at him.

The hospital entrance was a heavy double door beside a metal sign featuring a caduceus and red star. Henry followed Anya into a dim lobby, stale air reeking of alcohol and gangrene. An empty gurney stood against a wall, its sheets soiled and wet.

A bloated nurse sat slumped behind the front desk, under a photograph of Ceausescu. She wore a dirty smock and babushka, her puffy vampire face mottled from red to purple. Her bleary yellow fish eyes glowered at Anya and Henry.

"You will direct me to the blood bank," Anya snapped in Russian. When the nurse only gaped stupidly, Anya repeated herself in Rumanian.

Snarling, the nurse exposed rotted brown fangs. "Show me your authorization papers, comrade."

Anya whipped out an ID inscribed in Cyrillic, and a gleaming badge featuring a hammer & sickle over a red star and dagger.

"I can't read that!" the nurse snapped.

"KGB, you stupid pig," Anya retorted.

Trembling, the nurse replied, "My apologies, comrade. But I am sure you appreciate my need for verification from my own immediate superiors. This will not take long."

"But I am thirsty *now.*"

The nurse arose, shakily. "One moment, please, comrade."

"Forget your blood bank, *comrade,*" Anya spat her words. "If it is too much trouble, I will drink here instead." Anya spread her lips, revealing a mouthful of startlingly long fangs.

Before Henry could faint or run, Anya gripped his wrist, her eyes still on the nurse.

The nurse sank back down. "No trouble, comrade. Our blood bank is in the subbasement. Very fresh blood. *Children's* blood. Not like mine. Please, help yourself. Here, I will draw you a map. Please, drink all you want."

The nurse's pudgy fingers trembled as she scribbled.

Anya snatched the map. "I do not ever again want to see you, or hear you, or even know you exist. If anyone even mentions you to me . . . " Anya bared her fangs.

"Yes comrade. Please, enjoy your blood. I am not even here. I am busy with my work. Please, pay me no attention . . . "

Henry still heard the nurse babbling long after Anya dragged him away from the front desk and around a corner.

The unlit halls reeked of a sour blood stench, discernible even beneath a suffocating odor of ammonia, alcohol, and gangrene. And the waiter's blood had been potent enough so that, although engulfed in darkness, Henry saw the unswept green and gray linoleum floor tiles, the grimy walls, the cracked frosted glass on doors haphazardly open or closed.

Anya released his wrist and he followed her shadowy figure, her cape billowing and concealing her movements.

"You heard?" she asked. "You understood? The blood bank is in the subbasement. Doubtless near the Securitate tunnels. Her map should help you locate the entrance."

Henry didn't know how to begin. "You're a vampire."

Anya stopped, then laughed. "They are fake." She opened her mouth, displaying pristine toothpaste commercial teeth. No fangs.

"They're gone," said Henry.

"Yes. I removed them."

"You didn't . . . retract them?"

She laughed again. "Look at my face."

"I'm looking."

"See any blood clots?"

"No." Henry wanted to believe her. "That vampire out front didn't have any problems with it. You looked okay to her."

"I told you, vampires are stupid. And yes, there are variations. Upper *nomenclatura* are better fed. They appear healthier in a certain light. Doubtless that cow had no idea what a KGB officer was supposed to look like." Anya locked eyes with Henry. "Let us say I am a vampire. What do you do now?"

"Run?"

"Then I catch you. Anyone in Rumania can catch you." Anya gripped his arm. "Who would you rather catch you? Me or Securitate?"

Henry wondered how strong her grip really was, if tested. She looked normal. Beautiful, even. Strong and healthy. Very unlike Rumanian vampiredom's parasitic dullards. Assuming she was not gonna peel off her face and reveal a KGB monster underneath . . .

"Well I'm with you, of course," he said. "And I mean that whoever you are. Makes no difference to me. If the KGB has a beef with the local Reds, that's your business."

"I am not KGB. You must trust me. If I intend to kill you, I would have done so by now."

"Sure. Good point. That makes sense." *Unless you need me,* Henry thought. "You convinced me. You're not a vampire."

He wanted to see her fake fangs, wanted her to place them in his hand so he could see for himself, but what if he asked and she couldn't comply . . . ?

Anya was already hustling him along. "You saw me wield silver. That should reassure you."

"Yeah," he nodded. "Another good point." She had wielded silver. A silver cigarette holder. While wearing gloves.

Anya glanced at him, as though his assurances were unconvincing. Or maybe he just imagined the suspicion in her eyes.

They came to an ancient elevator cage, no elevator in sight. She tried the button, without response.

"Looks like the stairs," said Henry.

Anya approached a metal door that might have led to a stairwell, but it was locked. Upon closer examination, it also turned out to be bolted and welded shut. Anya continued down the hall, presumably in search of another stairwell.

Henry followed because he had nowhere else to go. His own embassy had turned him out. At least Anya wasn't loathsome to behold. And if she was KGB, which was likely, at least she was liquidating Rumanian Reds rather than Americans. A good thing, these cracks in the Evil Empire. He should encourage it, encourage her. Do his part to widen those cracks.

Trailing Anya's dark billowing form, Henry planned and strategized. He was probably safer under her KGB protection than he'd be with the CIA, this being Commie turf. Especially if the CIA was run by idiots like that Auster at State. And so Henry formulated a plan whereby he'd play along, use Anya as she used him, until he saw his chance for escape . . .

If that was even necessary. Anya might just release him after she terminated Ceausescu. Might even put him up for an Order Of Lenin. He'd pretend to be pleased, of course, then spill everything to the CIA once he returned to the US.

Might be his foot in the door to a whole new career . . .

Henry was still formulating and strategizing when the skulls appeared.

Skulls, floating in the night.

Henry halted.

A half dozen skulls, tiny and hollow-eyed, gliding low to the ground. Floating toward him.

As they neared, Henry saw they weren't skulls, not really skulls, but faces. But with flesh so taut and pale, excepting the shadowy rings under their sunken eyes, that they resembled skulls more than living faces.

They were children.

They padded silently toward Henry on toothpick legs, their groping stick-like arms both pathetic and menacing.

Henry had no idea what to say, so he said, "Hey kids."

Silently they closed in on him, encircling him.

Henry backed off, not wanting to fear, or appear frightened, but not wanting to touch or be touched.

The children raised skeletal hands, tugging his jacket, gripping his stomach and waist and legs.

Henry pushed them back, gently at first, but they pressed in and groped ever more aggressively. He shoved their hands off his body. More children poured from a room and their numbers swelled to over a dozen. They crowded ever more tightly around him. He raised his voice, then cursed them.

A child bit his hand.

Henry yanked his hand away, smacking the child. It snarled. Henry punched it. Another dozen tiny hands pulled at his jacket, his pants, his belt. He felt teeth along his arms. He pummeled the ravenous children with his fists. They shrieked and snarled and cursed.

Henry was only vaguely aware of running footsteps, the flash of silver, the sparks erupting from the back of one child's head. Panic spread through their pack, but the shrieking children were unable to conceptualize or locate the source of danger.

Anya swept her arm like a scythe, silver sizzling and crackling against flesh, littering the ground with writhing children, smoke hissing from their burnt flesh. Those uninjured ran toward the walls, cringing and crying, shrieking and screeching, baring their broken baby fangs. Frightened but feral.

Anya aimed her riding crop at Henry. "Do not lag behind!"

Henry now noticed that her riding crop, with which she had menaced Stanescu, was capped with silver. He also noted that Anya gripped its leather handle with a gloved hand.

"They were just kids," Henry blurted.

"Orphan ghouls, abandoned by their parents and raised by the state."

"State should teach them some manners."

"A state cannot teach, only indoctrinate. A school cannot instill love. A village cannot raise a child." Anya swung her crop, keeping the snarling ghouls at bay. "These unwanted spawn live only because Ceausescu prohibits abortion."

"Surprised he gives a damn."

"It was his wife's idea. Elena thought it would increase the slave supply, so they outlawed abortion and stationed DSS officers in delivery rooms. But instead, another vampire miracle. Rumania's population is plummeting. Not only from black market abortions, but also suicide. Nobody wishes to be alive."

Henry eyed the ghouls baring fangs, edging closer. "Careful—"

Swinging her crop, Anya pounced and scared the last of the ghouls away. Then she readjusted her cape. "Chinese vampires mandate abortion to limit their large unruly slave population. Naturally their slaves grow more numerous every year."

Henry nursed his arms. "I didn't know, I didn't expect—"

"You must beware everyone! In socialism's final stages everyone is a bloodsucker, all innocent flesh long since drained. Many of these orphans will soon die. The survivors will have known no family loyalty, only loyalty to the state. Securitate recruits heavily from their ranks."

"Okay. I'm sorry."

Anya sighed. "Did they bite you?"

"Yeah."

"Show me."

Henry held out his arms. Saliva stained his jacket sleeves, but there were no holes. Anya examined his hands. The flesh was unbroken.

"You are fortunate," said Anya. "You drank vampire blood. If now they drink yours, you may turn. Then I must kill you." She said it casually, without smiling. A joke?

Henry forced a grin. "Then you'll never find the tunnels."

"I will. After I kill you, I will drink your blood. Then I will know what you know."

Henry searched for a flaw. "That can't be as effective."

"You think not?"

"You'd have done it by now. KGB doesn't pull punches."

"Very true. You can recall your own blood memories better than someone who merely drinks your blood."

They continued down the hall, until an orderly emerged from a ward up ahead. Anya pulled Henry into a room, then peered into the hallway, waiting for the orderly to depart.

Henry glanced about the room. Crowded with beds, two children per bed. Twenty pairs of hollow eyes staring at him.

"Pass the silverware," Henry whispered.

Anya shushed him without turning.

As Henry watched, a doctor and nurse materialized, misty and ethereal, shimmering with the same pale glow as the fog he'd seen near the onion dome.

Ghosts.

The ghostly pair hovered over a bald girl, slitting open her foot with wispy shades of dulled and dirty scalpels. The girl's spirit writhed within her corporeal body, pulling against ghostly straps. The doctor and nurse were still performing surgery when they vanished. Their ghostly scalpels vanished. The girl's ghostly foot and leg vanished. Both legs.

Henry blinked, his eyes readjusting to the dark.

He saw a solid living bald girl, lying in bed, both legs amputated below the thigh. She stared back at him with numbed soulless eyes.

Anya tugged Henry. They left the room.

"I am not overly concerned with the hospital staff," Anya whispered as they strode down the hall. "But as we near the tunnels, we shall encounter even more dangerous vampires. Smarter, stronger, crueler."

"I just saw a ghost," said Henry. "Two ghosts."

"In the room just now?"

"Yeah."

"What did you see?"

"Two adults operating on a little girl's foot."

Anya frowned. "Why do you say they were ghosts?"

"They were white, or bluish-white. Transparent. They appeared. They disappeared."

"You saw a blood memory."

"Huh?"

Anya hustled him into a dank stairwell smelling of rancid meat. "Someone witnessed this surgery, an orderly or a nurse. Then someone drank that witness's blood, then someone else drank that person's blood, and so on down the line to our waiter. When you drank his blood, you drank from all his prey and from all their prey." Anya pulled him along with one hand, gripping her violin case in the other. "As for the images in your memory, they were likely triggered by that room. Something the first witness saw."

"The little girl was there. In the flesh."

"Mystery solved."

"Not entirely," said Henry. "The ghosts were operating on her foot, but in reality she had no foot. Not even a leg."

"She likely contracted a post-operative infection and they amputated. Rumanian doctors frequently use unsterilized instruments due to shortages of antiseptic."

"What about beds? Two kids to a bed. Must be fun, sharing a bed with another sickie."

"They are lucky to have a bed. Ambulances no longer collect the old or retired. *Nomenclatura* excepted." Anya slowed as they neared the subbasement, her boots echoing upon stone.

Despite the cold, the rancid stench intensified with their descent. Henry tried breathing through his mouth. "Something else, though. Those ghosts, or whatever, operated on one foot. But the girl was missing both legs."

"Perhaps they erroneously amputated the healthy leg, then returned for the infected one. It happens."

"In the US, that'd be the mother of all malpractice suits."

"The people and Ceausescu are incapable of malpractice."

As she said it, pale phantoms materialized in Henry's mind, his own blood memory of Ceausescu on TV at Otopeni, pummeling his little fists, the assembled bureaucrats chanting, "The people and Ceausescu! The people and Ceausescu! The people and Ceausescu!"

Henry now knew what they had been chanting.

Anya shook him and the phantoms faded.

"I know what a blood memory is," said Henry. "What I saw up there was different. They were ghosts, like on the moonscape."

"What ghosts? What moonscape?"

"The ruined churches. I saw ghosts there too."

"We have no time for this." Anya withdrew the nurse's map. "Yes, maybe you saw a ghost. This nation is full of them. But to me it sounds like blood memory."

Henry noticed the metal door before them. They had reached the subbasement level. Discarded carrion meat lay piled in a corner. "So that's what's been stinking up the place."

Edging closer, Henry saw bloated rats gnawing on tiny human limbs, bluish-black and drained of blood. He spun away and held his breath.

Anya indicated the map. "Through this door and left. That will take us to the blood bank, over in this corner. That should be near the tunnel entry. Does that correspond to your memory?"

"Yeah, maybe."

"Are you ill?"

Swooning from the putrid stench, Henry croaked, "I'm fine."

"I need you to direct me once we enter the tunnels. Illness is not an option. Do you understand?"

"Sure. Where are we going?"

"The Presidential Palace. Ceausescu will be working late tonight." Anya tucked the map into her greatcoat. "Get a grip. You will see worse before this night is through."

Still clenching her violin case, Anya helped Henry heave open the door.

SEVEN

Heavy pipes hung underneath the subbasement ceiling. Heavy machinery crammed the floor. Boilers, generators, refrigerators, meat lockers. Heavy cables and tangled wiring spilled from the machinery, snarling about the floor, connecting electronic cabinets, passing through holes in the wall, entangling about pipes. Some machines droned and rattled and hissed with crippled life. Others sat silent with death. Everything was caked with greasy sludge, dripping oil and brown water.

Anya led, occasionally stopping to listen. Henry wondered how she might expect to hear anything amidst the machinery. He couldn't, despite the waiter's blood, but perhaps some vampires had sharper ears. Maybe not Rumania's socialist sloths, but an elite KGB assassin . . . ?

Anya halted and pointed. Henry saw a white figure moving past some freezers up ahead. They ducked behind a smoking generator, weaved a circuitous path toward the white figure, then peered from behind some pipes.

A woman in white was shuffling past rows of flickering incubators, a sickly infant within each box. She unplugged them one by one, until they flickered no more. When all incubators were dark, she opened one, removed a squirming purplish-brown infant, and carried it to a freezer.

Anya nudged Henry and they proceeded toward the subbasement's corner wall, now within sight.

The wall opened.

Anya yanked Henry behind a freezer.

A large vampire in a black leather trench coat emerged from the hole in the wall. His face was bright crimson with only a few blue splotches, as though he enjoyed his blood fresh and often, its hemoglobin oxygen-rich and all-you-can-drink. Behind him emerged a vampire in a black leather jacket. And behind him, a vampire in a steel blue Militia greatcoat, heavy with braids and medals.

All three creatures were burly and ponderous, crimson-faced and purple-lipped. Their yellow eyes glowered from dark sunken eye sockets, glowing catlike.

The trench-coated vampire led them to the incubators. Henry could no longer see them from behind the freezer, but he heard one bellow, "You shut them off already?!"

"Yes comrade," replied a female voice. "Just now."

"Comrade Ceausescu wants fresh blood."

"They are still warm. Still fresh."

"You were freezing them already."

"Incubators waste electricity. I have my orders, comrade."

"You needn't freeze them all," grumbled another male voice. "You can leave a few on."

"I have my orders," the nurse insisted. "They would die soon anyway."

Henry heard an incubator door squeak open, an infant squeal, the crunch of meat and bone. A male voice slurped, "It is still warm."

"We came just in time," grumbled the first male.

Anya tugged Henry and led him to the hole in the wall. The hole turned out to be a large hatchway, wider than a manhole, its hinged steel door still open. Entering, they descended a brief flight of stone stairs and exited into a concrete tunnel.

The tunnel was narrow, extending in two directions. Cables, pipes, and wires ran along the walls and ceiling. Dim bulbs glowed at distant intervals.

Henry ran with Anya for what felt like several city blocks. Then a branch tunnel appeared and they ducked into it.

Anya leant against the wall. "We must establish our bearings. But beware, those Securitate vampires may reemerge from the hospital at any moment."

"I thought one was Militia."

"The one in uniform, correct. The Militia is closely linked to Securitate. Police and secret police. Securitate is somewhat akin to 'making detective.' Not quite, but somewhat."

Something scurried around the corner, pattering in the dark. Henry became still. Dripping water echoed amidst wet scampering.

"Rats are safe down here," said Anya. "No one tries to eat them. Tunnel vampires are too fussy and well-fed."

Henry moved away from the wall. "Any special kind of rats they got in this country? Any vampire rats or . . . ?"

"We should be advancing toward the Palace. I want you to confirm and provide details."

"How?"

Anya grasped his shoulders. "Concentrate on your memories of the map. Locate the hospital as before, and the tunnel connecting it. Follow it toward the Palace, stopping at the first branch tunnel. That is our location. Do you see it?"

Henry strained to recall the map. "I sort of remember it."

"Sort of is unacceptable. Ceausescu presides over a meeting at the Palace tonight. He may already be there. But he will not be there forever." She squeezed his shoulders, her voice softening. "Take your time. Tell me when you see clearly."

In concentrating, Henry recalled the waiter's viscous blood slide down his throat like dirty oil, its rancid taste burn his stomach, blasting stars across his vision. The map hovered in his memory, floating in his mind. He strained to see and capture it like a fading dream.

"I sort of see it. I mean, I do see it. Sort of."

Anya sighed, then nodded. "Which way toward the Palace?"

Henry rotated the Bucharest map in his mind, attempting to overlay it upon the hospital and tunnels. Then he began threading forward, slowly, uncertain, seeking other branches. Now Anya followed, clasping his arm, a huntress yielding the lead to her bloodhound.

Henry envisioned a branch tunnel up ahead to his right, and when it was so, his confidence grew and the map became clearer in his mind. His pace quickened. Light bulbs were dim and few, but they sufficed. He saw all he needed to see. Darkness alive with shifting shades of black, as nocturnal creatures might see night, and within that shimmering blackness the blood red lines on the Securitate's Bucharest map.

In time they entered a broad tunnel, which Henry believed to run parallel under The Boulevard of the Victory of Socialism. He envisioned the Presidential Palace straight ahead several blocks. Then Anya's grip tightened and she was pushing him forward. Then she was ahead, pulling him along, running, her boots echoing from all directions. Henry quickened his pace, running after her.

"I'm losing concentration," he said.

"Remember your spot."

Henry saw clearly now, the tunnel rather than the map.

Anya pulled him into a narrow branch tunnel, smaller so that it muffled her boots, yet boots still thundered and echoed behind them.

"We're being followed," said Henry.

"No, we are being chased."

"What do we do?"

"You will remember your spot." She pulled him into another tunnel. "Where you left off. Remember its location relative to the Palace."

"Easy. Straight ahead."

They ran another two blocks, then Anya yanked him into still another branch tunnel, stopping just inside. Crouching, pulling him down beside her, Anya faced the tunnel they had just exited. "Straight ahead the wide tunnel?"

"Yeah—"

"It runs under the Boulevard?"

"I think so."

Anya bustled with something under her cape. "Good. I think I can find the Palace from here on."

Henry wondered if maybe he had said too much. "I think I'd probably have to show you. Some of it looked complicated."

Anya gave Henry a silver pistol that looked like a ray gun. A fat silver ray gun.

"Is it loaded?" he asked.

"Not a gun. A flame thrower."

"It's got a trigger."

"You know how to use a trigger?"

"Sure." Henry bobbed the gun and found it heavy. So she trusted him enough to give him this? Maybe she was CIA after all. "Pretty small flame thrower."

"A small fuel tank. Do not waste your fire." Anya continued fidgeting beneath her cape. "It has a short range but wide spread, so you need not be a good shot, not in close combat."

Henry swung the gun to and fro, aiming swiftly, James Bond style. Readying for an onslaught of vampires.

When Anya saw him, she said, "Give it to me."

"Why?"

"You will hurt yourself."

Reluctantly, Henry surrendered it even as bootsteps echoed from the tunnel. "I should have *something*."

Anya pocketed the pistol and handed him a silver cross.

A heavy item, its edges hard and sharp, its silver warm to the touch. Henry fingered its three bars, the top one slanted. "Always thought these looked kinda weird."

"Weird?"

"What are these extra bars for?"

"It is a Russian Orthodox cross," she scowled. "Christian Orthodox."

"I know, I've seen them."

"Show it to them, then run."

"I know how a cross works."

"And it will work as well as any Western cross."

"I'm not doubting you." Henry regretted offending her. He

needed a friend. Still, could this thing really be considered a cross? Did it really work as well?

He'd soon find out. Bootsteps were approaching, Rumanian voices bellowing in the dark.

Anya flung back her cape, revealing a crossbow with multiple arrows fed from a magazine. Wooden arrows with silver tips. She stood by the tunnel entry, peering past its edge.

Henry came beside her, raising his cross. He placed a comforting hand on her shoulder.

Anya jerked her shoulder. "Out of the way!"

Henry stepped back, lowering his crummy little cross while she stood tall with her killer crossbow. He felt useless and unappreciated and didn't much care for it. He hadn't asked to come to this miserable backwater nation, jerked around by Goff, lied to about the film's financing, mocked by his own embassy. And now, perhaps, soon to be dumped by this odd Russian woman, who may or may not be with the CIA, or KGB, or a countess, or even a vampire.

Stone shattered and burst behind Henry's skull, shooting shrapnel into his neck and ear. Machine gun blasts exploded within the tunnel, echoing within its walls. Henry fell and gripped the ground, neck and ear aching, burning. Anya was down too, slumped near the entry, head and shoulder just past the edge, exposed to gunfire.

Henry crawled toward her, bullets blasting against masonry, shooting sparks, his shouts to her drowned by deafening gunfire reverberating within the tunnels, filling its darkness with lightning and thunder.

Henry grappled Anya's ankle, was still pulling and tugging when she kicked free. She sprang past the edge, crossbow shooting silver. Three shots. Then she ducked inside again.

A single machine gun shot its load for a few seconds more, then became still.

All quiet save for one lone vampire screaming in the dark, shrieking, howling, pounding the walls and floor, dying yet not dying.

Anya gazed down on Henry, sitting with her back against the wall, him lying in the dirt. They eyed one another for what felt like minutes as the vampire hollered in the dark, just around the corner. Anya's eyes were hypnotically bright, her irises almost white, almost glowing. Maybe all KGB vampires looked like that, beautiful because they drank the very best blood. Or maybe CIA operatives came to look like that after one drink too many.

Was it possible Anya was no Commie, but still a vampire?

"We must destroy him," said Anya.

"We can't just move on?"

"When they find him, he will inform."

Henry listened to the cries, part human fear and self-pity, part beastly rage. "You wounded him?"

"Do you not hear?"

"Yeah. I guess his bark is worse than his bite?"

"A wounded beast? Surely you know better." Anya paused for the implication to sink in. Dangerous to go back, yet they must. "Can you locate the Presidential Palace from this branch?"

"You mean from the map?" Henry rose to his hands and knees. "My concentration's all fucked up."

"Then we must backtrack to the tunnel under the Boulevard."

Henry patted the back of his neck. It didn't feel wet. He touched his ear. It stung, but seemed in one piece.

"Are you injured?" asked Anya.

"Guess not. I thought you might be."

She ignored his chivalry. "I miscalculated. These tunnel vampires are very high *nomenclatura*. Excellent vision. Highly developed hearing."

"Hearing too?"

"Yes. I knew that, but forgot. The vampires detected me before I expected them to. It was an error."

"That's too bad." Henry realized he had begun to think of Anya as error-free. Her admission made her seem more human. Of course, vampires also screwed up, as witness the animal screams around the corner.

Henry rose to his feet, dusting off his safari jacket. "You know, I tried to save you."

"Did you?"

"I grabbed your leg. I was gonna pull you in."

"You nearly ruined my aim. As it happened, I struck two in the heart. My third was the flesh wound."

"I did that?"

Anya paused, considering. "No. My error."

"We all make mistakes."

"I think I grazed his aorta, very near the heart. I expect he is disoriented, perhaps even partially paralyzed. Prepared, we should destroy him without incident." Crossbow poised and ready, she crept toward the entry. "You may carry my case."

Henry lifted her violin case, feeling perhaps more important than the job entailed. "He sounds just around the corner."

"Two, three hundred feet. This crossbow has a good range." Anya crouched, peeking around the edge, Henry behind her.

A 25 watt bulb burned a hundred feet distant, another bulb a few hundred feet beyond that. Neanderthal screams emanated from the darkness between the two lights, mindless, primitive, tribal. Henry strained to see into the darkness, and the darkness came alive. Maybe his night vision was sharpened by his recent attempt to visualize the map? Even so, he saw only a shifting blackness within the dark, its movements indistinct.

A crimson dot materialized, gliding through the dark, sliding across tunnel walls, trailing a red beam to Anya's crossbow. She had a laser under her crossbow, a scope mounted atop. Henry wondered if the scope had night vision, or if Anya saw into the dark with naked vampire eyes. She had killed two vampires with two shots, both in the heart, and in neither case had she used her scope. He was sure of it.

The crimson dot floated onto a blacker shade of black.

Anya lowered her crossbow. "He hides behind his comrades' corpses."

"I don't see that. All I see is black."

"You should drink more blood."

Henry wanted to ask, *how much blood to see as you see?*

For the first time, Anya peered through her scope. "His night vision is highly acute. Sharper than mine. And he has cover. I do not. My sole advantage is the extent to which I crippled him."

"Maybe he'll bleed to death?"

She lowered her crossbow. "Follow me, several paces back. Stay low. If he shoots, drop. If he kills me, use the cross. It will protect you."

"That'll be enough?"

"No," Anya grinned. "Securitate will kill you, and soon. But armed, you die fighting. You die joyfully."

Before Henry could decide how serious she was, Anya disappeared into the dark and was gone.

Henry hurried after her.

Her boots were perhaps amplified by his sensitized ears, but even without heightened senses he'd have seen her silhouette in the dim light, flapping cape crouched low, barely weaving within the narrow tunnel. He could only imagine what the wounded vampire saw and heard. Maybe nothing except its own screams.

Anya reached the light bulb, ran past it, Henry behind her. A shot exploded. Henry crouched lower. Anya did likewise, yet ran on. Another shot, a pistol. Then another.

A red laser pierced the dark, silver flashing, sparks in the distance, an inhuman roar, boots racing, silver flashing, another scream.

Henry half ran, half crept, shoulder against a wall, probing the dark with outstretched hand, wondering how much farther . . .

"Done!" Anya shouted.

Henry arrived to find Anya perusing three vampires, all dressed in plainclothes DSS black leather. One vampire still lived, squirming and shrieking, an arrow piercing his eye. He was pushing the arrow through his brain, its silver arrowhead smoking from the back of his head. Another arrow lodged near his heart, a raw cavity gouged around it, exposing several ribs.

Anya indicated the cavity. "He did it, trying to push the arrow through."

"Why didn't he pull?"

"He did not wish silver to pass through his chest again, not so near his heart. He inadvertently broke the arrow, then gouged his chest to reach the shaft so he could push further."

Henry watched the vampire clumsily shoving the arrow through his eye, through his skull. Fumbling left-handedly.

"He's not very good at it," Henry observed.

Anya indicated the vampire's right hand, smoking and disabled. "I aimed for his pistol flash."

"Good shot."

Anya stepped toward the vampire, braced her legs and aimed her crossbow.

The vampire glared at her with his one eye, wheezing blood through clenched teeth, hissing hate.

Anya fired.

Silver pierced the vampire's chestbone, searing his heart and anchoring the arrow's wooden shaft. Black blood erupted from his heart, yellow saliva foaming past his fangs.

Anya accepted her violin case from Henry and took him back to the main tunnel, then on to the Palace. Henry followed in a daze, not noticing her or his surroundings. This was the first vampire he'd seen die. Expire. Whatever. Something was wrong.

"Did you notice . . . ?" he finally asked.

"What should I notice?"

"Maybe I'm wrong. It's dark in here. But I think all three of those vampires wore leather."

"They did."

"But back at hospital, one wore a uniform."

"Yes," Anya nodded. "These three were not those three."

"So where are those three? The three from the hospital?"

"These tunnels are extensive." Anya smiled at him. "Why else would I require your help?"

"I see. So they could be anywhere down here?"

"Them and others."

Henry scanned a darkness mitigated only by an occasional weak light bulb and his own weak night vision. He stiffened as they approached and passed a branch tunnel, stiffening whenever he thought he saw a branch tunnel.

They entered a chamber that blocked their path, but split into several smaller side tunnels.

"We made it, Henry!" Anya exclaimed. "We are under his Presidential Palace."

"How do you figure?"

"We cannot proceed forward, and you said the tunnel terminates at the Palace."

"That's what I saw." Henry enjoyed hearing Anya use his first name, and took pride in that she so readily trusted his memory. He also felt that same rush of fear and excitement as when they'd entered the hospital, but less fear, more excitement. He had a formidable ally. Look how far they'd come already.

"Any of these forks should lead to an entry," Anya continued. "The Palace would likely have several."

They entered a tunnel at random, Anya creeping silently, as if aware of her noisy boots and the likely presence of Securitate near the Palace. But they met no vampires and reached the tunnel's end without incident.

Stone steps led to another hatchway, its steel door shut and locked. Anya placed an ear against the door. Satisfied, she spun its steering wheel locking mechanism and the door eased open, apparently never locked.

"Not unexpected," she whispered. "The outlying entries are locked and the tunnels full of Securitate. We are not expected to get this far. No enemy ever has."

They entered the Presidential Palace.

EIGHT

The Palace of Versailles in shades of red.

An ornate white ceiling loomed overhead, its Louis XIV coffers golden-trimmed and dazzlingly lit by massive crystal chandeliers. White walls behind pinkish-red marble columns. White marble busts on fluted pinkish-red pillars. Tricolor national flags of blue, yellow, and red. Red flags bearing a gold emblem: a hammer & cycle framed by wheat under the letters PCR. Henry had seen that emblem on Ceausescu's podium on TV. Blood memory informed him that it was the Rumanian Communist Party's flag and emblem.

Henry was scurrying upon gold-fringed red carpeting, so plush he felt he was floating on air. Anya's boots made no sound. They had ascended some service stairs and were now above the basement levels and ground floor, having yet to see anyone. The Palace was more mausoleum than home.

"He lives here?" whispered Henry.

"The House of the Republic? This is an office building."

"You said it was his Palace."

"His Presidential Palace. Headquarters for his government."

"These are all offices?"

Anya nodded.

Henry glanced about the extensive hallways, branching off in all directions. The Palace was huge. "We have a destination?"

"I know the outlay."

"Glad to see the CIA knows its—"

"Shut up," she whispered.

Henry shut up, noting that the KGB more likely had access to such information than the CIA. Still, he 90% trusted her, and only partly because he wanted to trust her.

Anya halted, again handing him her violin case. "We are now past the front security. If anyone sees us, they will assume we are cleared by Securitate. They do not expect tunnel incursions. If they detain us, they will be suspicious but lax. Say nothing. Do not panic."

Henry bristled that she thought it necessary to tell him so. He was getting good at this spy business, no?

Anya pulled her cape's collar over its silver clasp, obscuring it completely. Henry noted that it, too, bore her coat of arms.

They hurried past silent offices. No overtime tonight, not on this floor. Yet despite a citywide blackout, every empty inch of the Presidential Palace was warm and brightly lit, dazzling to behold even with no one to behold it. No one but Ceausescu.

Ceausescu gazed across every hallway at himself, gazing from towering oil paintings, embroidered rugs, murals, mosaics, photographs, and busts. Always, he was the virile visionary with jet black hair, his gaze combining wisdom and fortitude and benevolence. Sometimes he gazed alone, sometimes alongside Lenin or Marx, sometimes alongside his wife Elena, but most often he gazed before undifferentiated masses of people. Ceausescu and the peasants before bountiful wheat harvests. Ceausescu and the workers atop gleaming oil rigs. Ceausescu beside cheering rosy-cheeked children. Ceausescu crowned in laurel.

Ceausescu also gazed in stark marble, alongside marble busts of other national and socialist heroes. Including one bushy-mustached man in a peaked velvet crown. Henry recognized him as Prince Vlad Tepes. Vlad the Impaler. Vlad Dracula.

Seems Ceausescu considered Dracula worthy of a marble bust.

Henry thought to point it out to Anya, maybe impress her with his own knowledge of Rumanian history, but now seemed not the time.

They turned a corner and faced a broad circular marble staircase. A Militia vampire sat slumped in a chair, blue tunic, black jackboots. He perked upon their approach, yellow bloodshot eyes squinting. He rose, gripping his machine gun.

"Long life to the General Secretary, comrade," he said.

Anya smiled, fangs exposed.

Henry waited for her to whip out her KGB badge.

Instead, Anya said, "Long life to the President, comrade."

"Your identification papers, please?"

"Of course, Comrade Captain." Anya reached for her pocket, then spun and lashed out her boot, smashing the vampire's chin.

A dry snap. The vampire collapsed, head askew.

Henry stared at the crumpled corpse.

Anya grasped the vampire's shoulders. "Do you intend to help or watch?"

Henry helped her seat the vampire in his chair. "They teach that at CIA school?"

"Decapitation?" Anya positioned the vampire's head so it wasn't noticeably askew. "Vampire hunters have been decapitating socialists long before there was a CIA."

Henry wondered why she didn't just flash her KGB badge. Or use her crossbow. For that matter, he hadn't seen the crossbow beneath her cape when she did her jump-kick. Not that he saw much beneath her heavy layers of cape and greatcoat and skirt.

"But you picked it up at the farm," he suggested, pleased to show off his knowledge of CIA arcana.

"I was never at the farm. I studied at School of the Americas. And Juilliard." She tapped her violin case, cuing Henry to take it and follow her up the thickly carpeted staircase.

"You really play this?" asked Henry.

"And other instruments."

As they ascended, a pair of fat vampires in brown suits descended. Henry tightened his grip on the violin case. Heavy. A good weapon, if necessary.

"Long life to the General Secretary," said Anya.

"Long life to the President," said one of the vampires.

When the vampires were gone, Henry asked, "What's Ceausescu? General Secretary or President?"

"He has many titles and likes to hear them all."

They ascended to the top floor, then entered a lavish marble and mahogany hallway. Raucous noise emanated from around the corner. Female screams. Male shouts. Laughter. Music.

Anya slowed, scowling.

"What's the matter?" asked Henry.

Anya shook her head, uncertain.

"What?" Henry insisted, scrutinizing her for clues.

"Ceausescu is a workaholic," she said.

"So he's having a party. We'll catch him unprepared."

They turned the corner. A stern Militia vampire stood guard down the hall. Loud gypsy string music emanated from the double doors behind him.

Henry glanced at Anya, striding purposefully beside him. An assassin, pumped and ready to kill. No turning back.

Just then the doors opened and another Militia guard joined the first. Then a third and fourth. Henry glanced at Anya. She was still striding resolutely, yet he sensed her trepidation.

The four vampire guards were shouting boisterously, each one tall and strong and alert, each cradling a machine gun. The odds looked bad. Henry heard Anya breathing deeply, calculating, preparing, flexing and unflexing her fingers. He wondered what surprising new skills or weapons she had planned. What might enable her to break through and kill the most heavily guarded vampire in Rumania? And afterwards, to escape.

Then Henry knew.

Anya was on a suicide mission.

It could not be otherwise. Assassinate a foreign leader on his home turf *and* escape? Impossible. Only a suicide mission was feasible. That should have been obvious from the start.

A fifth guard emerged, machine gun ready.

Henry wanted to run but needed Anya for his own escape. Yet if he assisted her, there was no escape for either of them. Odds were better if he ran and took his chances. Yet he'd seen the vampires, knew them for what they were, as did she. As his own State Department did not. Whoever or whatever Anya was, she was one of the good guys. He couldn't desert her, she needed him even if she didn't think so. And hell, maybe his chances *were* better with her.

Then a guard saw them and it was too late to run.

"Long life to the President," shouted Anya.

"Long life to the Supreme Commander," the guard replied. The florid red and gold insignias on his epaulets indicated he was the group's leader. "Your papers, comrade?"

"Of course, Major." Anya reached for her breast pocket.

Grabbing her arm, Henry shouted, "We're with the band!" He raised the violin case toward the closed doors behind the guards, toward the source of music. "Hope we're not too late."

Even as Anya glared at him, Henry was stunned to realize that he was speaking Rumanian for the first time in his life, speaking it fluently, without thought or effort.

"Five hours," said the Major, casually training his machine gun on them. He glanced at a guard. "Inform Comrade Ceausescu."

The guard opened the doors and disappeared into the room.

Anya yanked her arm free of Henry, then smiled at the Major. "I was so hoping to meet the Comrade," she purred, her deep silky voice now less cold, more sultry. "He is my hero."

"He is hero to all Rumanian people," said the Major, now keeping his machine gun on Anya.

"He is inside now?"

The Major ignored her question.

Another guard waved his machine gun at Henry's safari suit. "No costume?"

Henry forced a laugh. "Rumanian dry cleaners. What a joke."

The guards exchanged suspicious squints.

Henry cleared his throat. "I mean, they should be reported to Ceausescu. If Ceausescu knew about the dry cleaners in this city, wow, he'd fix things. I'd be wearing my costume right now, all spic and span. In fact, clothes would never get dirty in the first place. Ever. That Ceausescu, he really knows how to run a country. I'm gonna go in there and tell him."

The Major curled his purple lips into a grimace. "Musicians are all deviationist anarchists."

Henry stared at the machine guns trained on them. He sensed Anya beside him, tense, coiled, her quarry just behind the doors. She was ready to spring into action. Brave and suicidal action.

"Yeah well, a lot of musicians are," Henry agreed. "Western rock artists, man, they are the scum of the Earth. MTV, garbage. Deviationist garbage. Like you said. Now, gypsy music, that's what I go for. Listen to it all the time. Can't get enough."

"You play the *hora?*" the Major asked.

"I do," said Anya.

"Yeah, she's the musician," said Henry. "I'm with the band, like I said. I'm sort of her groupie. Actually, I'm her roadie. I got promoted."

The Major pointed to Henry's violin case.

A guard grabbed it, then screamed and dropped it, clutching his smoking hands. "Silver!"

"To prevent theft," said Anya.

Henry now saw that the clasps were indeed silver. The guard would have been safe had he merely touched the handle or case.

"You carry silver?" the Major asked Anya.

Anya raised her gloved hand. "I am cautious."

"And you possess a weapons permit?"

"I do."

"You will show it to me now. And I must again insist to see your papers."

The double doors opened and a tall vampire emerged. He wore a gray Italian suit, French silk shirt, English knit tie, gold Rolex watch. A New York yuppie, aside from his fangs, yellow bloodshot eyes, and bloated crimson face.

"Comrade Ceausescu demands immediate execution of the tardy bastards!" he bellowed, swooning, laughing, his breath heavy with alcohol. Boisterous laughter emerged from the room behind him.

"Tell the shits nobody comes late to my party!" a man shouted from the room, followed by more laughter.

Laughter. A joke. Henry wondered how far they'd carry it.

"A potential problem, Comrade Andrei," said the Major to the well-dressed drunk.

"Stefan Andrei?" asked Henry.

The drunk squinted at Henry.

"I'm Henry Willoughby. We have a film deal. Greg Goff sent me from New York."

"Goff?" Stefan Andrei pondered the name.

"Ion Stanescu booked me at the Hotel Intercontinental."

"Ah, Ion! Yes. Henry Willoughby! The most highly esteemed American film director from Hollywood, California."

Henry nodded. Nice to know Goff lied to everyone.

"But what are you doing here?" asked Andrei.

"Ion dropped me off. Thought I should meet you."

"Ion brought you here?" Andrei scanned the hall. "Where is Ion?"

"He had an appointment. Just dropped me off."

"Ion is an idiot!"

"Comrade Andrei," the Major interrupted. "This is most unusual."

"Surprised me too," said Henry. "I sure never expected to drop by the Palace and meet Ceausescu."

"The House of the Republic," Anya interjected.

"Yeah, House of the Republic," said Henry. "Ion called it a Palace."

"Ion is a fool!" Andrei added.

"They carry silver," the Major insisted, showing the violin case to Andrei. "My man burned his hand."

"To discourage theft," purred Anya.

Henry smiled. "My friend's a musician."

"Ah, you have already found a friend," Andrei leered. "Did we not assure your esteemed Mr. Goff that ours is the friendliest nation in all of Europe?"

"Very friendly," said Henry.

"Thank you, Major. You have done your duty." Andrei transferred the violin case to Anya, then escorted both humans inside. "Perhaps you will honor us tonight with your music?"

"It is every musician's highest honor to perform for our beloved and esteemed President," replied Anya, already scanning the room for her quarry.

NINE

A cavernous conference room, dark wood panels, lofty windows overlooking the Boulevard. A dozen bloated red vampires slumped about a long table draped in sparkling white linen, newly stained with blood and alcohol. Most of them wore expensive suits, a few wore heavily decorated brown or blue uniforms. Off in a corner a folk-costumed band played vigorous gypsy music. Mottled waiters and waitresses bustled about in crisp white outfits, serving food and drink on golden trays with golden utensils. No silver.

"May I perform for the General Secretary now?" Anya shouted to Andrei, straining to be heard over the loud music.

"Where are your drinks?" Andrei shouted, bleary-eyed.

"Where's our food?" Henry shouted. He wanted to ask if they might eat at the table, however nauseous the prospect of dining amongst drunken malodorous red bureaucrats with food stuck between their fangs. But the Central Committee Secretary for Economic Affairs had already departed, leaving the humans unattended.

A vampire pointed to Henry. "A spy! A spy in our midst!"

Henry tensed, but when several vampires laughed, he realized it was another joke.

The jokester sat at the head of the table. Tall, thirtyish, dark-haired. Open silk shirt revealing a hairy chestful of gold chains and medallions. Hairy arms laden with gold bracelets and watches. Hairy fingers thick with bejeweled gold rings. Despite his expensive suit, more than anything else he resembled a discount electronics merchant.

"A spy in our midst!" he shouted again, grabbing a waitress. "Are you a spy too? Are you hiding a tape recorder in your cunt? Show me what you're hiding, you bitch."

He reached under her skirt. She screamed, struggled, but no one moved to help her.

He shoved her to the ground. "Shut up you bitch. You think your cunt is such a treasure? We have ten million cunts in Rumania and they all smell better than you. Get me a Scotch before I piss on you."

Although the waitress was already crawling away to bring him his drink, a tall vampire in dark gray pinstripes and gold-rimmed glasses leapt to his feet, fingers snapping. "Scotch for Comrade Ceausescu!"

Another waitress rushed into the kitchen.

Comrade Ceausescu sniffed his fingers, grimaced, then shoved his hand under the tall vampire's nose. "Hey Oprea. Isn't that the stinkiest cunt you ever smelled?" As Oprea nodded, Ceausescu got up and kicked the crawling waitress's ass, shoving her out of the room with his foot. "Get your smelly cunt out of here before I vomit!"

Henry shouted into Anya's ear, in English yet no louder than necessary, "He doesn't look like his picture."

Anya replied, "His son Nicu."

"As in Crazy Nicu's Video Asylum?"

Anya smirked. "Nicu Ceausescu is Candidate Member of Political Executive Committee, Rumania's Politburo. Also Minister for Youth Problems, and First Secretary of Union for Communist Youth. And Nicolae Ceausescu's heir apparent. Crown prince of Communist Rumania."

"What about the big guy next to him?"

"Gheorghe Oprea, First Deputy Prime Minister." Anya smiled sultrily as Andrei returned with drinks. "Will the President be here tonight?"

Andrei only replied, "With warmest fraternal wishes from the most highly esteemed Comrade Nicu. Johnny Walker Black Label."

Henry swirled the ruddy gold liquid in his glass. Leave it to vampires to spike Scotch.

"Taste it," Anya shouted. "See as they see."

Henry sniffed his Scotch, rancid with blood. "Guys in here must have great night vision."

"I think not. Vampires are forever trying to kill their minds, their perception, their ugly reality. They steal blood then kill its taste with vodka or pills, as if killing its taste will erase its origin. Blood without reminders of a bloodline. They deaden their minds with mindless sloganeering. 'The people united shall never be defeated.' 'Four legs good, two legs bad.' Vampires cannot bear to think. Thought is agony to a vampire."

Henry indicated Andrei, wobbling near enough to hear.

Anya sneered. "Do not worry. These master vampires grow fat and lazy. Ghouls are lazy with despair. It is Securitate you must watch for. Vampires who have both hunger and hope of fresh blood. The revolutionaries and executioners. Too hungry and fearful and hateful to always be drunk."

"They're here?"

"Most likely the serving staff."

A waitress set a tray before Nicu, then turned to leave. He drank a long swig from the bottle then hurled it across the room, shattering it against the dark wood, showering glass and alcohol onto the assembled guests. Some laughed. Most gaped, stupid and oblivious.

"Come here you bitch!" Nicu screamed, stumbling toward the waitress, pinning her against a wall, squeezing her breasts. He tried to bite her neck, but she struggled. He bit her ear, threw her down, then spat her ear lobe across the room.

"Not always a glamor job," Anya shouted to Henry.

Anya turned to Andrei. "I was hoping to meet General Secretary Nicolae Ceausescu. He is my hero."

Andrei shouted over the revelry, "Comrade Nicolae Ceausescu is hero to all Rumanian people!"

Upon hearing it, several vampires began pounding the table, drunkenly chanting, "Ceausescu and the people! Ceausescu and the people! Ceausescu and the people!"

Andrei wobbled back to his place at the table, struggling to finish. "And also Rumania's most esteemed scholar—"

Oprea sprang to his feet, shouting, "To Comrade Elena!"

Anya turned to Henry. "Microphones."

Even as some vampires rose to contribute toasts, the others continued chanting, "Ceausescu and the people! Ceausescu and the people! Ceausescu and the people!"

A sixtyish vampire raised his glass, shouting, "And to Comrade Nicolae Ceausescu, Comrade President of the Socialist Republic of Rumania, Supreme Commander of the Rumanian Armed Forces!"

The table chanted, "Ceausescu and the people! Ceausescu and the people! Ceausescu and the people!"

The old vampire screamed louder, "This most Rumanian of men, raising our motherland up to join the great family of the most civilized and most highly esteemed countries of the world!"

Anya shouted to Henry, "Ion Coman, Central Committee Secretary for Armed Forces and Security."

"And to Comrade Elena!" Andrei seemed determined to establish a record of his praise for Elena. "The most highly esteemed and world-recognized chemist, scientist, and scholar, whose invaluable contributions to the world of chemistry and science are of the most highly esteemed and inestimable value, and who has single-handedly raised Rumania up to the forefront of international leadership in the world of science!"

"Ceausescu and the people! Ceausescu and the people! Ceausescu and the people!"

Another vampire raised his glass. "Comrades, as someone who has coordinated the Department for Cults, I have been told that priests and rabbis must pray to their god, whoever he may be, in the morning, in the evening, and at least once during the day. We, however, are atheists, comrades. We believe only in the most beloved, esteemed, and illustrious son and daughter of the Rumanian people, Comrade Ceausescu and Comrade Elena!"

"Ceausescu and the people! Ceausescu and the people! Ceausescu and the people!"

Shouting to Henry, Anya strained to be heard over the chanting and gypsy music. "Emil Bobu. The Department of Cults supervises all religious activity within Rumania."

"And to Comrade Minister Nicu Ceausescu!" Oprea added. "Who is so sensitive."

"Ha!" Nicu slammed Oprea's back. "When my old man croaks, I'll make you prime minister, Oprea."

Several vampires exchanged nervous smiles, reluctant to endorse Nicu's irreverence, yet reluctant to contradict him, daring only to chant, "Ceausescu and the people! Ceausescu and the people! Ceausescu and the people!"

All the while the band played on, frenzied and without rest, their joyful music belied by the musicians' tense expressions.

Henry wondered how long he and Anya would be ignored. Nicu and the microphones seemed the center of attention, all vampires courting one or the other. How long before they discovered the dead vampire a few floors below? Or the ones in the tunnel? How long before the Major took the initiative and contacted the front security desk? How long before somebody phoned Stanescu?

Henry shouted to Anya, "Maybe we should leave?"

"Andrei has not answered my question."

"He's not here. And it doesn't look like he's coming."

"Then where is he?"

Henry shrugged. "Home?"

"He has forty-four residences."

"You mean, the Company doesn't know?"

She ignored his bait. "Nicu might."

"I doubt Nicu gives a damn about dad."

"Drink your Scotch. But do not get drunk."

Henry held his breath and took a sip. The blood was bitter, but smoother than at the café. And more potent. One sip and his head swooned, the room exploding in red and gold, colors becoming more vivid, stark, saturated. He glanced at Anya, a silver glint from under her collar piercing his eyes. He turned away, squinting. The clasps on her violin case gleamed. Not so bright as to burn his eyes, but bright enough to bother him.

"Powerful blood," said Henry.

Sipping her drink, Anya nodded. "Another security breach. Stupid creatures. Conspicuous to anyone who cares to see them."

Henry decided he'd had enough to drink. He looked away from the violin case and at the solitary guard by the door. The guard glared at Henry with yellow bloodshot eyes, squinting suspiciously. Henry turned away. Must be someplace he could look comfortably.

He noticed the tall windows overlooking The Boulevard of the Victory Of Socialism. He hadn't seen the famed Boulevard yet so he approached a window, its ledge low to the ground.

The Boulevard lay some dozen stories below, glowing ghostly white, stretching off into infinity, disappearing in a black void dotted with cranes and moon craters. Apartment blocks lined either side of the Boulevard, facing a broad street utterly devoid of cars. Bisecting the Boulevard were concrete islands containing gardens, fountains, and quasi-modern baroque street lamps.

Every lamp shone, bathing the Boulevard in stark bone white. Colossal crimson banners draped every building, shimmering in the night. Blood banners draining buildings, drying stone into bone, bleeding their occupants, bleeding onto sidewalks, blood soaking through the pavement and into the dark tunnels below.

"Oysters, you scum," Nicu screamed at a waiter.

Oprea was already snapping his fingers needlessly. "Oysters for Comrade Nicu Ceausescu!"

Nicu finally noticed Henry, apparently forgetting his earlier joke. "Who's the shit by the window? He's gawking like some stupid peasant never been up this high before."

Andrei quickly answered, "He is the esteemed Henry Willoughby, a Hollywood film director and a most highly esteemed guest of your father."

"Is that true?" Nicu asked Henry, then to the band, "Shut your noise before I kick you shitholes out the window! All your songs sound alike! I'm sick of it!" Nicu turned to Henry. "You want to put me in a movie? You think I could be a movie star?"

"You would be a marvelous actor," Oprea insisted. "A bigger star than anyone in Hollywood. You are so sensitive. Don't you think so, Comrade Andrei?"

"Yes, I do," Andrei agreed. "I think Comrade Nicu would be an excellent actor."

Nicu waved for silence. "I want to hear what the American thinks."

Henry perused the vampires about the table, most so drunk they barely noticed him. "I was just thinking that's a very nice street you got down there."

"Truly!" Coman interjected. "Yet the Boulevard was the bold vision of only one man!"

"Let me try and guess," Henry began.

But Coman would not be denied his brownie points. "Comrade Nicolae Ceausescu, whose unique genius and daring spirit single-handedly engineered this great Boulevard for the Ages, at which end he raised this building, this Acropolis—"

A dumpy vampire squeakily interjected, "This symbol of our Age of Pericles!"

Coman never paused, "—in the heart of Bucharest, cleansing our city of the bourgeois vestiges of the past!"

"Churches and synagogues are poison," another vampire interjected, "and Comrade Ceausescu has eradicated this poison and replaced it with his own unparalleled gift of a revolutionary urban achievement!"

"It all sounds great," Henry interjected, hoping to cut them off. The vampires did not seem to be listening or responding to one another, determined only that their praise make the record.

Anya first pointed to the dumpy vampire, then the other one. "Ion Avram, Minister of Electric Power. Mihai Florescu, Minister State Secretary of National Council for Science and Technology."

Henry wondered if it was such a good idea for her to display her knowledge, now that they had the vampires' attention.

"Who's the new skirt?" Nicu asked.

Anya responded, "Esteemed Comrade Nicu, I am the daughter of simple workers and a student at the Gheorghe Enescu Conservatory, but as you can see I read *Scinteia* religiously." She smiled as Bobu laughed at her joke, then continued, "So naturally I recognize all here who serve your most highly esteemed and beloved father. My highest ambition is to someday perform for the Rumanian National Philharmonic, but I would gladly surrender that goal if only once I may perform for the most beloved son of the Rumanian people, for he is truly the source and inspiration of all music."

"What a sensitive observation," said Oprea. "And so true."

Anya added, "If you would grant me this wish of playing for your illustrious father, I would be infinitely and eternally grateful."

"Granted," said Nicu. "Now show me how grateful. Let's see what's under your skirt."

"Certainly," Anya responded. "And far greater pleasures for the esteemed young Minister. After I perform for his father."

Henry wondered if anyone else noticed her almost imperceptible pause before answering, or heard the tension in her voice, or saw the strain in her smile. Truly, a suicide mission.

"What am I, a fucking pimp!?" Nicu shouted. "First let's see if you're worth it. I want to hear you play. I want you playing before me, grease naked on this table, with stuffing up your ass, playing the *hora* while I eat potatoes out of your cunt."

Oprea snapped his fingers. "Stuffing for Comrade Nicu Ceausescu! And potatoes!"

One waiter hurried into the kitchen. Another exited with a tray of oysters, setting them before Nicu.

Nicu indicated the gypsy band. "If a grease naked bitch can play better than those shits in dresses, then maybe I'll pass you on to my old man."

Henry came beside Anya. "Actually, esteemed Comrade Nicu, I mean highly esteemed, most highly esteemed. And beloved, beloved and esteemed. All of it most highly. This lady is my friend."

"To hell with her!" Nicu shouted. "I'll give you another friend. As many Rumanian friends as you want."

"Esteemed Comrade Nicu," Andrei nervously interjected, "perhaps we should allow this honored guest of the Rumanian people to the friend of his choice."

"Why?" Nicu demanded. "Doesn't he have any friends in Hollywood?"

"But as a representative of the esteemed Mr. Goff—"

"This bitch is Rumanian, no? We own her. We can do what we want."

"But perhaps our esteemed guest—"

"Don't be such a prude, Stefan. You sound like an old woman. You too." Nicu pointed to Henry, having forgotten his name. "I know! We'll stuff her with oysters. Stefan will eat out of her cunt. The American can suck oysters from her shithole."

Several vampires laughed.

Nicu sniffed the oysters piled on the golden tray. "Idiots! These oysters are raw! Where's the seasoning! This isn't a cathouse, it's a VIP club!"

Henry took Anya's arm, whispering, "We should go."

Anya nodded.

Nicu clambered atop the table, unzipped his pants, and began pissing on the oysters. Henry was so stunned, he didn't hear the door open, bootsteps rushing into the room.

Anya spun and lashed out, dropping one guard. Henry turned too late. Militia overpowered them both, pinning their arms behind their backs.

"Comrade Minister Nicu," the Major saluted, careful to avoid staring at Nicu's naked red penis, still dribbling pee. "Captain Codurescu has discovered three dead officers in the security tunnels."

"Are the fresh babies here?" asked a groggy vampire.

They were. The uniformed vampire from the hospital subbasement entered carrying baby corpses hooked on a rod like sausages.

"Another officer dead in the lobby," the Major continued.

"Why tell me?" Nicu demanded. "Can't you shits do your job without my help? This cunt is about to regale us with her music, I'm seasoning oysters for her pleasure, and you shits come breaking in here because you can't do your job."

"I am sorry, Comrade Minister," the Major said. "But I have reason to suspect your guests are the spies and saboteurs responsible."

One guard grabbed Anya's violin case and slammed it onto the table. His hands protected by gloves, he opened the clasps, then flung open the case.

Henry squinted against the sudden burst of light, presumably worse for the vampires. The guards weakened their grips and Anya struggled, but they quickly reasserted themselves and twisted her arms back. The gloved guard shut the violin case, extinguishing its blinding glare.

The case had held no violin. It contained an array of weapons, all gleaming silver. Silver crossbow, neatly folded. Silver cylindrical gun, longer than the one Anya had shown Henry in the tunnels. Silver canisters, cases, shells. Silver-tipped arrows, stakes, spikes.

Purple lips baring his fangs, the Major pointed to the case. "There! The weapon that killed my men!"

TEN

Although Anya made no sound from between her clenched teeth, blood and saliva streaked her chin. Henry realized that while he was merely being held, Anya was being hurt. She had possession of the murder weapon from the tunnels. And the guard she had struck was even now vomiting blood onto the bright red carpet, his mouth foaming yellow. His comrades were returning the favor.

Nicu spun upon a partygoer in a heavily decorated blue uniform. "You shitty idiot! You let these assassins get this close to me! What sort of general are you? You ought to be on duty for the government! For the people! Not getting drunk like some lazy capitalist shit!"

The General turned neon pink, which was perhaps how red vampires paled. "But, Comrade Minister, but, as you can see, my men stopped her before she could do anything—"

Nicu threw the tray of oysters at the General.

The General daren't respond, sitting motionless, tray in his lap, oysters covering his face and uniform.

Henry turned to Anya, whispering in English, "You okay?"

Anya smirked, eyes bitter but defiant.

Henry wondered if she had a plan. "Should have kept it under your cape."

"The strap chafes my shoulder," she whispered.

A brave joke? It didn't seem like a good reason to go weaponless. Henry asked, "You have a plan?"

Anya remained stone-faced.

"Mind if I try?"

Before she could respond a guard shouted, "Shut up you two!"

"And what say you, Stefan?" Nicu threw a glass of Scotch at Andrei. "What an idiot! Importing assassins from the CIA!"

"Comrade Nicu," Andrei protested, "it is the duty of the CIE to screen foreigners, and CIE gave both Goff and Willoughby clean recommendations. The most highest recommendations."

"The CIE's been run by imbeciles since before Pacepa defected! Now they've let the CIA into The House of the Republic!"

"We're not CIA," said Henry.

"Indeed." Andrei looked hopefully at him.

Henry tried to glare at Nicu, still exposed atop the table. "Man, you just made the mother of all mistakes, Comrade Asshole. May as well run to Switzerland now, Comrade Shitface. Cash in those Cayman Island bonds, esteemed Comrade Motherfucker."

Startled gasps from around the room. The guard pinning Henry weakened his grip, as though feeling faint.

"The lady is not CIA," Henry continued. "She's KGB."

More gasps. Henry glanced at Anya, still stoned-faced.

"Yup," Henry continued. "You just pissed off your masters in Moscow. I wouldn't want to be in your babushkas for the world."

"Is that true?" Nicu asked Anya.

Anya only glared at him. Even so, the guard set her arms to a more comfortable position.

"Yeah it's true," said Henry. "And the lady's got the badge to prove it."

"If she is KGB," said Nicu, "then perhaps you are KGB?"

"I've been with the KGB for quite some time," said Henry, assuming the past few hours qualified. "Quite some time."

"You hear that, you scum?" Nicu bellowed to all the vampires from atop his perch. "You let these spies past all your security and I get a confession from them in under a minute. Major! Torture the details out of them, then execute them both."

"Wait a minute!" said Henry. "We're KGB! You can check her ID."

"I know you are KGB," said Nicu. "I want to know why the KGB is sending assassins into Rumania."

"A coup attempt, no doubt," Coman suggested.

Henry didn't have an answer, so instead he said, "We demand to see the Russian ambassador."

"Why?" Nicu demanded. "So they'll know we have you? Better you should disappear."

"They already know we're here," said Henry. "Check this lady's ID. It's pretty high-ranking. They keep tabs on her."

"Maybe we should consult President Ceausescu," a general in brown suggested.

"Yes, perhaps we should discuss it with your father," Oprea told Nicu. "He is so sensitive about these matters."

"He'll say the same thing," said Nicu.

"Why aren't they afraid?" Henry asked Anya in English.

"They are," Anya replied. "But vampires prey on each other. The weak obey the strong only so long as disobedience appears infeasible." Then Anya shouted in Rumanian, "Why not *show* them *your* ID?"

Henry hesitated. "My ID?"

"Yes. *Show* them your ID. Your very special ID."

"What is so special about his ID?" asked Nicu.

"*Show* it to them," said Anya.

At Nicu's nod, the guard behind Henry released his grip.

"Okay," said Henry. "I think your ID is more important, but okay." Uncertain, Henry reached into his pocket and produced his crumpled letter from Stanescu.

Anya groaned.

The Major grabbed the letter and handed it to Nicu.

"A letter from Ion," said Nicu.

"Yeah," Henry replied, then got an idea. "Yeah, Ion's part of our KGB network. See, it's not just us. We got KGB in every level of Rumanian government. KGB all the way up to the top. In this room, even. I see KGB everywhere I look."

Ministers, generals, guards, even the serving staff and band members, all exchanged nervous or suspicious glances. Nicu eyed everyone from atop the table. Everyone tried to avoid his eyes while appearing not to, lest they seem to have something to hide.

"Nobody leaves here tonight," said Nicu. "Not before full interrogation by DSS Third Directorate, Special Service Unit."

"What a sensitive idea!" Oprea exclaimed.

"A brilliant maneuver!" Andrei concurred.

All vampires agreed that it was indeed a sensitive and brilliant idea reflecting unparalleled genius.

"We begin on them!" Nicu pointed to the humans. "Their interrogations will be over quickly, as we can use torture."

Wondering how they'd come full circle so fast, Henry asked, "What about the KGB listening in on your microphones?"

"Microphones!" Andrei exclaimed. "What microphones?"

"Your microphones," Henry insisted. "The microphones your Securitate's got planted all over this nation. The ones you've been playing up to all night."

"You are mistaken," said Bobu. "Article 17 of the Constitution of the Socialist Republic of Rumania guarantees every citizen's right to privacy irrespective of their ethnic origin, race, sex, or even religion."

"Comrade President Nicolae Ceausescu himself guarantees it!" added Coman.

"Indeed!" said Andrei. "I have never 'played up' to microphones but have always expressed only my sincerest admiration for the esteemed Comrade Ceausescu and Comrade Elena."

"Good for you," said Henry. "But I say this room is crawling with mikes, and some of the people at the other end are KGB, and Chebrenkov's gonna be really pissed—"

"Chebrikov," corrected Anya, arms still pinned, albeit more comfortably.

Henry nodded. "Yeah, see why she's the boss? She's a real Russian, not Rumanian at all." Henry pointed to Nicu. "Big mistake, thinking you owned her. Lady knows Chebrikov in person. The KGB's main man. In fact, they're an item, if you know what I mean. And Chebrikov, he's gonna be pissed big time when he hears how you disrespected his lady. Dropping your pants, flashing your dick, badmouthing her. That's disrespect, man. You don't do that to somebody else's lady."

Nicu shouted to the microphones. "All DSS Unit T to remain at post until they are interrogated by DSS Fourth Directorate."

Every vampire marveled at Nicu's highly estimable command to the nonexistent microphones.

"Now. Finally." Nicu pointed to the humans. "We can begin their interrogations and torture."

"Why do we always come back to that?" asked Henry.

"*Show* them your ID," Anya insisted.

"My ID?"

"Your *weird* ID. The very *weird* ID. *Show* it to them."

"What is she talking about?" asked Nicu.

Anya glared at Henry. "*Show* them that very *weird* ID that I gave you in the tunnel to *show* to Securitate if confronted."

Henry gawked at her.

"The *weird* ID," said Anya. "The ID that you thought looked *weird*, but that I said you should *show*, because it was a good ID even if it looked *weird* to you."

"Show this to me!" yelled Nicu.

"Oh," said Henry. "Oh yeah. Forgot about it."

All vampire eyes were on Henry, scrutinizing his every move.

Henry reached into his pocket and withdrew the silver Russian Orthodox cross.

The shape of a cross must possess a special ability to bend or magnify light, for the cross blazed many time brighter than all the silver weaponry in the violin case. It shined with the blinding radiance of a thousand silver suns.

ELEVEN

Henry shut his eyes against the sudden silver glare, against radiance so bright it concealed rather than revealed. If he were dazzled, the vampires must be blinded.

Shouts, screams, gunfire.

Henry hunkered low at hearing the first bullets, cross still upheld. He squinted his eyes open. The cross worked as a lighthouse beacon, shining intensely in all directions yet casting its brightest beams wherever it faced.

Anya was burning Militia with the pistol flame thrower that she'd shown Henry in the tunnels. She'd had it all along. She also wore a pair of shades, dark and stylish.

Henry's ears exploded with gunfire.

"Stay low!" Anya shouted.

Henry turned to see a guard, eyes shut tight, blindly firing a machine gun over him. Flames roared past Henry and the guard erupted into a fireball.

Screaming fireballs lay thrashing throughout the room, former guards filling the air with black smoke and burnt carrion stench. Bureaucrats and generals cowered blindly beneath the table. Nicu lay prone on top, hands shielding his eyes as he barked orders at nonexistent Militia. Anya had flamed them all.

Anya seized her crossbow from the violin case, unfolding it with a flick of her wrist, snapped in a magazine of arrows. She tossed the crossbow's leather strap over her shoulder.

"Cover the doors," she told Henry.

Henry rose and aimed his cross at the entrance, keeping his eyes averted. Like welding without goggles. Be nice if Anya carried an extra pair of shades.

Anya had her pistol in Nicu's face when the First Secretary of the Union for Communist Youth peeked through his fingers. She cradled her crossbow in her other arm.

"Where is your father now?" Anya demanded.

Nicu only stared at her, unable to comprehend obedience from his end.

"You or your father," said Anya. "Who shall die?"

Machine gun bullets shattered a wall.

"Down!" Anya screamed.

Henry ducked.

Anya fired her crossbow at the entrance, piercing a guard's arm so he swung his machine gun in wide arcs, firing randomly. A second guard leaned in, shooting blindly at the glare, aiming for the cross, which Henry held toward the table.

"Watch your fire, you idiots," shouted a vampire from under the table.

Anya shot again, impaling the first guard's skull, throwing him to the floor, grappling with the arrows in his head and arm. Another arrow grazed the second guard's cheek, sent him shrieking, clutching his smoking face. All along Anya kept her pistol aimed at Nicu. Two more machine guns edged past the doorway, blindly spraying the room with gunfire.

"Do not shoot!" Nicu finally managed to scream.

The gunfire ceased.

"Withdraw or the Minister dies!" Anya shouted.

"Get out you idiots!" Nicu shouted.

The gun barrels withdrew from the room. The first guard remained on the floor, clawing at the arrow in his head.

"Your father!" Anya demanded.

"I am a very important government official," said Nicu. "I can grant you immunity. Otherwise, you will beg for death—"

Anya stepped back and fired a quick burst, spewing blue and orange flames over Nicu, searing his hands, singeing his hair.

Nicu cried hysterically, "I don't know! How should I know?"

Anya leaned into him, but spoke without whispering. "Be reasonable. I only wish to kill the President. And Comrade Elena. Then you will be boss."

"I don't know where he is!"

"Then I must kill you instead." Anya pressed the gun barrel against Nicu's chubby neck. Its silver burnt his flesh, the sizzling mingling with his screams.

A waiter rushed from the kitchen, pistol firing.

Anya shot her crossbow. The waiter collapsed, blood already erupting from his pierced heart.

Anya pressed her gun down upon Nicu's hands. Nicu screamed.

"No shooting!" Anya ordered.

"Do not shoot, do not shoot, do not shoot!" Nicu screamed.

Anya turned to Henry. "I told you serving staff was Securitate. The band too. Watch everyone."

Henry swung the cross in an arc, its blazing beacon covering entrance, table, gypsy band, kitchen, then back to entrance. The cross warmed his hand. He could well imagine it burning vampire flesh.

"You wanted an interrogation," said Anya to Nicu. "And torture."

"I can pay you!" shouted Nicu. "Not *lei*. Hard currency. Whatever you like. Swiss franc, pound, dollar. Gold. I give you gold." He fumbled with his Rolex.

Anya pressed her gun upon his hands.

"He's at home!" Nicu screamed. "My old man's at home!"

"Bucharest residence?"

"Yes. Yes, of course."

"I do not believe you." Anya pressed her gun briefly against his neck, drawing screams. "You would not betray him so quickly. But now that I know where he is *not*, I know exactly where he is."

Anya extracted what looked like a fishing reel from her violin case, snapping it under her crossbow. She replaced the magazine of silver-tipped wooden arrows with one steel grappling arrow, hooking it to the reel's cord. She shut the violin case and turned to Henry.

"My case," she said.

Cross held high, Henry lifted the case and followed Anya to the windows overlooking the Boulevard.

Anya stepped onto the window ledge. She turned to face all the vampires, wounded or dying or cowering under the table. "I can shoot the esteemed Comrade Nicu as easy as a grease naked turkey from here. Do not follow or he is dead."

"Do as she says!" Nicu screamed, hands covering his face.

Anya shattered several glass panes with her crossbow, kicking aside their frames with her boot. Arctic wind gust into the room, billowing the red draperies.

"Out," Anya ordered Henry.

Henry stepped onto the window ledge, gingerly easing himself through the broken windows. Outside, upon the narrow outer ledge overlooking The Boulevard of the Victory Of Socialism, he gazed down at what seemed a long drop. The Boulevard was not directly below. The Presidential Palace was a layered building. Directly below was the roof of another portion of the building, some seven or eight stories down.

Anya came to stand beside him, her cape flapping and billowing against him. Henry inched farther down the ledge, icy wind cutting through his jacket.

"Can I put this cross away?" Henry shouted over the wind.

"Yes, you will need a free hand."

Henry pocketed the cross and the deep drop disappeared from view, becoming a bottomless black hole. Then his eyes adapted to the Boulevard's cold white light.

By now Anya had removed her shades and unhooked her crossbow strap. "Slide the handle through here."

Henry slid the violin case's handle through the strap. When Anya rehooked it, the case hung from it. She turned her back to the drop, facing the broken window. The room inside appeared dim without the cross.

"One arm over my shoulder," Anya said, "the other around my waist. Clasp your hands. Do not let go."

"Why am I doing this?" Henry asked, wrapping his arms around her, gripping his wrists.

"Behind me. Feet along the edge."

Henry was teetering on the ledge.

"When I jump, you jump." Anya raised her crossbow. "Tighter, unless you wish to die."

Henry tightened his grip, feeling her bodily contours underneath her heavy layers. She felt small and fragile. "Maybe I should carry you? You hold me. I think that'd work better. I don't know what you're planning, but I think—"

"Shut up. Hold tight. Jump at my command." Anya aimed her crossbow into the room, at the wood paneling. Nicu no longer lay on the table. "I shall count three."

Henry tightened his grip.

"One, two—"

Militia tore into the room, machine guns blazing, shattering windows beside Henry. Anya fired, steel arrow puncturing a guard and striking the wall.

"Jump!" she shouted, shoving herself against Henry and over the ledge, plummeting past windows, frigid wind screeching, crossbow reel unwinding, slowing their descent ...

The cord broke.

They plunged the remaining stories, striking concrete, mind splitting pain, Anya upon him, pain shooting stars into darkness, glass shattering overheard ...

Anya shouting, grabbing Henry's hair, his ear, dragging him, pulling him to his feet, running ...

An explosion ripped the night.

Anya yanked him to a stop. They stood together on the roof, coldly lit by moonlight and Boulevard lamps. She pointed.

The guard she had shot lay sprawled where they had originally landed. His body had impeded the grappling arrow, slowing it, rendering it unable to properly embed itself into the wood paneling. The arrow had loosened from the wall, yanking the guard out the window with it.

Henry gazed upward. Silhouettes gazed back down at him from the topmost windows.

Anya rolled the guard over with her boot. He groaned, still alive. Bracing her foot against his chest, she yanked and pulled the arrow through his torso, finally freeing it in an eruption of dark pulpy flesh. She stepped away from the moaning guard and fired her pistol. He exploded into an orange fireball.

Anya curtsied to the above partygoers, then hurried to the roof's edge, already resetting her arrow. Henry saw they were still four or five stories above ground. Soldiers and Militia milled about below.

"They don't seem to have called down," said Henry.

"Even as we speak," Anya replied. "Seeing that the fall did not kill us."

Anya skirted the roof's edge, away from the Palace entrance, until the roof ended, facing a Palace wing. They continued along the narrow ledge bordering the wing, which now hid them from the partygoers. Henry wondered why they didn't break into one of the darkened windows behind them, but instead Anya walked the ledge until they came to a small roof. They looked down.

Mounting commotion over by the entrance from whence they had come, soldiers and Militia agitated, fanning out. Some hurrying in their direction, doubtless tipped off by the partygoers.

No one directly below. Not yet.

Anya turned her back to the drop, aiming her crossbow into a darkened window. "Grip me," she said.

Henry embraced her as before.

She fired her crossbow, shattering window, piercing drapes, striking something solid. She pulled the reel and found the cord taut. She counted. They jumped.

Plummeting, wind whistling, reel unwinding without incident. Henry struck pavement, Anya against him. Neither tumbling.

Anya detached the cord, left it dangling against the Palace, marking their trail. She handed the violin case to Henry. Then they ran.

A block away they entered a parking lot that looked more like a Dacia dealership. Everywhere, color segregated Dacias. The darker the Dacia, the more privileged its spot. White Dacias sat farthest back, despite many empty spaces nearer the Palace. Pastels in the middle. Black Dacias nearest the Palace, except for a few black Mercedes. And one black Audi.

Anya went straight for the Audi.

Henry assumed she'd know how to break in and she did. By the time he was in the passenger seat with the violin case she had already hot-wired the car.

Anya tore through the lot, spinning the Audi in suicidal loops, screeching past the exit several times. A soldier watched from the guardhouse, cradling a machine gun. Henry struggled to fasten his seat belt. Anya spun dangerously, then sped for the exit, which was blocked by a candy cane striped gate and steel road teeth. Henry watched the soldier watch their approach. Anya blared her horn and increased speed.

The soldier withdrew into the guardhouse, the gate rose, the teeth retracted.

Anya sped past the guardhouse onto the Boulevard, zigzagging down broad empty lanes, hogging two at a time, driving upon sidewalks while blaring her horn at nonexistent pedestrians. Then she careened into a side street and out of the soldier's view.

Anya stop zigzagging but increased speed.

"Maybe you should slow down?" Henry suggested.

"I am driving an Audi," said Anya. "We should not waste the opportunity."

"Nothing special about an Audi."

"Yes. It is a very special car."

Anya raised her cape's collar, now clearly exposing its silver clasp. Having imbibed stiff vampire blood at the party, Henry saw her clasp gleaming starker and brighter than ever, emblazoned with what he assumed was the Amasovich family coat of arms.

"You're not a vampire?" asked Henry.

"No. I am not a vampire."

"Not KGB?"
"No. I am not KGB."
"You're really CIA?"
"Yes. I am really CIA."
Henry sighed. "I thought so."
Anya glanced at him, smirking. "Did you?"
"I ninety percent thought so."
"And now?"
Henry shook his head. "You must be CIA. You were wrong about Ceausescu."
"How so?"
"You said he'd be at the Palace tonight."
"Ceausescu was at the Palace tonight. Nicu Ceausescu."
"Big mixup."
"Yes. It is a big mixup." Anya careened around a corner.
Henry grabbed the car door with one hand, clutching the violin case with the other. "You really should slow down."
"No. I should speed up. Before they find this car stolen."
"Slow down before they pull you over."
"They will not pull us over." Anya increased speed. Apartment blocks became a gray blur. "You mentioned two maps."
"Did I? Slow down."
"A map of Bucharest. A map of Rumania. You saw subways in Bucharest."
Henry braced himself as the Audi careened, its tires bouncing upon the sidewalk. "No subways in Bucharest."
"I know that. What did you see in Rumania? In red?"
"Different stuff. Barbed wire. Missiles. Test tubes."
"I could almost love you!" Anya laughed. "For your mind."
"Yeah, me too. I mean, I love your mind."
She grinned. "Not my mind, I think. But I love what is in your mind."
"Why? What did I see? Slow down."
"Prison labor camps. Military bases. Chemical weapons test

laboratories. All secret. Did you see a red star over crossed rifles? Think carefully."

Henry watched the gray blur outside. "Hard to concentrate on a map when we might crash any moment."

"Crossed rifles denote MI Troops. Ministry of Interior's elite military unit that is also Ceausescu's personal bodyguard. Also called Securitate Troops. The main body is always stationed near Ceausescu. If we know their current location, we can approximate Ceausescu's location."

Henry tried to recall the map, but only envisioned a complicated red mess. "It was covered in insignias. Hard to remember the details. How much military does this guy have?"

"There is the regular army. Then there are his MI Troops, which supplement the DSS Fifth Directorate Presidential Protection Group and plainclothes DSS. The Militia has its FOI military unit, that is, Forces for Internal Order. There are the 'anti-terrorist' USLA Troops. Perhaps you saw USLA at Otopeni? Also Patriotic Guards, which is a part-time 'worker's militia' composed of loyal factory hands, roughly analogous to a national guard and reserve."

Henry gripped the car as it careened though a narrow street. "Be easier on me with only one insignia to remember."

"Ceausescu is very paranoid. I told you he rotates his ministers to prevent them from establishing independent power bases? He also subdivides all authority beneath him as much as possible, much like Hitler and Stalin, so that no one vampire can command a large enough department to overthrow him. He especially does not trust his army. Army officers are forbidden to carry firearms near him."

"But he trusts Securitate?"

"No, but he must trust someone. MI Troops get better equipment and richer blood." Anya smiled at him. "Vampires respond to incentive however much their Marxist faith decries such Western superstition. Ceausescu knows a well fed vampire is a reliable vampire. Which is why you must concentrate and locate the MI Troops on the map. They will lead us to Ceausescu."

"I'd concentrate, but I think we're about to be stopped."

"Why do you say that?"

"Militia up ahead."

"Routine checkpoint. They will not bother us."

They were speeding toward a candy cane stripped gate, guards milling about. Henry waited for Anya to slow but she only blared her horn. Henry waited for the guards to aim their guns but they only ran aside. The gate rose.

Anya ignored the open gate, swerving, striking a guard, tossing him into the windshield, bouncing across the car roof, rolling down the trunk and into the street.

Anya sped from the accident scene.

Henry stared out the rear window, waiting for the Militia to give chase.

TWELVE

Henry watched the Militia checkpoint recede into the night. Then Anya turned a corner and it was gone.

Henry waited for headlights, but behind them was only darkness. Of course, vampires drove without headlights as they could see in the dark. Then again, so could Henry. And yet he saw no pursuing black Dacias against the black of night.

"They don't seem to be following us," said Henry.

"No, they are not following. We did nothing wrong."

"Maybe you killed him."

"I hope so."

"They won't ignore that." Henry turned to face a spiderweb of cracks, their windshield shuddering against wind as Anya sped at 130 kmph.

"Yes, they will ignore it," she said. "Only one Audi in all Rumania. We shall be accorded complete deference."

Understanding dawned on Henry. "Nicu's car?"

"We can drive into anything or anybody," said Anya. "No one shall stop us."

"No tickets?"

"No tickets. Not for us."

"They can't see it's us?"

"Tinted glass."

Henry realized the entire Audi was black. Outside, inside, glass and all. "Vampires can't see through tinting?"

"Not most, I think."

"Well as long as you're sure," Henry groaned. "I think you killed that guy."

"Yes. I had to hit and run. It is suspicious not to drive Nicu's car as Nicu does." Anya smiled. "And yes, I enjoy it."

Drab apartment blocks gave way to older houses. But unlike the building facades along the moonscape, these houses were well maintained. Bourgeois vestiges of a more genteel past.

"He's had other accidents?" asked Henry.

"He has driven into people, accident or not. When at fourteen he first raped a girl, he was not punished. He was praised for attaining manhood."

"So. His folks spoiled him."

Anya smirked. "And his bodyguards, who were his childhood playmates. Nicu is groomed to succeed his parents. Toward this end, Ceausescu assigned his upbringing to Cornel Pacoste, now Deputy Prime Minister. And to your Stefan Andrei."

"He's not *my* Stefan Andrei."

"He thought you most highly esteemed," Anya smiled, teasing. "Nicu is no different at thirty-five. Expect no good from a vampire. Not even gratitude or loyalty to their own kind."

"That why you expected him to squeal on his dad?"

"I expect nothing. I was feeding disinformation. Let him think I was leaving Bucharest." She smiled again. "And yes, I enjoy interrogating him."

They were passing stately manors protected by stone walls and guardhouses. Henry watched greatcoated guards whizzing by, waiting for one to point and sound the alarm. "They must know this car is stolen by now."

"At the Palace, yes. They know."

"Word travels fast."

"Then we must travel faster." Anya increased speed to 140 kmph. "Ceausescu has 44 residences. A Bucharest mansion. A former royal palace. Guest residences in each of Rumania's 39 districts. Dachas at Snagov Lake, in Neptun by the Black Sea, and in Predeal in the Carpathian Mountains. Also his Presidential suites in Rumanian embassies, but I am ruling those out." Anya slowed as she guided the Audi along curving cobblestoned streets. "Ceausescu makes many foreign state visits, hoping Rumanians will be so impressed with his international prestige they will not mind to freeze and starve. His dream is to win the Nobel Peace Prize. Yet he is now in Rumania, otherwise *Scinteia* would be full of tedious praise concerning his latest foreign affairs 'victories.'"

"*Scinteia*'s the local rag?"

Anya grinned. "A daily. Its front page always reports what Ceausescu did the day before. The rest is mainly articles praising Ceausescu's leadership in every facet of Rumanian life."

Henry touched the windshield and felt frigid air seeping through its fissures. Just as long as it held. "If *Scinteia* covers him that well, it should report what city he's in."

"*Scinteia* lies."

"About what city—?"

"I told you, Ceausescu is very paranoid."

Henry fell against the door as Anya made another sharp turn. He was becoming carsick. Between her driving, and all the rancid blood and alcohol he'd drunk, and all the petrochemical air he'd breathed, he would have vomited right then if only his stomach had something solid to offer . . .

"You don't feel like going home?" he asked tentatively. He vaguely remembered her promising to spirit him out of Rumania. Or at least she implied it. "Say we forget Ceausescu and return to the US?"

"I thought you wished to join CIA?"

"Well yeah, but we did our job. Made a damn good effort to terminate the target with extreme prejudice. It was the boys at Langley who screwed up. Gave us bad info. Target wasn't at the Palace. Not our fault." Henry's head was throbbing, worse than before. No longer excited, no longer pumped, nothing mitigated his fears except nausea. Good thing he felt so sick. "CIA can't expect you to continue alone."

Anya smiled at him. "I am not alone."

"Well no, of course not."

"Then I can count on you?"

"Sure. Absolutely." How could he say otherwise? The lady looked like a fashion model, was gutsy as hell, and had saved his life several times tonight. Always after first endangering it, but that was her job, and a noble job at that. "Still, we could use a breather," Henry continued. "Don't you have a safe house? A place to lie low, contact your bosses, get some accurate info on Ceausescu's whereabouts?"

"Accurate operational data? From the boys at Langley?"

Henry sighed. "Good point. But we need food and sleep."

"No time. The Palace knows this car is stolen. You said so yourself. By the time we have rested, the district Militia will have been informed. We must hit Ceausescu tonight."

Henry's stomach knotted and swooned, nerves trembling, fear overwhelming his nausea. They were gonna do it again, engage and attack the enemy, and soon, very soon. He tried to get pumped up about it, but felt only queasy and afraid.

"Great, let's do it," he barely croaked. "Only, we don't know where Ceausescu is."

"If not in Bucharest, we proceed to Predeal. He often winters there, hunting in the Carpathians."

Anya careened past another sharp turn.

Grabbing the dashboard, Henry noticed a button. Could it be? He pressed it and the heater blasted hot air. Finally!

Anya parked by a curb and shut the engine. The heater went silent.

"Now I am not speeding," she said, "so you have no excuse. I want you to concentrate on the map of Rumania and locate the red MI Troop insignias."

Henry pressed his hands against the vents. "I just turned that on!"

"You should not have waited." Anya gripped his shoulder so he faced her. "You must locate the MI Troops. Several of Ceausescu's district residences provide winter hunting lodges, but Predeal is his favorite. The main body of Troops are stationed in the Carpathians whenever Ceausescu is in Predeal or Sinaia. In Baneasa when Ceausescu is in Bucharest or Snagov."

Sighing, Henry shut his eyes, straining to visualize the map he'd seen at the hotel. Maybe it was hunger, maybe nausea, maybe fear, but he saw only a red, white, and black jumble. "It's no good. Map isn't clear. Even if it was, I don't read Rumanian."

"Of course you do. The blood gave you that knowledge."

"I don't know. Maybe. My head hurts."

"Open you eyes." Anya withdrew a map of Rumania from her greatcoat. "Visualize the map you saw, then compare it to this one. Point to the location of the MI Troop insignias."

Concentrating, eyes half shut, Henry gazed at the map in her hands, his mouth tasting memories of Nicu's bloody Scotch, strong and bitter, red subway lines filling his mind, Bucharest map . . .

He didn't want the Bucharest map.

He continued concentrating, Anya breathing patiently, careful not to disturb or rush him. Bucharest dissolved into Rumania, red lines into glittering red stars. Red stars atop barbed wire, test tubes, gas masks, atoms, tanks. The secret machinery of an evil empire. Including Securitate Troops.

Henry pointed.

Anya nodded. "Baneasa. As I suspected. Ceausescu is in Bucharest. We strike tonight."

"Or Snagov. You said Bucharest or Snagov."

"No, Snagov is a summer resort. Its lake freezes in February. Ceausescu is at home in Bucharest."

"Unless they moved him to a safe house."

"Immediately after our attack?"

Henry nodded.

Anya smiled. "Very good, Henry. But I already considered that possibility. I told Nicu I had a specific target in mind, other than the Bucharest residence. Now there is nowhere Ceausescu would feel safer."

"Assuming he bought your story."

Anya pocked the map. "His very paranoia circumscribes his moves. Whenever he travels abroad, air conditioning ducts must be sealed against poison gas. Radiation detectors installed in every room. His clothing, bedsheets, and food, all brought from Rumania, sealed and guarded. He does not eat at dignitary functions, but rather drops his food under the table and kicks it away. What a pig. Trust me Henry, Ceausescu will not easily depart the reliable security of his residence. If he was there an hour ago, he is there now."

"If he's so paranoid, what makes you think he bought the line you fed Nicu?"

"Certainly he has doubts. But stay or flee, either move jeopardizes his miserable skin. I admit, when I saw I had tracked the wrong Ceausescu to the Palace, I worried the father was in Predeal. But you, Henry, confirmed my first suspicion. He is in Bucharest. And he will not bolt for Predeal while his Troops are in Baneasa. Ceausescu is in Bucharest, in his home on Primaverri Street." Anya pointed. "Around that corner."

THIRTEEN

They left the Audi parked by the curb, in a street otherwise devoid of cars. Around the corner a high brick and concrete wall lined Primaverri Street, baroque street lamps casting prison gray shadows. Anya stood motionless before the wall, eying its top.

Henry wondered what she found so interesting. Did she hear things on the other side? He alternated the violin case between his frigid hands, its silver clasps reflecting moonlight.

"They'll spot the car," he finally whispered.

"Shhhh. We will be in and out long before then."

Henry sighed. Famous last words.

Despite winter, a nearby tree bloomed with blighted leaves and tiny limes. Upon inspection, Henry saw the limes were genuine rather than painted imitations. But when he picked one, he found it rock solid. Frozen dead. Inedible.

"Henry," Anya snapped. "No time to smell the flowers."

Henry pocketed the lime. "I haven't eaten—"

"Come give me a boost."

"What about guards on the other side?"

"Less likely than at the front gate."

Henry didn't think that very encouraging. Sighing, he took her foot and lifted, his fingers numb and stiff.

Anya wobbled in his grip, stepped on his shoulder, tottering. "You have no black bag experience, I see." She gripped the wall and heaved herself up.

"I'm not wearing gloves."

Anya gazed down on him. "Yes, you are poorly dressed for Rumanian winter. You dress like . . . " She sighed, unable to characterize his safari outfit.

"Like a Hollywood film producer."

She laughed. "Your Stefan Andrei said you were a director."

Henry passed up her violin case. "He's not my Andrei. And I'm neither."

"In any event, your hands must be freezing. We will correct that at first opportunity." Anya removed a cord from her violin case and wound it around herself. She dropped its end to Henry, then lay down and gripped the wall. "Climb."

Henry recalled her soft body beneath all those gray layers. "I'll pull you off."

"You prefer to wait here? I can return when finished."

"You know I don't—"

"Then quickly!"

Henry gripped the cord and climbed, tugging Anya nearer the edge. Yet her grip held even as Henry's white Reeboks fought for traction against the wall. He soon lay atop her, then edged off, whispering, "Sorry, don't mean to get fresh . . ."

She sat up without comment.

He sat up and looked down.

Ceausescu's backyard stretched before him, a Versailles-like garden extending several acres. Cadaverous white lights illuminated marble statues and artesian fountains. Trees loomed over sculpted shrubbery and exotic flowers. Soft pink lights tucked beneath rose bushes outlined curving paths.

The garden was devoid of vampires. No guards, no Ceausescu.

Anya jumped in, immediately opening her violin case. Henry dropped beside her.

Anya slung on her crossbow. "You still possess the cross?"

"Sure."

"You know how to use it."

It wasn't a question. Henry made no reply.

Crossbow poised, Anya darted into the garden, glancing back only once to ascertain that Henry was carrying her case. He had taken it without being asked, his other hand pocketed, gripping the cross. Away from light, it had cooled considerably.

Anya avoided the glowing pink paths, running instead beneath heavy trees and around bushes and through flower beds. The night shimmered in shades of black, leaves and stems distinctly visible thanks to all the blood-spiked rotgut Henry had drunk in the past several hours; on the TAROM flight, at the café, at Nicu's party. Shadows bounded beside them, just beyond his periphery of vision. Any moment, Henry expected to see MI Troops drop from trees or leap from bushes. But the shadows only dissolved into the night.

They crossed the garden without incident, reaching the rear of a brightly lit mansion. Warm yellow light flooded through its sliding glass doors, exposing white stucco walls and oaken balconies. Anya halted in the shadows, just beyond the stone patio.

"We lucked out," Henry whispered. "No goons in the garden."

"They were there."

"Where? Behind us?" He looked back, saw only subtle shifting shadows amidst the shrubbery.

"Around us. I sensed them."

"I didn't. I don't think I did."

"I have been drinking blood for many years now. Many years. I sensed them."

"Really?" Henry glanced at her teeth. No fangs. Not right now. "Surprising they didn't sense us."

"Yes. It is puzzling."

"You think they did?"

"I wonder." Anya sighed. "What do you suggest?"

"You asking me?"

"Your advice," she smiled. "Which I may not accept."

Henry saw no vampires past the sliding doors, left curiously ajar. A bit too convenient. As in a trap. Surely she realized it too, especially after drinking blood for . . . how many years?

"I see three options," Anya continued. "Advance, retreat, or wait."

Henry sighed. "If this is a trap, the jaws lie ahead."

"Most likely. You counsel retreat?"

"Well if you sensed right, we got bloodsuckers behind us."

"Do we wait?"

Henry watched his breath in the cold air. If this were a trap, they were already surrounded. At least indoors the light would empower his cross. Gripping it now comforted and emboldened him, its feeble warmth reminding him of its blinding potential. And if a silver gun scorched vampire flesh by mere touch, imagine the kindling power of a silver cross . . .

"Waiting changes nothing," said Henry. "If we're in a trap, we're screwed as of now. Sooner or later, we gotta fight our way out. Waiting will only weaken us."

"My thinking exactly," Anya smiled. "Though I hoped you may conceive a fourth alternative."

"Nope. You covered every base. Sorry."

She nodded. "You know what Ceausescu looks like?"

"I've seen his picture."

"If you forget, you will find him in your blood memory."

Henry grimaced. "How can I forget that?"

"I hope you never will," Anya grinned. Then she took his shoulder and looked him in the eye. "This is important. If I die before I destroy him, you must promise to finish the job."

"Sure . . ."

"You promise?"

"Yeah. Absolutely." Feeling suddenly queasy, Henry tried to steel himself, clenching the cross tighter. Anya had always sounded confident, even hubristic. He now realized how comforting that had been. If she was certain of success, then it must be so. If not . . . "It's a promise," Henry added. "But don't worry. You won't die."

Anya squeezed his shoulder, her eyes conveying a grim idealism, at once both young and world-weary. "Tens of millions have died resisting vampires this century. Better dead than undead."

"Sure. I agree. But you promised to get me out of this hellhole. So you can't die."

"I never . . . " She paused briefly, then smiled. "Yes, I will try to keep my promise."

"Okay. Me too."

Letting him go, she poised her crossbow. "Stay close and watch my back."

"Yeah. Good luck."

"And you."

They rushed past the sliding doors into a spacious living room adorned with Persian rugs and Ming vases and immense oil portraits of the Ceausescus. Anya scanned the room, spinning and darting, refusing to be a motionless target for any hidden snipers. Henry wondered if he should withdraw his cross, thereby blinding any such snipers. He wanted to ask, but suspected Anya preferred to maintain silence.

They hurried through wide hallways, Anya swinging her crossbow in SWAT team fashion, expecting attacks from every doorway.

Angry voices bellowed from just around the corner. A heated argument, intensifying, getting ugly. Anya edged along the wall, creeping toward the unseen vampires. She spun the corner, Henry behind her.

They saw no one. Just an empty corridor plushly carpeted in red. Shouting emanated from a room at corridor's end, its padded double doors wide open.

They rushed in, Henry withdrawing the cross, saturating the room in light, squinting against its radiance.

Telly Savalas continued arguing with his supervisor, however washed out his image.

They had raided a screening room.

Anya dashed down the aisle scanning empty rows. Finding no one, she shouted to Henry, "Put it away!"

Henry pocketed the cross. His vision readjusting, he saw a spacious theater upholstered in light gray velvet. Despite the *Kojak* episode playing on the movie screen, the lights were on.

"Warn me before using it," Anya shouted from the front row. "Unless an emergency."

"Sorry," Henry whispered, then realized she couldn't hear him over Kojak's pontificating. He hurried down to meet her.

The front row comprised only two easy chairs, wide and deep, behind two low tables. One table held an opened bottle of what looked like yellow sunflower oil, a glass of the same oil, and a plateful of tomatoes, onions, and feta cheese. Blood tinted the oil and outlined the fang marks in the cheese. The other table held a bottle and glass of pink bubbly.

Anya examined the bottle of oil, calmly inspecting its label and scent. She jiggled it. Dark ruby streaks swirled within its viscous liquid. She hurled the bottle, shattering it against the wall, darkly staining its gray velvet.

Cringing against the noise, Henry scanned the empty theater.

Anya picked up a bit of bloody cheese with a napkin and inspected its fang marks. "He was here. But no longer."

Henry pointed to an easy chair. "His?"

Anya nodded. "The peasant still eats with his hands. What a pig."

Henry was tempted to sit in the chair, but lacked the nerve. He instead examined the bloody meal. Hungry as he was, he wasn't that hungry.

"The guy drinks cooking oil?" he asked.

"Odobesti Yellow, a sweet Moldavian wine produced especially for him."

Henry nodded. "So where is everybody?"

Anya picked up the bottle of bubbly. "Cordon Rouge. Elena was here also." She hurled the bottle against the cinema screen, drenching a black pimp in bloody pink.

Kojak was just asking him, "What's the word on the street?"

"Show's not over," said Henry.

Anya nodded. "Yes. They left in a hurry. And recently."

They exited the screening room, running through deserted hallways, dashing up thickly carpeted stairs. On the second floor they entered a private study, its heavy mahogany furniture inlaid with ivory, bookshelves laden with volumes of Marx and Lenin bound in blue leather, Ceausescu's tomes in red leather.

Behind a large desk, framed by red drapes, French doors led to a balcony. Anya mounted a platform behind the desk to check under it. Seeing Henry's perplexed gaze, Anya explained, "Ceausescu is only five five."

Henry nodded at the platform. "Does he also wear elevator shoes?"

Anya laughed. "Napoleon and Stefan the Great are his idols. His role models. Stalin was five four, Napoleon five two, Stefan under five foot. So beside them, Ceausescu is a giant. He likes to remind everyone of that."

"Think it's safe to talk in here?"

"Nowhere inside the socialist bloc." Anya was ransacking Ceausescu's desk, sifting through papers. "But we are alone. And no microphones record Ceausescu."

"So where do we go now? You said maybe Predeal?"

"Shut up!"

Henry shuddered under her fury.

Glaring at him, Anya rolled a wade of documents into a tube and slipped them under her cape. "I *assume* no microphones," she hissed, her words barely audible.

She strode wordlessly past him, her face an icy mask of contempt. Henry followed her downstairs, eager to make amends. She was right, he should know better by now.

Anya halted at the bottom of the stairs, suddenly still, uncertain, breathing silently. Raising her crossbow, she finally crept forward, toward the living room.

Henry clutched his pocketed cross. He was supposed to warn her before using it, unless an emergency, presumably so she could apply her shades. But she wanted silence. Great. Now he'd have to decide if whatever happened next, if anything, qualified as an emergency. An attack on an empty theater apparently did not.

They paused at the living room threshold. All was calm. No vampires in sight. Henry strained to see past the sliding doors, saw only empty night, heard only the rustle of leaves. He waited for long moments, Anya motionless beside him, the violin case becoming heavy in his hand. All seemed well.

An icy breeze blew past the open sliding doors, ruffling the red drapes, carrying a faint scent of sour blood.

Anya nudged him and began a slow retreat down the hall, soon scurrying, then running from the rancid vampire stench blowing in from the garden.

Sound of bootsteps rushing across patio stone, door sliding, bootsteps thundering across thick carpeting . . .

Anya was halfway up the stairs when she turned to aim, Henry struggling with the violin case behind her.

Brown uniforms dashed into view, two dozen MI Troops padded in riot gear, helmets, shields.

Anya shot a rapid succession of silver, striking sparks upon the Troops' armor or grazing their faceplates, all to no serious effect. The Troops formed a phalanx, creating a wall of shields, helmets peering over the edges. One arrow penetrated a heavily padded shoulder, another pierced a calf. But these flesh wounds emitted only thin whiffs of smoke, the arrows easily pulled free. Some troopers raised machine guns, yet none fired.

Squatting behind Anya, Henry shouted, "Now?"

"What?!" she screamed, lowering her crossbow and drawing her pistol flame thrower as the phalanx advanced.

"The cross?"

Anya flamed the Troops, roaring streams of fire singeing the carpet, melting oil portraits. Yet the Troops appeared impregnable behind their shields and faceplates, however discomforted. Inching inexorably forward, several fired aluminum gas canisters, their casings spewing thick pink clouds.

One canister landed on the stairs. Hoping it was only tear gas, not poison, Henry flung it back. He shook Anya's shoulder and shouted, "I'm using it!"

Anya nodded even as he withdrew the cross, setting the hall ablaze in white radiance.

And still the Troops advanced, wading through rising pink

clouds, clouds lit by Henry's cross, clouds gusting aside from Anya's roaring furnace blasts. From the stairs, Henry had the eerie sense of floating over a desecrated Heaven. Looked like Heaven, except the clouds were glowing pink and spitting hellfire.

The troopers' faceplates had blackened, polarized against whatever light frequencies the cross radiated. MI riot armor protected them from fire and silver. Their ordnance had neutralized Anya's entire arsenal. Black tubes attached to their faceplates indicated they were also safe from tear gas.

Anya shoved Henry upstairs, tears streaming from under her shades, both of them coughing as they retreated to the second floor, escaping to Ceausescu's study. Anya locked the door.

"That won't hold them," Henry coughed.

Anya ran to the French doors. "Stay down. They may or may not be in full gear outside."

She flung open the doors. They ran onto the balcony, Henry's cross turning night into day. They peered past a wooden beam railing and saw a circular driveway exiting toward a gate. Black Mercedes and Cadillacs were parked nearby, Dacias in the distance.

No vampires in sight. Nor any time to make certain.

Anya climbed the railing, clambering halfway over...

A dark form swooshed up from below, snatching Anya, carrying her into open air, rising with her, black wings spreading out from behind the MI Trooper...

Henry leapt and grabbed Anya, the trooper lurching from the added weight. Anya clawed at the trooper's neck and faceplate, Henry clung to Anya, violin case abandoned on the balcony...

They rose higher, icy gusts tossing them about as they spiraled up over the courtyard. Henry saw the mansion grow smaller, dark helmeted bugs pour onto the balcony and out the front door, pointing at the trooper weaving overhead, Anya clawing at his thickly padded turtleneck, his leathery wings flapping desperately, yet Anya's gloves preventing her nails from drawing blood...

Henry slipped and grabbed Anya's crossbow strap, yanking

her body with his sudden drop, all three beings lurching in the wind, Anya's cape flapping about Henry, who clung to the strap and nothing else, one hand on the strap, one hand on the cross . . .

Henry saw other MI Troops spread wings and rise from the balcony, swoop in close, pawing and grabbing. He swung his cross in silver arcs, flashing moonlight, striking thickly gloved hands to no apparent effect. They might have seized him with ease, yet the trooper clutching Anya was spinning and reeling in the wind, his frenzied flight hindering his comrades' attempts to snatch Henry . . .

Henry hammered his cross against the trooper's faceplate but it proved shatterproof, the faceplate attached to a thick rubber gas mask tightly sealed upon his face . . .

Henry raked the cross against the trooper's neck, trying to shred and peel away the padding. Anya must have seen and realized what Henry was attempting because she clawed away the reinforced turtleneck, stripping away a piece, took the cross and shoved its silver against the trooper's exposed red skin . . .

Face behind the faceplate exploding in a burst of fire . . .

A conflagration blasting and vaporizing the faceplate, liquefying its rubber mask . . .

The entire armored uniform disintegrating under internal combustion, another Hindenburg transformed in an instant from flight to fireball . . .

Anya bore the brunt of the blast . . .

Henry was stunned, dazed, unaware they were falling, unaware until he hit the branches, crashing through twigs, breaking limbs, smashing against boughs, finally striking the cold packed earth . . .

The last thing he felt was Anya's limp body upon him.

FOURTEEN

Henry awoke to heavy crunching bootsteps, confused shouting, his body aching in a dozen spots, rough hands grab his shoulders, drag him along the ground. A painfully bright but familiar white radiance lit the trees overhead. Turning aside, he saw dark silhouettes moving through the light. The hands yanked him upright, some gripping him while others frisked his pockets, searched under his jacket, pawed his legs and crotch.

An MI Trooper was shouting at him, rubber tube detached, gas mask off, faceplate lifted just high enough for Henry to see yellow fangs and dark purple lips, red mouth spewing a putrid stench of diseased blood and sour bile into Henry's face.

Turning aside from the vampire, Henry saw his cross lying in the distance encircled by bulky forms in radiation suits. Two of them grasped the cross between pincers and transferred it into a thick metallic or lead box. When they shut the box day returned to night, a complete blackout descending upon the garden.

As Henry's eyes slowly readjusted to the sudden dark, he saw troops detaching gas masks and raising faceplates, if just a bit. Seemed the Securitate enjoyed fresh night air as much as the next guy. Or maybe they savored Bucharest's benzene odor, pungent even within this garden oasis.

Henry was still too woozy to comprehend what the vampire was shouting at him, mainly threats and invectives. When the vampire finished his tirade he strode away and Henry was allowed to sit down, but not lay down. When he tried, a boot against his back pushed him back up. Several helmeted vampires stood about him, machine guns aimed low.

Henry wasn't sure how long he'd been unconscious after landing on solid ground. Not long, he supposed, as the cross was still not boxed and sealed when he awoke. After tonight's Palace raid, the Securitate knew about the cross and likely arrived here with radiation suits. There being no additional delay in sending for suits, Henry couldn't have been unconscious too long.

He scanned the garden for Anya but saw only troops tromping about the trees, shields set aside, wings withdrawn. He wondered if they'd frisked Anya too, and as thoroughly, hands up her crotch. If so, was she at least groped only by female vampires? Unlikely.

Pocketing his hands against the cold, Henry wondered if Anya had been allowed to keep her warm attire.

A trooper kicked Henry's arm. Henry got the message and unpocketed his hands.

A tall gaunt vampire approached. Instead of riot gear, he stooped under a heavy brown greatcoat, sharply cut and trimmed in dark violet. Instead of helmet, he wore a peaked cap encircled with a dark violet band. Red stars on his cap and collar twinkled bloodily in the moonlight.

The troopers encircling Henry saluted, one of them shouting, "Long life to the President!"

"Long life to the Supreme Commander," the vampire morosely replied. He motioned and the troopers dragged Henry to his feet.

"Long life to the General Secretary," said Henry. It seemed the thing to say.

The vampire's bright yellow bloodshot eyes glared at Henry from beneath a visor heavy with golden laurel wreaths. His leathery red visage featured a long and narrow beak of a nose, so that he resembled *Nosferatu*'s Max Schreck. He scowled for what seemed minutes, finally stating in English, "I am Colonel General Iulian Vlad. You may address me by my rank."

Thereupon Vlad turned and strode through the garden, machine guns prodding Henry from behind. Despite Henry's fluent Rumanian greeting, Vlad had responded in English. Perhaps he wanted Henry to know that he knew that Henry was not Rumanian. Either that or he was being hospitable to a foreign guest. Not very likely.

Every part of Henry ached as he trudged along, searching for Anya along the way, failing to spot her, seeing only helmeted MI Troops milling about. Maybe Anya had escaped. Maybe he'd broken her fall and she'd run. Or maybe she died in the explosion. As a worst case scenario, Henry imagined Anya lying paralyzed with a broken neck in some socialist snake pit, lying helpless and alone in excruciating pain with burns across her body. At the mercy of whatever passed for "doctors" in this nation. At the mercy of other desperate patients.

Anya was right. Illness was not an option.

Although Henry doubted Vlad would be forthcoming with information, he might let slip a clue. Clearing his throat, Henry began, "I came with a lady friend. Any idea where she is?"

Vlad said nothing, his tall figure plodding before Henry.

"Colonel General," Henry quickly added. "I was wondering if some of your men might have seen her?"

Vlad did not turn around. "Who?"

"Anya—" Too late, Henry realized he probably shouldn't reveal her name. No telling what the Rumanians knew or didn't know that might be important.

Yet Securitate Colonel General Iulian Vlad appeared uninterested, almost ignoring Henry. Soon they exited the trees and entered the lawn, approaching the extended driveway.

"You were not mistreated?" Vlad asked Henry.

Nonplused by the question, Henry said nothing.

A trooper prodded Henry with his gun. "Answer the General!"

"Ah," said Henry. "What?"

Vlad bid the trooper to stay calm and asked again, "You were not mistreated during your capture? All of your civil and human rights were respected?"

Vlad's breath was so foul, Henry missed Bucharest's benzene stench. Even the gangrene and ammonia of the children's hospital was preferable.

"Ah, yeah," Henry replied, almost reflexively. "Of course."

"Very good. You will say so to whomever asks, yes?"

"Yeah. Sure thing."

Satisfied, Vlad said no more.

Henry was not eager to smell the old vampire's breath again, yet he had to ask, "So what about the lady? Would you say her civil and human rights were also respected?"

Ignoring the question, Vlad led the way to a black Mercedes limousine parked amidst other black cars. "Please to remember your previous statement," he said.

"What's that?" asked Henry.

"Concerning your treatment after capture."

"Oh yeah," said Henry. "Sure. I'll remember."

Gripping Henry's lapel, leaning into his face, Vlad murmured with rancid breath, "We have your admission on tape."

"Okay. Glad to hear it." Were his stomach not empty, Henry would have vomited right then.

Vlad released Henry's lapel. Someone opened the limousine's door. Vlad's lopsided grimace was probably his best attempt at a warm and friendly smile. Was he trying to be hospitable?

Henry got into the back seat. Somebody shut the door behind him.

"Been off to adventure, have we?" asked Robert Auster.

Henry stared at the US State Department trade attaché seated beside him, warm and snug in a spotless camel hair coat. Still pale and sandy-haired. At least he wasn't a vampire.

"Well, well," Auster continued, "you've created quite a mess for us, haven't you? Been a bad boy. That's what comes of falling in with a bad woman. Anything to say for yourself?"

Henry gaped at Auster. They were alone in the back seat. A chauffeur sat on the other side of the glass partition.

"Nothing?" asked Auster. "Well that's gratitude for you."

Henry finally asked, "Where is she?"

Even in the dimness of the limousine, Henry saw Auster raise a smug eyebrow. "Any idea who she was?" asked Auster.

"Was?"

"Any idea at all? You've nearly provoked an international incident. A crisis even, or close to. May help ameliorate matters if you told me what you knew of her."

"You should know. You met her tonight."

"Did I?"

"I saw her at the embassy. And you were the only staff member on duty."

Auster scowled. "Be careful about leaping to conclusions."

Although the windows were tinted, Henry could see MI Troops outside guarding what was supposedly a US embassy car. He scrutinized Auster's skin, eyes, teeth. No hint of vampirism.

"What are you doing here?" asked Henry.

"In addition to cleaning up your mess? Pulling your ass out of the fire is what."

"You knew I was here? I find that odd."

"Odd? I received a call from Minister Postelnicu this evening." Auster patted down his coat's creases. "A most upsetting call."

Blood memory informed Henry that Tudor Postelnicu was Minister State Secretary in the Interior, chief of Securitate. He nodded warily. "So the Securitate called you. Very odd."

"You know who Postelnicu is?"

"You'd be amazed. Very odd that an American official should get a personal phone call from the head of Securitate."

Sighing wearily, Auster massaged his eyes. "Mr. Willoughby, if the President of the United States were attacked by a Rumanian national, one seen leaving their embassy only hours earlier, would you deem it odd if the Secret Service or FBI were to contact that Rumanian embassy?"

Henry remembered the Militia outside the US embassy. They'd probably seen both him and Anya leave. Maybe even followed them to the café. Could be why Stanescu arrived on cue, why a Militia captain waited by Anya's Mercedes, why Militia Dacias trailed them through the moonscape. How long had they been followed? Surely not beyond the moonscape.

"Yeah, okay," Henry nodded. "That makes sense."

"Finally. Reason dawns. Didn't hurt, did it?"

"Anyway, you don't look like a Commie."

Auster raised an eyebrow. "Well, thank you so much for your vote of confidence."

"I can see them, you know," said Henry. "They look different than us."

"They certainly don't dress as well," Auster chuckled.

"Not the clothes. It's their lips and . . . Never mind."

"Gets chapped in this winter weather, I know."

Henry stared at the back of the chauffeur's thickest bullet head and ill-fitting peaked cap. The head had turned, as though listening. Unlikely through this partition. Yet the beefy head reminded Henry of the Marine's disdain when Henry had described the bloodsucking microphones. Merely telling the truth had made Henry sound like a paranoid extremist.

But if Anya was dead, and Henry unable to fulfill his pledge to terminate Ceausescu, the least he could do to honor her memory was bear witness to the truth.

"Communists have red skin," said Henry.

Lowering the tray from the seat before him, Auster paused to scrutinize Henry. "Really?"

"Not Indian red. Bright cherry red. Red devil red."

"I see."

"Not all of them. Just the leaders, the well-fed ones. The underlings have purple splotches on their skin, like the blood in our veins. Old used blood. And their underclass is so anemic, they're a pale bluish-green, like zombie cadavers."

Auster furrowed his brows. "Oh dear."

"Commies also have purple lips and black tongues."

"Dear dear."

"And fangs."

"Oh my." Auster clucked his tongue. "Surely not."

"I could show you, but you have to drink their blood."

"My my."

"It's true. Ask your own CIA."

"I will indeed. I will ask the CIA." Auster set his briefcase on the tray before him. "Now, Mr. Willoughby, you may help me help you by recounting everything you know of your former companion."

"My *former* companion?" Henry paused for it to sink in.

Auster snapped on a dim interior light, its glare obscuring the chauffeur behind the partition. "Fangs excepted, of course."

"I know she was the best agent you'll ever have."

"That I will ever have?"

Henry shrugged. "Our government then. Smart move, sending her out on wet work when you got Militia crawling outside the embassy."

"Wet work, Mr. Willoughby?"

"Sure, I know the jargon. She was gonna put me up for a job with the Company."

Having unlocked his briefcase, Auster paused before opening it. "Mr. Willoughby, understand this right now. We do not sponsor lunatic terrorists or crazed assassins. Any actions engaged in by your companion tonight were on her own initiative."

"Oh, I get it. Nice. *Mission Impossible.* Should she fail, the Secretary of State will disavow any knowledge of her existence."

"Enough!" Auster snapped. "Mr. Willoughby, you may rant all you wish about red devils, but get this clear in your delusional brain. Anya Amasovich has never been in the employ of any branch of the US government."

"She said she was CIA."

"And I will not tolerate you repeating her lies to the Rumanian government!" Auster gripped his briefcase, straining to regain his composure. "Do you wish to leave this country, Mr. Willoughby?"

"Who doesn't?"

"Then please permit your embassy to be of assistance. Contingent, of course, upon your cooperation."

"You can grease the wheels? Just like that?"

"And arrange transport." Auster opened his briefcase. "By car or train if no flights are immediately available."

"No one's that slick. We tried to kill their President."

"Don't flatter yourself. The Rumanians have pursued Amasovich for quite some time. They are satisfied she acted on her own accord. More importantly, acting independent of Washington."

"You convinced them of that? You've been a busy bee."

"Indeed I have." Auster began sifting through documents and filling out forms. "Secretary Andrei contacted me shortly after the disturbance at their House of the Republic. He informed me of the First Son's graciousness concerning the incident."

"Nicu? Oh, he's a gent."

"Andrei states the young Ceausescu has generously offered to overlook everything. All he requests in return is that we assist them with any information we have concerning Countess Amasovich."

"And you agreed?" asked Henry.

"I offered your full cooperation to Minister Postelnicu."

"Sure. What the hell. She's dead, right? Be easy to disavow her. Just dump her. Chuck her down the memory hole."

Auster stopped writing. "We cannot dump her because she was never ours. Understand that now." Instinctively, he lowered his voice. "This is neither here nor there, but frankly, I think the Rumanians suspect her of being KGB."

"Suspect? She's alive?"

Auster perused several forms. "Do you have your passport?"

"Is she alive?!"

"No, Mr. Willoughby. She is not." Auster produced a rubber stamp. "Do you have your passport?"

Numbed and shell-shocked, Henry searched his pockets. "Reds must have stolen it when I was passed out."

"I'll prepare one now." Auster pulled a blank passport from his briefcase. "You're a lucky man. Amasovich was seen exiting our embassy followed shortly thereafter by yourself. You rendezvoused at the café. Whereupon she assaulted Minister Stanescu and mortally wounded a local waiter."

"That what they said?"

"Do you have another version?"

"You want to hear about vampires?"

Sighing, Auster continued processing Henry's passport.

"You must admit," said Henry, "it'd be funny behavior for a KGB officer."

"Perhaps she's a rogue? Even KGB officers go insane." Auster spoke without looking up from his work. "Granted, her actions, and yours, greatly upset and confused the Rumanians. I suggested to them that Amasovich took you hostage at the café."

"How do you explain the KGB visiting our embassy?"

"If the Rumanians wish to believe Amasovich was KGB, they'll have to explain it themselves. Our position is that she was a random lunatic off the street. Embassies get them all the time."

"Securitate will never buy that."

"Andrei has. Or at least he trusts that she was not one of ours. Fruits of our long-standing policy promoting good relations with all host countries." Auster smirked. "Either way, Amasovich won't be contradicting us."

Henry wanted to smash that smile off his face. "So the Commies trust you. Interesting. And you trust them?"

"Some more than others. We at State term it *differentiation*. You see, rather than constituting a faceless red monolith, the complex reality is that the socialist bloc comprises many nations which embrace liberal democratic values and are even enthusiastically pro-West. Differentiation is the policy whereby which we reward open pro-Western socialist societies such as Rumania, and withhold rewards from the more rigid socialist bloc states."

"What kind of rewards?" asked Henry.

"Both economic and diplomatic. Chiefly under the rubric of MFN."

"Sounds like a load of Commie rubbish. That can't be Reagan's policy."

"Sadly no. Nevertheless, it may encourage you to know that differentiation was developed under a Republican administration. Developed by Nixon and Kissinger. The policy remained in effect through Ford and Carter, and continues to be State policy despite troublesome efforts to the contrary by that embarrassment in the White House."

Henry ached to beat the crap out of Auster, but only said, "The White House sets foreign policy. That makes Reagan's policy your policy."

"Yes and no. But why so surly? The MFN incentives provided by our differentiation policy have clearly benefited you. You're being expelled rather than prosecuted largely because, aside from a recognition that Amasovich was the instigator and you the pawn, the Rumanians wish to encourage future Hollywood film investment. President Ceausescu greatly values economic ties to the West."

"You think we got an open liberal society here?"

"The State Department enjoys excellent relations with President Ceausescu. Secretary Andrei has already unofficially accepted my suggestion that Amasovich kidnapped you."

"Unofficially?" asked Henry.

"Naturally, under tonight's special circumstances, your visa requires Ceausescu's personal signature. Andrei assures me it's a mere formality. Contingent, of course, upon your cooperation with Postelnicu. Another formality. A few questions."

"An interrogation."

"Not at all." Auster tensed. "They didn't interrogate you before now, did they? Andrei assured me you would be permitted to first consult your embassy."

"Yeah. All civil and human rights were respected."

Auster relaxed, smiling. "Differentiation at work."

"Didn't work too good for Anya."

Auster leaned close. "Two things to remember. One, Amasovich kidnapped you. And two, she never worked for any branch of the US government. Your exit visa depends on your answers."

Auster gave Henry his new passport.

Henry flipped through it. No photo, no visa. Not yet. He wondered how much of Anya's memory and honor he'd need to betray to buy his own safety.

"Andrei and Nicu both saw me help Anya," said Henry.

"Stockholm syndrome."

"No way. Commies won't forgive and forget what I did."

Auster shut his briefcase. "What did you do?"

"Brandish a cross."

"What else?"

"Nothing."

Auster smiled again. "I think they'll overlook a cross."

"Not a silver cross."

"Oh, I think they will. The Rumanians are not unreasonable. Not at all the red devils some extremists in the US make them out to be. They're tolerant of religion. Certainly tolerant enough to overlook a cross. Besides, the Rumanian CIE likely vetted you before your arrival. I suspect you have a clean record. No extremist conservative contacts."

"I voted for the Gipper," said Henry.

Auster chuckled. "We needn't tell them that."

"Great. I'm safe as long as I hide my politics. This county's about as free and open as an American campus."

Auster reached forward to shut the car's dim interior light. "Mr. Willoughby, I cannot describe what pleasure it has been assisting you in your foreign travels. If there's anything else I can do to expedite your exit from this nation, please don't hesitate to ask."

Auster shut the light. The partition became transparent and glare-free. Henry saw the chauffeur glowering into the rearview mirror with yellow bloodshot eyes.

"Who's the guy up front?" Henry demanded.

"Teodorescu? An embassy chauffeur."

"Sounds like he's got a Rumanian name."

"Yes, most Rumanians do," said Auster.

"You crazy? Hiring local vampires?"

Sighing heavily, Auster turned away from Henry, as though it were painful just to look at him. "So long as the vampire can do the job."

Too late, Henry realized Teodorescu probably read lips. And there had been no glare on his side of the partition.

No point in shutting up now.

"Look at him," said Henry. "Staring. Watching. He knows I know. He knows I see his face, all red and purple."

Auster glanced at his watch.

"A face like Gorbachev's blotch, only more purplish," Henry continued. "Funny, how everyone sees Gorby's blotch. Might mean the Commies are losing it. Wonder if they'd have lost their powers by now if we didn't keep propping up their economy or letting their spies into our embassies?"

"Naturally, Mr. Willoughby, our security screens all hires."

"Why hire them at all?"

"You can't expect us to import janitorial or cleaning staff from the States. Besides, the policy generates local goodwill."

"Bet the Commies don't have that policy."

Auster smirked. "Yes, well, some socialist bloc leaders are as paranoid as certain Americans."

Something tapped Auster's tinted window. He opened the door to reveal a short pudgy vampire outside.

"Ah, Minister Postelnicu!" Auster smiled warmly, shaking the vampire's hand.

"Hello my esteemed American friend," said Postelnicu. Then he looked past Auster at Henry. "And how is our young Hollywood film director after his ordeal? Well, I hope?"

Henry glared at the Minister State Secretary of DSS. Black leather trench coat wrapped tightly around his grossly overweight body. Black fedora atop his oily black hair. Dirty fangs drooling bloody spit. Beady ratlike eyes darting behind fatuous folds of flesh. Greasy red face leering.

"Well enough," Henry answered. "Better than Countess Amasovich."

"Aaaahh," Postelnicu drooled noncommittally. Then he turned to exchange whispers with Colonel General Vlad, who loomed behind his boss. Auster glared at Henry.

Postelnicu turned back to Henry. "If your most highly esteemed Robert Auster has not already so expressed, please to accept our most sincerest apology that such misfortune is to have befallen you in our beautiful country."

Henry snorted contemptuously. "Yeah, whatever." He glanced at Teodorescu's eyes in the rearview mirror, the vampire glaring back.

"Mr. Auster," said Postelnicu. "For your own record, and so as to reaffirm the great mutual friendship and goodwill and trust between our two great peoples, please to examine this evidence for the benefit of your own eyes."

"Certainly." Auster winked at Henry.

Henry groaned. Auster only cared about not rocking the boat of international relations, however much he must appease an evil empire. Anya was expendable.

And Postelnicu was no dummy. His DSS probably knew Anya was CIA. And even if they figured her for KGB, they still knew that Henry acted voluntarily and with full mental capacity.

But DSS also knew that whatever else she was, Anya was the brains behind the attacks. And now Anya was dead. Arresting Henry would only embarrass the US and threaten Ceausescu's MFN candy, whereas quietly expelling Henry protected MFN, and possibly advanced Auster's career at State. Not for the first time, Henry wondered if Auster was a Rumanian mole. Maybe it didn't matter, the result was the same. Either way, Postelnicu would play along with Auster's face-saving game if it got Ceausescu whatever goodies came with MFN.

A trooper passed a large object to Postelnicu, who displayed it for Auster.

Anya's violin case.

The most prominent weapon in the case was the long cylindrical gun, looking like a silver bazooka. It lay amidst an assortment of silver canisters, shells, and daggers, and silver-tipped stakes and arrows. Missing was the flame thrower and crossbow. Anya had those when she perished.

Might she still? Was she alive? Henry had seen no body.

"These were found on the criminal Amasovich," said Postelnicu, his tiny rat eyes squinting against the silver glare.

Auster clucked his tongue. "Madness. Sheer lunacy."

"No shit," said Henry. "Country seems to be infested with vampires."

"Just some Hungarians in Transylvania," Postelnicu joked.

Auster was scowling at Henry.

"Look at him!" shouted Henry, pointing at the DSS chief. "He can't look at silver. Can't even hold it without gloves."

Postelnicu was squinting too much to read his expression, but Vlad glowered at Henry from the darkness behind the Minister. Teodorescu glared at Henry from the front seat.

Postelnicu barked an order and a trooper passed an object to Vlad, who displayed it for Auster.

Anya's flame thrower and crossbow.

Henry felt sick again.

"Absolute lunacy," clucked Auster. "She appeared emotionally disturbed when she barged into our embassy this evening, but I never suspected the depth of her insanity."

"Our most sincerest apologies," replied Postelnicu, "for not providing sufficient security to prevent such intrusion into your privacy." His eyes almost shut, he addressed Auster while facing away.

Yet Auster noticed nothing. Vampire expressions and mannerisms, like fangs, yellow eyes, and red skin, were too subtle for him to detect. Maybe if he saw one fly, then surely . . .

But what were the chances of that?

Returning the violin case to the trooper, Postelnicu said to Auster, "For your own record, and the benefit of your own eyes, please to come see the destruction caused by the criminal Amasovich."

Although nobody invited him, nobody objected as Henry followed Auster and Postelnicu back toward the mansion. Vlad wordlessly came beside Henry, still gripping Anya's flame thrower and crossbow. The trooper on Henry's other side clutched her violin case. Henry saw no point in disputing ownership. Both creatures were bigger and better padded than he. Besides, Henry was already the luckiest man in the country. He had a ticket out. Out of this nation of fear and lies, of paper food and benzene air.

What time was it? He checked into the hotel at about seven. By now it must be around midnight. He might be back in New York before noon today, EST.

In exchange for that escape ticket, Henry could forget the aches in his bones, the gnawing in his stomach. He could leave Vlad the flame thrower and crossbow. He could tell Auster and Postelnicu whatever they wanted to hear. Let them tell Andrei and Nicu and Ceausescu whatever they wanted to hear.

For a ticket out of here, Henry could overlook all that. In time, he might even forget it.

What Henry would never forget was that while returning to the mansion, he saw a Dacia surrounded by MI Troops.

Anya in the back seat.

FIFTEEN

Anya's face was black.

She looked like she had been smeared with soot, apart from the area around her eyes. She sat in the Dacia, arms behind her back, looking like an inverse raccoon, black face in white mask. The "mask" was a silhouette of the shades she had worn.

For one dread moment, Henry feared that Anya's face had been burnt black. But her black skin was smooth, unmarred by scars. She did not seem in pain. Her clear eyes gazed stoically, apparently unharmed. Yet if Anya saw Henry watching her, she gave no notice. She gave no notice of seeing anything. Maybe she was in shock?

Henry considered flagging Auster, now chatting amiably with Postelnicu. But would Auster see Anya? The Dacia was parked far away, windows tinted. Henry saw through the tinting, but perhaps such visual acuity required vampire blood? If Auster saw nothing from here, he would hardly insist on an inspection that might embarrass his Rumanian hosts.

Or did Auster already know? Maybe Auster and Postelnicu had reached an "understanding" about Anya. Could be Nicu himself had plans for Anya. Maybe her sacrifice was the price for continued good international trade relations, with Henry's freedom tossed into the bargain as an afterthought.

Or maybe Auster was ignorant of Anya—and wished to remain so. Henry's pointing to Anya, alive and well, might embarrass Auster (what didn't?) by compromising his plausible denial and exacerbating this "international incident." Everyone, Auster included, would pretend to see no Anya, hear no Henry.

And if the vampires knew that Henry had seen Anya, his own

visa might be jeopardized. The smart move was to wait till he was safely back in the US, then write to his Congressman and Senators. As had myriad MIA families over the past decade. With the same rapid result.

They entered the wooded area and left the lawn and driveway and Anya behind. About a half dozen MI Troops trudged alongside Postelnicu's retinue as Henry brainstormed for another smart move. Something better than simply dumping Anya.

Henry was unarmed. Beside him Vlad carried the pistol flame thrower and crossbow. Without arrows the crossbow was useless. But the pistol should still contain gasoline, lighter fluid, whatever.

Step One was to secure possession of the pistol. Henry deliberated on how to knock it from Vlad's grip. The Colonel General was big, but not so young anymore. His greatcoat and gloves provided some protection, but he wore no padded armor.

Henry was still evaluating all his potential moves when Postelnicu bellowed and Vlad scurried forward to the Minister.

Henry considered following Vlad, but then Vlad gave the pistol and crossbow to a trooper who disappeared into the darkness with them. Along with Henry's nascent plan.

A car engine started.

Glancing back, Henry was relieved to see that Anya's car was silent and still. But it might depart next. Even now, Henry was leaving Anya. Every step jeopardized her eventual rescue.

Henry perused the trooper beside him, the one carrying the violin case. It mainly contained ammunition. Magazines, shells, cases, canisters, arrows. All useless without a delivery system.

Also some old-fashioned wooden stakes.

Only delivery system a stake needs is a good strong arm.

But if MI armor could stop arrows, it should stop a stake, no matter how strong the vampire hunter's arm. True, the stakes were silver-tipped, but so too the arrows. So it seemed silver had no special armor-piercing power.

Then there was that long cylindrical gun. Fat and tubular like a bazooka, as opposed to small and tubular like the pistol flame thrower. What was it? A bigger flame thrower, one with combat-strength firepower?

By now, most of the troopers had detached their gas masks and lifted their faceplates, exposing their faces . . .

Or maybe not a flame thrower at all, but a shotgun loaded with silver pellets? Or even a machine gun? A few arrows had pierced MI armor, if only slightly. A shotgun might go further. A machine gun might pulverize every vampire in sight.

Or prove utterly useless.

In which case Henry's grab for the gun would deteriorate into a suicide mission.

But if Anya could brave a suicide mission, then so could he. Not to kill a Commie, he wasn't that generous with his life, noble cause though it was. But to save a lady's life. Or at least, to save this particular lady.

Henry glanced at the trooper carrying the violin case. His padding would likely protect him from Henry's piss poor karate skills. So Henry conceived another maneuver . . .

Trudging past a tree, Henry leaned down and snatched a dry winter branch. The trooper glanced at Henry, eyes hidden behind his tinted faceplate. Henry briefly fretted over his plan. If the polarization filtered out silver rays, what else?

Henry snapped several pieces off the branch, hoping the full moon was sufficient illumination. He said nothing to the trooper carrying the case, gave no warning. When moonlight broke through overhead Henry set two branches against the trooper's faceplate.

Sign of the cross.

The trooper flinched. It was enough.

Henry grabbed the violin case and raced into the woods.

Shouting, footsteps behind him, Auster calling . . .

Henry flung himself down, snapped open the case, grabbed the silver bazooka, aiming at onrushing troops, pulled the trigger.

No gunfire, no explosion, no flames.

Hissing.

Gray smoke spewing and hissing from the gun's nozzle, across a wide spread, concealing everything before Henry, smoke spilling back toward him.

And he wore no gas mask.

No, not smoke.

Warm mist enveloped Henry, the fog spreading rapidly through the garden. Henry swept the gun in a circle, surrounding himself with a malodorous cloud. It stank but did not sting. Seemed the gun's purpose was defensive, its function to provide camouflage. In which case vampire eyesight, however acute, was presumably unable to penetrate this mist.

Must be a pretty special mist.

It felt hot and steamy, and reeked of rotten eggs at a waste treatment plant. Henry licked the moisture on his lips and immediately spat out what tasted like used toilet water.

The gun was powerful. The fog thickened quickly.

Maybe Auster saw no mist, its vapor too subtle for his unsophisticated Ivy League eyes. Maybe all he saw was Henry waving an impotent gun while blinded troopers stumbled about for no apparent reason. But having tasted vampire blood, Henry saw the mist, and was unable to see beyond a few feet. Yet he continued spraying in circles even as he ran to where he believed Anya was parked.

Henry stumbled and crashed upon the ground, still firing his gun, refusing to stop. Through the fog he saw the trooper he had tripped over, shrieking in the dirt and fumbling with a gas mask, its rubber tube clogged with bloody vomit.

Henry rose to his feet, the garden so thick with mist he saw little else. Maybe the occasional faint outline of nearby trees. As he left the retching trooper he became aware of other screams, silhouettes of troopers tearing at their faces and eyes, fumbling with gas masks or ripping them off to avoid drowning in their own vomit.

Ceausescu's garden had become a scene out of the Great War.

Gulping the foul air, Henry became nauseous, though not so sick as the vampires. Eventually he no longer saw trees. Soon he stumbled against the rear of a car. A black Dacia.

Like the one holding Anya.

Like a dozen other Dacias in Ceausescu's driveway.

Henry fumbled around it and peered into its back window, up close so he could see.

For once he was lucky on his first attempt. His heart leapt when he saw the Russian aristocrat, safe in the back seat. Anya was staring back at him, wide-eyed, apparently too incredulous to display joy or gratitude.

Henry tried her door. Locked.

He tried the front door. A driver glared back, crimson eyes more bloody than bloodshot, eye sockets bleeding tears and blood, deranged eyes welling terror as Henry yanked the door. Locked.

Yet the driver was relocking it, slamming the lock, twisting in his seat, craning his neck to check every window, panicking as mist enveloped the car.

Henry struck the gun's butt against the driver's window.

The frenzied driver pressed the window, uselessly buttressing it, coughing it up with blood and foam.

Henry struck again. The window cracked.

The driver fumbled with his holster.

Henry struck again. The crack widened.

Frothing at the mouth, shrieking Rumanian, the driver jabbed his pistol at Henry, pointing Henry away, indicating Henry was to leave.

Henry stopped slamming the window, yet continued spraying gas. The driver pointed him away more vigorously. Henry ignored the order. Obviously the gas was more than mere camouflage. The driver wasn't gonna shoot and break that window, not with the fog outside, not unless he went completely insane.

Which, from the way he looked, was not unthinkable.

The driver fumbled with the ignition and started the engine.

Anya swept her handcuffs over the driver's head and pulled from behind, choking him, tugging the chain so hard that within seconds the driver's red vampire face darkened to purple.

Henry tapped the window.

Ignoring him, Anya dragged and pulled the handcuffs back and forth, its chain sawing into the driver's neck, steel links traveling to and fro across his torn throat, cutting through meat and cartilage, severing his jugulars and exploding dark blood onto Anya's clenched gray gloves, finally slicing the spinal column and hacking head from body.

His head tumbling into his lap, the driver's neck became a blood geyser, splashing dark streams against the window. Anya unlocked the front door. Henry opened it.

The flaccid corpse tumbled out of the car, its neck spraying Henry's pants with blood, its head rolling off into the mist.

Anya exited the car. She stood erect by the door, long hair blowing past her face. Having been cuffed from behind, she must have slipped her legs over the chain. A difficult feat in high-heeled boots and heavy layers of skirt and coat and cape.

Anya nodded toward the car, stating, "My hat." Then softly adding, "Please."

Henry leaned into the back seat and retrieved her fur hat.

As her gloves were soaking red, she let him brush aside her hair and gently crown her.

"No need to dirty your gloves," said Henry. "The gas would have killed him."

"I wished to do it." Anya was glowering with moist red eyes. Was she sick or angry? Had she been abused, violated? Was she herself a vampire, suffering from the gas?

Henry dropped the gun and hugged her. She felt stiff in his arms, but made no motion to resist. Henry buried his face in her hair, wanting to kiss her, but only held her tight, until her body was shaking and she struggled away from him.

Henry let go.

Anya bent over and began retching, coughing bloody vomit and saliva, kneeling low to the ground, her small frame quivering.

Not the exact feeling Henry hoped to instill in a woman. He wondered if he should touch or comfort her. He also saw it was a while since she'd eaten any solids. Although she coughed extensively, she disgorged little.

"You okay?" he asked.

Rising, Anya wiped her mouth, her wrists still cuffed. "Get my gun. We are not free yet. They will follow the mist."

Nodding, Henry retrieved the gun.

Anya doubled over and hacked out a string of bloody phlegm.

"You sure you're okay?" asked Henry.

Anya nodded, her nose dribbling blood and mucus. "Damn holy water."

"They made you drink holy water?"

"This mist. Holy water vapor."

Henry sniffed the foul air. "Tastes and smells like an outhouse sauna."

Anya forced a smile. "Cool rainwater to some. But my veins carry too much vampire blood, too much socialism, and I foolishly drink more before my body can heal. And although vampire blood is already stolen, and so stealing it functions as a vaccine to socialism, still it makes me ill. Sometimes I feel so unclean, as though I lived a lifetime in New York, in a rent controlled apartment collecting food stamps." She sighed. "You know what Nietzsche warns to those who would fight dragons?"

Henry shrugged.

Anya was frisking the driver's headless corpse. "Take care you do not become one." She found the handcuff keys and gave them to Henry.

Henry removed her cuffs. "I don't know how to tell you this, but you're black."

She smiled. "And you."

Henry looked at his hands. Dirty, but still white.

"Your face," said Anya. She pointed without touching, her bloody gloves now also stained with phlegm and vomit.

Henry rubbed his face. His fingers became black.

"Vampire ash," Anya explained. "Fine residue of a spontaneous combustion. A consecrated silver cross is still the quickest, cleanest, purest way to destroy a vampire."

"My face been black all along? Auster never said nothing."

Anya scowled. "The State Department never sees what it does not choose to believe. Socialism's greatest strength is that no one believes its horrors."

A cold wind was fast dissipating the holy water mist, revealing retching troopers strewn across the garden. None had managed to reattach their gas masks before falling ill.

One lone figure was unaffected by the mist. Robert Auster, now running toward them, waving his arm and shouting, "Mr. Willoughby!"

Henry grinned. "Auster will have to believe those barfing vampire troops."

Anya shrugged. "Auster does not matter."

Auster did matter regarding Henry's visa, but Henry made no reply. Instead he silently awaited Auster, eager to tell him: I told you so. And so did the Gipper.

A dark winged shape burst through the fog, flying and pursuing Auster, gaining on him. An armored MI Trooper, still wearing his gas mask. Followed by two more. Three flying troopers.

Henry edged toward the Dacia. Its engine was still running, the driver's final act before decapitation.

The troopers soared over and past Auster, apparently not pursuing him at all. They were aiming for Anya.

"Better get in the car," said Henry.

"Fire the gun," Anya shouted.

By now Henry knew better than to argue. He grabbed the gun and fired, watching the foul cloud spread before him, wanting to grab Anya back as she dashed toward the troopers flying low to the ground . . .

Anya leapt and seized a trooper's rubber tube, ripping it off while hoisting herself into the air with him, slamming her boot into another trooper's faceplate, shattering it . . .

Anya dropped to the ground, the two gassed troopers briefly floundering in flight before crash-landing.

The third trooper had kept a safe distance. Although Anya had not breached his mask, he wobbled as though previously sickened by the holy water vapor. When he landed, Henry understood why.

The trooper was tall and wore a greatcoat rather than armor. Colonel General Iulian Vlad.

The fog was dense now, so Henry ceased firing, ready to resume if it dissipated. He approached Anya even as she approached Vlad, even as Vlad spread his wings, more for balance than flight.

Just then Auster arrived, screaming, "Oh my God!"

Anya reached under her collar and rushed Vlad, who raised a pistol as Anya stabbed him with silver, his greatcoat not thick enough to shield him from her clasp, silver needle piercing coat and flesh. Vlad slumped in pain as Anya tore off his mask, Vlad coughing as Anya unbuttoned his greatcoat, dragging it off him just before his first bloody disgorge.

"Oh dear Lord!" screamed Auster. "My word, my word!"

Anya handed Vlad's greatcoat and cap to Henry. "You complained of the cold."

Henry did not want to appear ungrateful, but nevertheless said, "I wanted gloves."

Anya tossed the gun into the Dacia's back seat. "For that you must help yourself."

Auster surveyed the winged vampires strewn about him. "Mr. Willoughby! What is the meaning of this?"

Henry watched Vlad retching blood and phlegm and vomit upon himself despite covering his mouth, the bloody disgorge dribbling between his fingers.

Henry followed Anya into the car. "Gloves were too big."

The last Henry saw of Auster, the trade attaché was wandering among the vomiting vampires, muttering, "Oh my God! Oh good Lord! I am so dreadfully embarrassed! Absolutely mortified!" Then Auster said to Vlad, assisting him up, "You must not allow this unfortunate event to tarnish your view of the United States. All peoples have their share of right-wing Neanderthal jingoists. Please allow me to express, in the strongest possible terms, my government's sincerest regret regarding this most unforgivable behavior by these extremist—"

As Anya drove along Primaverri Street, Henry wondered if Auster had seen the wings, or even cared to see.

SIXTEEN

They sped down dark curving streets, the crappy tin box of a Dacia squealing at every turn. Searching for a seat belt, Henry found his side generously supplied with three tongues but no buckles. Perhaps Anya's seat was hogging all the buckles. Or maybe this Dacia only came with tongues while another Dacia toured Bucharest with just buckles.

Clutching a strap as they careened around another corner, Henry noted this was his fifth ride since landing at Otopeni. A taxi to the hotel, another Dacia to the café, the Mercedes through the moonscape, the Audi to Ceausescu's mansion, and now this Dacia to—?

"Where we going?" asked Henry.

Anya watched the road through her windswept hair. She had lowered her window, maybe to conceal the dead driver's blood and vomit. If the cold wind bothered her, she didn't show it.

"To find and kill Ceausescu," she answered.

"Still?"

"He is still alive?"

Henry groaned, clutching Vlad's greatcoat on his lap, the Dacia's heater hissing uselessly. "What about weapons? They got most of your stuff."

"Vampires are hardly immortal. We have silver. Holy water. We can always carve wooden stakes. Or use fire. Or decapitate him with whatever's available."

"Lucky they didn't find your clasp."

Anya sneered. "Incompetent slugs. What do vampires know? They still believe redistribution creates wealth. As if draining blood from the healthy will nourish rather than kill a nation. As if bleeding with leeches can cure anything."

"Nicu didn't seem too keen on helping or curing anyone. Nor Vlad, nor Postelnicu . . ."

Anya nodded. "Yes, every vampire's primal concern is sinking his own fangs into the blood spoils. But redistributionist greed aside, most vampires truly believe they can conjure up blood, housing, fuel, whatever, by mere command. They imagine the state a god. They make a law, and it is so. All they need do is plan and manage and mandate, and someone else creates it for them, as though by magic. Truly voodoo economics."

Henry nodded. "So how'd the vampires miss your clasp?"

Anya grinned. "It is not all they missed. They cuffed me, patted me down, thought it enough. Even if they miss something, they saw I was restrained. Available for further search and interrogation on my arrival at Jilava."

"Jilava?"

"Underground fortress built by King Carol outside Bucharest, now a prison. I assume it was to be my immediate destination."

"Guess they didn't figure on me," Henry remarked, proud of his rescue, eager for her to recognize his feat.

Anya replied casually, "I was planning to escape en route to Jilava."

"You were gonna ditch me?"

"When I saw Auster, I presumed your trip home was secure. Auster is an idiot, but he is tidy. And I know how much you wish to go home."

"I do. But I figured you needed me."

"I can take care of myself." Anya increased their speed as the curving road widened to broad city streets. Not one window was lit, nor any street lamps. Only vampires with *nomenclatura* vision drove Bucharest by night. Cruising at an easy 125 kmph, Anya finally rewarded Henry with a smile. "I am glad you returned. Even if your attack strategy makes me nauseous."

Henry took that as high praise, coming from her. She didn't seem the sort who gave thanks or praise easily. Maybe it came with being an aristocrat. "So where we going?" he asked again. "Now that we know Ceausescu ain't in Bucharest."

"He was there. You saw his food, his movie."

"He was gone before we arrived. Which means they didn't buy the story you fed Nicu. They knew we were coming."

"My story was a gamble," Anya shrugged. "And possibly they staked out several targets. It does not mean they expected us at any one."

Henry had hoped this latest setback would induce Anya to finally quit her mission and flee Rumania with him. But he knew she wouldn't. And she was right, he could have fled courtesy of Auster, but he'd chosen to stick with her, and that meant sticking through her mission. And he admired her for it.

"Okay, so where now?" Henry asked. "Predeal?"

Anya considered it before she spoke. "Unless it was a ruse and Ceausescu was never there. The garden was full of Securitate. I sensed them when we arrived. They could have stopped us, yet they permitted us to enter and search. Why? What did they want us to see? And if they wanted us to disseminate disinformation, why stop us afterwards?"

"Maybe you sensed wrong, they arrived after we entered the house. Seems a lot of trouble, setting up all that food and movie just to fool us."

"No, Potemkin villages are standard Securitate procedure. They will erect an instant food market, even plant flowers and paint trees green. But food is forbidden to be sold. Ceausescu arrives to inspect, Securitate agents in crowd applaud him, media records cheering masses. Then as Ceausescu drives to next inspection, Securitate collects all food, unplants flowers, races to reset market at next site before Ceausescu's arrival."

"I've seen the painted trees," Henry nodded. "Weird guy."

"What is truly weird is Ceausescu knows the market is false, yet also believes it is true." Anya careened past a corner and began speeding along the embankment of a dark river. "So you see, fabricating scenarios is normal task for DSS. Possibly Ceausescu was never at his residence."

"Okay, so he's hunting in Predeal. His winter hideaway."

Anya sighed. "No, we saw too many MI Troops back there. If Ceausescu is in Predeal, the main body of Troops are stationed in the Carpathians. Yet the Troops we saw were fully equipped and in place *before* we arrived. I trust my senses. Which means they came from nearby. Baneasa, as you said. Which means Ceausescu is in Bucharest or Snagov."

"You said he doesn't go to Snagov during winter."

Anya slowed and parked along the embankment, the car facing the river below, its turbulent waters carrying ice floes reflecting cold moonlight. "Yes, Snagov lake freezes. So Ceausescu is in Bucharest. Or was. Because if he was at home, we scared him off. But to where?"

"A safe house?" Henry suggested.

"But where can he feel safe? Assassins have invaded his security tunnels, invaded his Palace, held a gun to his son, invaded his home. Ceausescu never feels completely secure, but he feels most secure in his chief residences, because they are most thoroughly vetted. He must have fled to another one."

"Unless he doubled back after we left."

"A sly maneuver, and he is that. But he is also a coward." Anya shook her head. "No, it may be shrewd to return home, but he could not feel safe there now, not until all Bucharest is interrogated. If I am KGB, who else in Bucharest is KGB? If I can infiltrate his tunnels and Palace, if I can access his DSS maps, then who in the Bucharest district DSS has aided me? No, Ceausescu will flee Bucharest. But to where?"

"Predeal?" Henry suggested again.

"But he needs his MI Troops close and they are not so easily moved, not overnight. If they are in Baneasa then Ceausescu can feel comfortable only in Bucharest or Snagov. And since we drove him out of Bucharest, he must be in Snagov."

"Okay, he's in Snagov."

"Possibly." Anya was still dissatisfied. "When he feared Brezhnev would invade Rumania in '78, Ceausescu barricaded himself at Snagov. And he must already suspect Gorbachev of plotting a coup."

"Okay, he's in Snagov," Henry repeated.

Anya again shook her head. "No, Snagov is too close. If DSS is corrupt then so too perhaps every Interior employee in Bucharest, MI Troops included. Ceausescu will certainly suspect them of allowing our escape. He will want to relocate far from Bucharest. And Snagov is closed for winter, sparsely staffed, unprepared. Predeal is fully staffed, vetted, its few MI Troops easily reinforced with local FOI Militia until Troops can be transferred. After rescreening, of course." Anya finally nodded, satisfied. "Yes, Ceausescu is in Predeal."

"Well that's what I said all along."

"Yes, I heard you. Ever since you entered the car."

"Car, hell, I been saying it ever since we left his study," Henry grumbled. "You nearly bit my head off. You're welcome."

Anya grabbed Henry's wrist. Her glove felt sticky with vomit. Henry grimaced, but said nothing.

She began laughing. "Henry Willoughby, I can almost kiss you!"

Henry considered her sooty face, smeared with vampire ash. Anya was more beautiful dirty than most women clean. Radiant even after having just barfed.

Henry leaned toward her . . .

"Obviously Ceausescu's residence was a trap," she continued, "however hastily arranged."

Henry groaned impatiently. "We know that. So what?"

"But why did DSS want us to see Ceausescu's food and movie, to convince us he was present, if they only intended to arrest us afterwards?"

"I don't know." And he really didn't care anymore.

"Because food and movie were not part of the trap. Ceausescu was there, then hastily evacuated. Securitate did not want to *show* us anything. They wanted to *hear* our reactions. We were permitted to search the residence so they could collect intelligence. Learn who we were and what we wanted. Which means they installed microphones prior to our entry."

"Yeah. Okay."

Anya laughed louder. "I warned you about microphones, but instead you opened your big mouth."

"Yeah, you bit off my head."

"Yes I did. After you opened your big mouth and said our next stop was Predeal."

"And I was right." Then Henry saw it. "Oh yeah. That means they'll be waiting for us."

"Yes, because of you a trap awaits us in Predeal. While Ceausescu hides in Snagov. Which is our next destination."

"When? Tonight?"

"Yes tonight. We must hit Snagov before they realize we will not show in Predeal." Releasing his wrist, Anya examined her glove, then pulled it off. "But first we bathe."

Henry perked up. "Bathe? Where? A hotel?"

Smiling, she affectionately wiped some soot from his chin. "Rumania has few hotels, and all staffed by Securitate. No, we will wash in the river."

Henry glanced at the black waters buffeting ice floes. But before he could argue, Anya exited the car and was striding down the mortar embankment's slope.

Henry followed her to the river, carrying Vlad's greatcoat for them to bundle in together afterwards. He still hadn't tried it on. Cold as he was, its coarse griminess nauseated him and he'd seen enough vomit for one night. But maybe after bathing in the frigid waters the coat would feel less repulsive, especially with Anya's soft naked body contributing to its warmth.

But Anya turned out to have an entirely different concept of bathing than Henry had imagined. Instead of skinny dipping, she merely crouched by the river, scrubbing her hands. This was the first he'd ever seen her bare hands; she'd always wielded silver wearing gloves. He didn't know what he expected, but again, no hints of vampirism. Anya's fangs probably had been false, just as she claimed.

"Do not stand gawking," she said. "You will not travel far with counterrevolution written all over your face."

Setting the coat aside, Henry crouched by the river. "What is this? The Danube?"

"Dimbovita River. It enters the Danube to the south."

Henry tested the Dimbovita, his hand soon stinging from the icy river. He sprinkled water against his face, trying to wash off the soot before his face froze off.

Having washed her hands, Anya was now scrubbing her face, vigorously, as if to compensate for lack of soap. Did vampire blood lessen one's sensitivity to cold? No, both the Palace and Ceausescu's mansion had been sweltering; vampires craved warmth same as humans. Which meant that, whatever she was, Anya ached from extreme cold, same as Henry.

"You're strong for a woman," said Henry, immediately disliking how that sounded.

"I am strong for a man," Anya smirked. "But yes, they are disgustingly weak creatures. Hysterical, hypersensitive, unfit for war. They join military for computer careers and child day care, not to fight and kill and die. And oh yes, the women are even worse."

"Uhm, I meant that as a compliment," said Henry. "I admire you for being strong."

"Perhaps you are not used to it?" Anya stood with her face spotlessly pale, scrubbed to perfection. "In West you live with softies. They cry about price of military buildup, but are glad to pay price of unilateral disarmament. Euro-pigs parading with their scummy *Ban Der Bömb* signs and skull masks. Mothers and students against this and that. They are all infiltrated by KGB, but they do not care, they would surrender now if possible."

"If Reagan and Thatcher let them," Henry emphasized, once again proud for having voted for the Gipper.

Snatching her gloves from the ground, Anya began washing its soft leather and fur. "I am sickened by these mothers who would rather their children grow fat than die free. If I were a mother, I would rather my child die fighting than survive in a gulag. Even if the gulag fattened him into a prize cow, I would not have him suckling vampires. Wretched souls survive at any cost, as if survival is a great virtue. Survival is a virtue for rats and roaches, not for men, and not for women. Roaches are the great survivors. I would not give birth to a roach. I would abort a roach." Wringing her gloves into a mess beyond repair, Anya flung them into the river. "Better one year as a lioness than a lifetime as a lamb."

Henry watched her gloves disappear into darkness. With the city in blackout, the road devoid of headlights, only moonlight glistened upon the river. He couldn't even see the Dimbovita's opposite bank. But having had enough of its freezing temperatures, and figuring his face was clean as could be without soap and hot water, Henry retrieved Vlad's coat and carried it as a muff, his hands tucked into its folds.

"My face clean enough?" he asked. By now his lips were numb and quivering.

"Put it on," Anya instructed.

As Henry put on the coat, he spotted two wing slits tailored into its back. Vlad had been tall, but thin for his height. The coat fit snugly over Henry's medium build, brushing his sneakers, almost touching the ground.

"So you are warm?" Anya asked. Despite her wool layers, her teeth chattered. She clenched them to steady her voice.

Henry shrugged. The coat was heavy and it stank. "Better, thank you. A bit long."

"No, the coat is fine. It hides your shoes. Westerners are always given away by their shoes. East bloc citizens all have shitty cardboard shoes."

"You don't." Henry pointed to her suede boots.

"Yes, but I have KGB papers. I can enter best Party stores. Though perhaps if Ceausescu thinks KGB is plotting against him, I should hide my boots." Anya adjusted the fit of his coat, brushing off twigs and leaves, smiling. "You wear a Securitate general's coat, one who is also Deputy Minister of Interior. You can buy smart Western leather shoes, but you would not wear white sneakers."

Henry smiled back at her. They were in grave danger. However isolated this spot, everything Ceausescu had in Bucharest, Securitate, Militia, maybe even the army, must be canvassing the city for them. Yet Henry was happy just standing here in the icy wind, admiring Anya's bright gray-green eyes, watching and feeling her warm breath escape past perfect lips and teeth, her naked hands enduring the cold just to adjust and clean his coat.

"You're very beautiful," said Henry.

"Yes, I am very beautiful," Anya replied curtly. "I know I am very beautiful."

Henry hesitated. "I know this is not a good time—"

"No, this is not a good time." She patted down his coat and stood back, pocketing her hands.

"Sorry, I didn't mean—"

"Why do men think if they tell a beautiful woman she is beautiful, then she should be grateful to them? Do men think beautiful women are ignorant of their looks? What have they given her by stating the obvious?"

"Ah, I only meant—"

"That I am beautiful. Yes, thank you." Anya began striding back toward the car, holding her hat against a sudden gust. "We proceed to Snagov."

Henry hurried after her. "Just a friendly compliment."

"Do you expect me to melt in your arms? Every day men tell me I am beautiful. In New York I was a Ford model. And in Rome. And a little in Paris, whose vampires are especially venomous despite their extreme cowardice. Perhaps you saw my picture? I was on cover of *Cosmo*, *Vogue*, all those rags."

"You know, that's very interesting, because when I first saw you, I thought you had a certain poise, and models—"

"Yes, I have poise," Anya cut him off, striding faster.

Quickening his pace to keep up, Henry tripped over the coat, his sneakers slipping on wet mortar. Great. This damn coat was gonna sweep the ground whenever he bent low or climbed uphill.

"Sounds exciting," he yelled, regaining his balance.

"No, it was very boring. I hated it."

"Really? What'd you hate about it?"

"The people." Anya spun around to face him. "Yes, I know models are stupid. Editors are stupid. Photographers and designers are stupid. I understand all this. But idiots should shut their mouths! But in modeling, idiots all think they must have opinions to prove they are not stupid. All the models and rock stars and society scum, when they are not sticking fingers down their throats over a toilet, they give cocaine parties for Sandanista butchers, and toast Che and Castro and Ortega." She spat into the wind, then continued striding up the embankment. "After Ceausescu, I think I shall next enjoy to kill Castro."

Henry followed her, careful not to trip over the coat's hem. "Sorry. Didn't mean to piss you off. I don't know what to say. I'm not used to talking to women who look like supermodels."

"Why must you say anything? Talk as you have. I do not need a boyfriend. We are amidst vampires. I require a comrade."

"Well sure, if you just wanna be comrades . . . "

Halting, Anya faced him again. "That is a great compliment I offer you. For me it is easy to find admirers. It is nothing. I do not respect them. But you I respect. You I call comrade."

"Well, that's great," said Henry. "Really, it is."

Anya grasped his shoulders. "Do you understand what it is to be comrades in the struggle against international vampirism? It transcends all differences of blood, birth, and gender. This is the great struggle of our century, our historic struggle." Tightening her grip, she locked eyes with him. "If necessary, I shall sacrifice you to the cause. But if it is only between us, I will sacrifice my life for yours. Because we are comrades, and you have earned the right to my loyalty."

"Sounds great," said Henry. He'd won her loyalty. They were comrades. All well and good. But he still wanted to win her heart. "Sounds really great. Most women just want to be friends."

"Yes, we can be friends. If you do not grope me like some photographer pigs, or not cry and be lovesick, which perhaps is more your style. If you can accept me as friend and comrade, then we may be friends."

"Okay, well, that's fine. That'd be great. Sure."

Anya scrutinized him, trying to assess whether he understood the import of her remarks, and if he truly accepted there'd be no relationship. Henry recognized that look in her eyes from other women who just wanted to be friends. It was universal.

She released him. "Come. We must hurry."

"I don't admire you just because you're beautiful," Henry added as he ran after her. "You're smart. Brave. In the CIA. I wanted to join but I never even tried. But you did it. International supermodel, cover girl, spy. How do you do it all?"

Arriving at the Dacia, Anya leaned into the back seat and retrieved the holy water gun. "It is because I am a model and musician that I am an effective spy. I can tour the East bloc with good cover." She finally smiled again. "Everyone thinks models are stupid." She shook the gun, its hollow rattle indicating little water left in the tank. "Henry, feel how warm."

Happy to hear her speak his first name again, Henry touched the silver gun. It was warm. Probably felt warmer to Anya. It would likely have seared Ceausescu.

"But low on fuel," said Henry. "Needs a refill."

"All in my violin case. We will not find many other sources of holy water in Rumania."

"No churches left standing?"

"Some, but most are Rumanian Orthodox. Except for the Lord's Army, which is underground, Orthodox clergy are salaried by the state. Collaborationist holy water will not burn vampire flesh."

Henry nodded, glad she was smiling, wanting to extend the moment, yet wary of saying the wrong thing. "So you're a musician?"

"Yes, I told you." Anya's smile broadened. "If we survive Snagov, and if we escape West, I will reward you with tickets to my next concert. Best seat."

"You'll be on violin?"

"Perhaps. Perhaps something else."

"What else?"

"Anything. Everything. I play many instruments. I am a prodigy." Anya raised a hand, displaying long delicate fingers. "I also compose. And have recorded."

"Well then you should do that, instead of modeling. If you hate modeling so much."

"Yes, but Mozart died in debt," Anya laughed. "But still I pursue music. Right now, I should be with New York Philharmonic touring Moscow, running errands for CIA."

Henry flinched. "But the CIA sent you here to kill Ceausescu."

Anya tossed the gun into the car. "Come. We are clean now. On to Snagov."

"The CIA sent you to assassinate Ceausescu, right?"

Ignoring him, Anya got into the car and shut the door.

Henry ran to the passenger side, reeling with nausea, wondering just who or what Anya was. CIA? KGB? Was she even a Ford model? He entered the car, almost shouting, "You do work for the CIA, right? You're acting under CIA orders, right?"

Anya was calm. "Yes, I work for CIA."

"And they ordered you to kill Ceausescu, right?"

Turning on the ignition, she peeled away from the embankment and sped down the road. "CIA usually assigns me to Soviet Union because I am Russian."

"And therefore?" Henry coaxed. "And therefore what?"

"What do you mean, what?"

"Why aren't you with your Philharmonic in Moscow?"

Anya replied, "My case officer is in Rumania."

"And he called you here?"

She paused briefly. "No, that is against security rules. I came of my own accord."

Henry was stunned. "You violated CIA security?"

"It is not such a big thing."

"The Militia saw you leave the embassy!"

Anya shrugged. "Yes, I took the risk."

"And you lost."

"I did not lose. They followed, we escaped."

Henry struggled for words while Anya drove serenely, staring stoically at the road, wind whipping her hair.

"But you broke CIA security rules coming here?" Henry asked again.

"I needed to know Ceausescu's location. My case officer was no help at all." Anya smiled at Henry. "You were more help, you and your maps. And your comradeship. And friendship."

Fearing he already knew the answer, Henry asked anyway, "Did your case officer order you to kill Ceausescu?"

"I thought I tripped him up when he admitted Ceausescu would be at the Palace tonight. Wrong Ceausescu."

"Did *anybody* in the CIA order you to kill Ceausescu?"

Clenching the air, Anya shouted, "Henry, ever since Senate Church hearings, CIA has no balls! Entire West has no balls! CIA does not execute vampires. Even before Church, their big plan is to spike Castro's cigar so his beard falls off."

Henry watched the drab apartment blocks speeding past, the Stalinist architecture a constant reminder that he was far from home. Although never certain of Anya's identity, at least a part of him had assumed that the long arm of the Company was protecting him. Now he knew otherwise. Another part of him had assumed that Anya was a professional for one side or another, backed by *some* powerful organization; if not CIA then KGB. Also not true.

"We're on our own," said Henry. "You're not CIA."

"Yes, I am CIA. I am a rogue agent. But I am still CIA."

"Well that's not quite the same thing, is it?"

Anya faced him, casually speeding without watching the road. "I did not lie to you, Henry. I said I was CIA and I am. I said I shall kill Ceausescu and I will. You assumed the two were related."

"A natural assumption."

"Someone must do it, Henry. You saw this country. Ceausescu needs killing."

Shrugging, Henry opened his mouth, but had nothing to say.

"You want to quit?" Anya asked. "I can do it myself."

Henry sighed. "I'd like us both to quit now and escape."

"I have ten thousand dollars in my coat lining," Anya flatly stated. "You may have half. Your Rumanian fluency should last a few days, enough time to bribe your way past the border. Communication will be no problem. Socialists understand greed."

Henry said nothing.

Anya cleared her throat. "I apologize. Socialist greed is directed at others' blood, and you earned this money. It is not your fault Ceausescu was not at the Palace. Go if you must."

Henry shrugged. "Thanks anyway. But no, I'm probably safer with you than with the entire CIA, KGB, and DSS combined. Anyway, I didn't save your life to quit now."

Anya laughed. "You still insist you saved me? But I know I would have escaped en route to Jilava. But thank you. If I did not say so, thank you for returning to rescue me. You proved I am right. We are comrades."

SEVENTEEN

Anya parked on the sidewalk behind a row of Dacias.

Exiting, she gripped her cape against the wind, every gust threatening to expose the holy water gun she cradled beneath it. Henry pulled Vlad's cap low, both to prevent it from blowing away and so its visor hid his eyes; green eyes lacking the bloodshot yellow of a Securitate officer.

Henry wanted to whisper but shrill winds forced him to shout. "The station might be watched."

"All stations are watched," replied Anya. "Always. But they expect us by car, so we go by train."

"They expect us in Predeal. And in a black Dacia." Henry began pointing. "Look, a white Dacia, a blue Dacia, a light tan Dacia. Take your pick. There's even a sporty red Dacia—"

"Which will be stopped at the first roadblock." Anya was already striding away. Henry hurried after her.

An immense building soon loomed before them. Henry would have guessed it for the North Station even without the sign over its broad entrance: *Gara de Nord.* Its dirty massive stones and rusted rococo lamps evoked the previous century's Orient Express, an expression of European power before the Great War and Bolshevism and Revolution crippled the continent. Everything in Rumania was either old and decrepit, or new and shoddy. *Gara de Nord* was the former. Its tall windows were opaque with grime, their faint yellow glow barely perceptible through the soot. Atop the building a large clock with curlicue arms and Roman numerals indicated it was well past one.

Militia greatcoats milled about the expansive stairs fronting the entrance.

"No hesitation," Anya instructed Henry as they ascended the stairs. "In Ministry of Interior they are mere beat cops, whereas you are FBI general."

Henry didn't correct her. He knew what she meant. Instead he whispered, "Our faces ain't cherry red. Maybe you look like a KGB vampire, if you stuck your dentures back in, but I don't look like any vampire."

"Do not worry. Vampires possess keen night vision but see a distorted image of themselves. Like certain insects. As you see them is not as they see themselves."

Lifting his greatcoat while hoping he needn't climb too many more stairs tonight, Henry eyed the guards atop the stairs by the station entrance. They were glowering back down on him.

"Whatever they see in us," Henry whispered, "they don't like it."

"No, that is their normal disposition. Utopian idealists of every race, of every socialist breed, hate all they see. Slavic vampires, Teutonic werewolves, Latin chupacabras, their eyes distort everything. Only visions of revolution and genocide please them. They see it as cleansing. Ceausescu is such a visionary."

As they passed the Militia near the entrance, every guard saluted. One exclaimed, "Long life to the Supreme Commander!"

"Long life to the General Secretary," Anya replied.

"Long life to the President," Henry added, keeping his head low, eyes averted.

The station's interior was cavernous and dim. Centered high above was a dusty portrait of Ceausescu—the virile visionary with jet black hair—draped on either side by a red Party flag and a Rumanian tricolor flag. Dark lumpen forms slumped or slept upon wooden benches lining the walls. The tiled floor was faded and filthy, the original colors in its mosaic impossible to determine.

The ticket counter was occupied by a solitary female hunched over a desk. Green epaulets hung from her shapeless brown tunic, her face mottled in shades of purple and blue with barely a trace of fresh blood red. Her waxen eyes gazed listlessly at Anya, but sparked fear when she saw Henry's uniform.

"The February log and timetable," Anya demanded in Rumanian. "Your complete version. Every arrival and departure. Passenger, freight, military, penal. Everything."

The clerk began sifting through her papers. "If the Comrade General can be more specific—"

"You were told all you need to know!" Anya snapped.

"Yes Comrade General," replied the clerk, answering Anya yet watching Henry. She gave Anya two heavy black binders.

Worried that the clerk might suspect his pale face and green eyes, Henry turned gruffly aside, trying to emulate a surly high-ranking vampire.

Movement within the shadows along the wall. A dark form detached itself, a shadow now separate and distinct, scurrying over to Henry, shifting shades of black against black, now coagulating into a shapeless pile of rags, slithering across the dingy floor.

Henry edged back, then saw the clerk scrutinizing him from the corner of her eyes. Best not show fear. A Securitate general did not fear shadows. Henry glanced at Anya for guidance but she was studying the binders, ignoring the approaching rags . . .

The edge of the rag pile slithered under Henry's coat, enshrouding his feet, stinking of blood and urine. Something touched his foot—

He jumped back.

The rags rose several inches from the ground and gripped the hem of Henry's coat, tugging at the coat, pulling the coat to itself. Henry yanked the coat free.

An old woman's face emerged from the rags, zombie gray skin, a bluish cadaver gray. The face of a ghoul. Kneeling low before Henry, the old ghoul clasped and shook her gnarled hands, imploring Henry with the universal sign of beggars.

Henry glanced at Anya, wondering if he should interrupt her perusal of train schedules.

Dry parchment bones gripped his hand, moist licking . . .

Henry yanked his hand from the ghoul's mouth. The bitch had tried to bite him. Must be really desperate for blood, trying to bite a Securitate general. Unless she had felt his sneakers and knew he was no DSS officer . . .

But the beggar was kneeling and swaying before Henry, pointing to her mouth. Henry saw only a black hole. The ghoul had no teeth. No fangs. Not even dentures. A citizen of a vampire nation devoid of fangs. It put the old ghoul at the very bottom of this classless vampire hierarchy.

She kissed the hem of Henry's coat. So that's what the tugging was about. And maybe instead of trying to bite his hand she had only tried to kiss it. What did she expect from him? Blood? Food? Cash? Henry supposed one could buy food on the black market with dollars but what could one buy with *lei*? A picture of food?

Henry searched Vlad's pockets but found no *lei*. Glancing at the clerk to make sure she wasn't looking, Henry searched his safari jacket under the greatcoat. Damn. Seemed all his *lei* had been stolen by the MI Troops who frisked him. All Henry found on his person was the lime he'd picked outside Ceausescu's mansion. A cold hard lime. Inedible.

Henry threw the lime aside. It struck the floor with a loud crack.

The ghoul snatched it up, licking and kissing it, clasping it to her bosom, swaying and rocking, raising her arms to the heavens. When she began grasping for Henry's hand, Henry pulled back. She snatched the hem of his coat, profusely kissing it before reaching to kiss his feet. Henry kicked her hands away.

She kissed his coat again, swooned in further gratitude over her lime, then scurried back into the shadows.

Henry scrutinized the darkness against the walls, trying to discern the lumpen shapes within the shadows. Then Anya took his arm and led him away . . .

Through an unlit tunnel, sound of rats scampering in water, they exited onto a platform, then onto the tracks, weaving past several lines of trains, most silent and dark. They approached an ancient black and green train hemorrhaging heavy clouds of smoke and steam, dribbling oil and water. Although the engine appeared about to explode, the attendant vampires seemed unconcerned.

A long line of soldiers sat by the train, slouching on their duffel bags, their faces young but not youthful. Army privates in green uniform, like those Henry had seen at the café, only now their embittered world-weary faces were mottled a sickly indigo. Henry caught one soldier glaring sourly at him, decaying fangs snarling at his sight. Or was he snarling at Henry's DSS uniform? It almost seemed so.

Either way, Rumanian soldiers seemed a uniformly surly lot, all sickly and unarmed. What good was an unarmed soldier? What was his point?

Inside the train's vestibule, a DSS officer was assisting an army officer check the soldiers aboard. Anya led Henry past the waiting line of troops and flashed a pass. The DSS officer waved them aboard, saluting Henry and adding, "Long life to the Supreme Commander."

"Long life to the General Secretary," Henry replied.

The train's interior was murky and musty, reeking of human waste and engine oil, dirty red paint peeling. Anya led Henry past wooden benches crowded with groggy privates, then through several other cars, flashing her pass as needed to gain access and information, eventually gaining entry to a private compartment.

After Anya shut the door, Henry whispered, "Mikes?"

"In here? Possibly. But doubtful."

"You used your KGB badge?"

Anya sat on the padded bench across from Henry. "High level train pass. From that silly cow."

Henry assumed she meant the clerk. "How far will that get us past Snagov?"

"This is train to Ploiesti. No stops at Snagov."

Henry groaned, sensing a long night ahead.

Anya smiled. "Security at Snagov will be extensive. We shall take a less direct route."

"Surprising we got this far. Pretty piss poor security for a military train."

"This train is not military. It transports labor."

Henry remembered the shabby green uniforms. "They sure looked like soldiers."

"They are, but Ceausescu does not trust his army. Not with guns. Instead military conscription is used for free labor. Soldiers work on construction projects, building agro-towns."

"No wonder they looked pissed."

Anya shrugged. "Better an agro-town than prison labor camp. Easier than for prisoners on Danube-Black Sea Canal project. Or in a mine."

The train jerked and jolted, nearly tossing Henry off his bench, then became still again. Crack of gunfire outside. An explosion, hissing steam. Henry peered out the window but saw only empty tracks and a dark neighboring train.

"Rumanian engineering," Anya smiled. "But no worse than driving a Dacia."

"Or riding a New York subway," Henry added. "Except that we're trapped on board this train. They question the clerk you talked to, they radio ahead, and we're dead meat."

"What can she tell them? I demanded the monthly timetable. I did not say why."

Henry glanced out the window. *Gara de Nord* was as busy as Otopeni. "Not hard to guess which train we took."

"They will not guess it from her. She knows nothing."

"Neither did those Militia outside the embassy. Until they saw you enter and leave."

Anya shrugged, unconcerned.

Jerking and jolting spasmodically, the train finally began shuddering out of the station, rumbling and creaking.

Henry gripped his bench until the shuddering became more even. "Like going up a dying roller coaster. Just hope we get off before we go over the hump." He leaned against the window, trying not to get soot on his face. "There time for a nap?"

"Sleep if you can. I will wake you." Her back against the window, Anya sat across the bench and faced the door.

EIGHTEEN

Sleep was difficult, elusive. Henry tried to keep an eye on Anya even as she watched over him, watching her through half-open eyes while he slept. Wasn't right, him sleeping while a woman sat guard. True, she was the pro, not him, even if she had gone independent. She claimed to have trained at School of the Americas; she could obviously handle herself. And she wasn't the one suffering jet lag after flying across seven time zones. No reason for Henry to lose sleep over any misplaced Catholic guilt.

Maybe he had slept. Maybe he even dreamed. He wasn't sure. The clattering vibrations kept jarring him alert, keeping him in a half state, never fully awake or asleep. He saw Anya sitting across the bench, facing the door. He tried to determine if he was actually seeing her or only fantasizing about her. Was he even awake? Did he only dream of guarding her?

In time Henry realized Bucharest was gone. No more featureless mortar housing blocks passing outside. Only cottages and drainage ditches and unpainted picket fences. Then the cottages abruptly ended. He tried to reposition his head less painfully against the shuddering window. Vast expanses of barren soil, strewn with rubble and bulldozers and ditches. A ravaged scorched earth.

Henry glanced at Anya. She was comfortably reposed, eyes half shut. She saw him and smiled.

"Just like Otopeni," Henry murmured.

"How so?" she asked.

"Piles of rubble. Empty soil."

"Systematization. Otopeni was a target. So too Dimieni and Odaile. We are now traveling through."

Henry watched the empty shell of a cottage passing by, as

hollow as the building facades on the moonscape. It was easy to see outside. Their compartment's solitary light bulb flickered dimly, while a full moon brightly lit the ditches and rubble in stark relief.

"Rumania contains 13,000 villages," Anya explained. "Ceausescu intends to demolish 8,000 of them, then expand the rest into agro-towns. Official goal is economic efficiency, but the true goal is domination and control. Vampires consider villages too scattered and remote. People are more easily controlled when concentrated, like pigs in a pen, like cattle in a corral. Systematization entails demolishing the smaller villages, then relocating their residents into cities or agro-towns."

Henry sat up groggily. "Those soldiers, they're the ones doing the demolishing?"

"Peasants must demolish their own homes. If they refuse, then yes, the state does it for them. In which case the state charges the peasant a demolition fee."

"So they lose their home, and pay for the privilege?"

Anya shrugged. "It is nothing new. Chinese vampires execute their enemies, then demand the victim's family pay for the bullet."

"Seems vampires have their own ideas about economic efficiency."

"Socialism was never about economic efficiency, always about power and control. Consider systematization. The peasant on his own land feeds himself and grows a surplus to feed others. Force that peasant into a city, and you turn a producer into a consumer. Economic lunacy in a nation already unable to feed its cities, yet vampires continue to systematize because it destroys peasant independence. Whereas before he was self-sufficient, now the peasant depends on the state for his subsistence. Whereas before he kept his own cottage, grew his own crops, raised his own livestock, now the state provides his job and housing. And the state can take it away."

"So he shuts up and obeys," Henry noted. "Of course, if state-owned housing is anything like their six star hotels, it can't be anything to brag about."

"Oh, but Rumanian hotels are built to attract Western hard currency. Naturally, they provide luxuries far beyond the reach of the ordinary citizen."

Henry recalled his filthy bathroom. "So what are the apartments like? Do they even have kitchens and baths?"

"No."

"No?!" Henry had been joking.

"Ceausescu says Rumanians are too fat, and so in keeping with his national 'scientific diet,' all new housing is built without kitchens. Ceausescu calls this an amenity, because workers will save time over a hot stove by instead eating in communal mess halls. And it will save them food and fuel."

"It'll save on food, if the mess halls are as well stocked as the groceries. They can't be any less stocked."

"Oh, but groceries have pictures of food," Anya smirked. "Mess halls have yet to be built. As for bathrooms, they are built one to a floor, which all apartments share."

"Sounds even worse than having the City of New York as your landlord."

"New York has more vampires than you may imagine. Vampires prefer urban dwelling. Apartment blocks are easier to monitor and control than outlying cottages. Every building in Rumania has a resident caretaker to register all comings and goings of tenants and visitors. Local DSS inspects this register every fortnight. And half the buildings in Bucharest, those constructed since the vampire infestation, have centralized heating so the state can shut their gas and electricity from a remote location."

Henry remembered the citywide blackout. He had assumed that no one dared violate the fuel conservation law. Now it appeared that none were able to. "So much for city life," said Henry. "I don't suppose agro-towns are much better?"

"In his home village, a peasant owns his cottage and plot of land. When he is forced to an agro-town, he gets a small room in an apartment block with a job on a collective farm. City life in miniature."

Henry nodded. "Like losing your own business and getting a corporate cubicle. I guess he doesn't get paid for his confiscated property?"

"Not if the land is used for agriculture. A token amount if the cottage is demolished to clear space for a building."

"And you think if you kill Ceausescu, it's gonna change?"

Scowling, Anya shook her head. "More likely the people will spawn another Ceausescu."

"After what they've been through?"

"Ceausescu is neither unique nor anomalous." Anya removed a napkin from her pocket. "Khrushchev advocated agro-towns while he was Secretary for Agriculture under Stalin. And a century earlier, Marx and Engels's *Communist Manifesto* advocated abolishing all distinctions between town and country by redistributing people evenly across the land. As though it were for them to dictate where people should live."

"Ironic, a Leftist advocating a nation of suburbs."

"They will advocate anything they think will increase their control. Marx envisioned an even spread of factories and collective farms. Precisely what Ceausescu is trying to create." Anya opened the napkin to reveal a bloody bit of feta cheese. "Henry, see what I have."

Henry grimaced at the pasty white blob, red fang marks still visible.

Anya grinned. "Ceausescu's blood."

"I'm not that hungry."

"When they searched me, the idiots missed the clasp under my collar and this cheese in my pocket."

"And the dollars in your coat lining."

Anya ate half the cheese, offering the rest to Henry.

Henry cringed. "You gotta be kidding."

"You wish to understand systematization? Then take and eat. See as he sees. Know what he knows."

"I'd rather not."

"Do not be difficult. You need to know and understand. And it will aid you in tonight's battle. Come, comrade."

Henry groaned. Seems if he wanted Anya to respect him as a comrade he had to eat the damn thing. Hoping her love would follow, he gingerly accepted the sticky goo.

Ceausescu's blood glistened darkly in the murky light. Henry popped the cheese into his mouth, tasting gamy flesh and sour blood, chewing and swallowing quickly, his stomach burning, sparks exploding, clouding his vision.

Henry gagged, "I'm gonna throw up."

"You may, but I doubt it."

Henry leaned over to vomit, the compartment going black, his body shivering, coughing, empty stomach wrenched into knots, disgorging air.

Anya threw open her cape, revealing the holy water gun in her lap, bathing the compartment in silver sunlight.

Henry turned aside, eyes burning, squinting against the dazzling silver beams, the rest of the compartment darkly invisible, train vibrating, himself dizzy and swooning, nauseous from blood, blinded by silver.

Anya draped the gun barrel with her cape, leaving its handle visibly radiating silver, her slender finger silhouettes gripping the handle, then letting go.

"Hot," said Anya, muffled and distant. "Too hot to hold for long without gloves. Not with Ceausescu's blood in my veins."

Henry shook his head, stars sparkling and swimming past his eyes. "Shouldn't have eaten that cheese."

"We shall require heightened senses to infiltrate his Snagov estate," her voice said from afar. "Vampire sight is adapted to darkness, however distorted."

"My senses are too heightened! I feel like that maniac in 'Tell Tale Heart.'"

"He possessed no heightened senses, he only thought he did." Anya sounded cheerful. "You see, I know my Poe."

"Everything's fucked up!"

"I have faith in you, Henry. A strong mind can correct for the distortions and recognize the true world. People succumb to vampiric infection because they want to, because it's comfortable and easy. But I have faith in you."

Henry scanned the compartment, seeing only sparklets swirling about the silver sun in Anya's lap, unable to determine where was up and where was down. "Guy can go crazy seeing the world like this," he shouted. "When will this wear off? I can't see anything!"

"You are experiencing an initial rush. That will abate in a few minutes, leaving you sharp and alert well past dawn."

Anya had eaten the cheese, had eaten Ceausescu's blood, yet her voice sounded strong, steady, unruffled. Henry supposed that she must have developed some resistance to vampire blood by now. She'd need ever stronger doses to be affected.

Henry shut his eyes, silver afterimages still glowing in his retinas, swirling germlike coils, forming ghostly images . . .

Henry saw an ancient man infected with vampire virus smash a stone against his brother's skull, bone splitting, blood surging, life force dissipating and useless, yet pleasing to Cain now that Abel no longer enjoyed life, envy marking Cain's face, scarlet mark of the vampire repugnant to men, shameful to the vampire . . .

Henry felt the train trembling uphill, his body swooning, he looked up, opening his eyes, saw the compartment's dim light bulb flickering into viral patterns, Cain's contagion spreading, infecting mortals, stalking at night . . .

The compartment blackened, Henry unsure if the bulb had died or if he was blind again, blinking as he fell, arms flailing air, germ sparklets exploding into an epidemic, Henry swooning amidst ghostly images of Parisian vampires screaming greedily for blood, fangs dripping venomous hate, jostling for blood dribbling down scaffolds, vampires grown arrogant in sunlight, safe, the vampire Robespierre carving a mask on a guillotine blade, mottled monster faces now hidden behind *liberté, egalité, fraternité*, envious mobs slurping blood en masse, multiplying exponentially, murderous envy masked behind the bright shining lies of The Revolution, genocidal hate masked behind utopian ideals . . .

Henry blinked back the images, Parisian phantoms fragmenting into newly resistant strains of socialist microbes, Napoleon carrying François-Noël Babeuf's germs into Russia and beyond, invigorating indigenous vampire lairs across the world . . .

Henry's guts wrenched and churned, train shuddering, stomach acid regurgitating and burning his esophagus, he fell against the window and saw red signal lights, taffylike red lights stretching ghostlike in the night, lengthening red communist specters haunting Europe, vampire masses swarming for hosts, no longer satiated by lone victims or defunct classes, Henry shouted but only heard the train's clattering as the 1848 plagues spawned ever more resistant grotesqueries, the vampire Karl Marx, embittered and self-loathing, fangs salivating resentment yet afraid to stalk, cowering in Paris while revolutions bled Europe . . .

Dizzily tumbling in darkness, groping for solidity, a silver beam cut through Henry's blindness, searing his eyes with vampire afterimages ravaging Russia, utopian socialists and nihilists and syndicalists and anarchists bombing and bleeding, trains blasting and blaring, the blood red vampire Lenin coagulating from dynamite smoke to butcher Kerensky's tribe, fangs drooling blood onto his black Satanic goatee, making terror official state policy of the vampire nation, devouring more mortals in five months than had a century of tsardom, while beside Lenin the vampire Trotsky scribbled *In Defense of Terrorism,* and the vampire Stalin . . .

Rubbing his sightless eyes, trying to clear away the phantom images, Henry saw ghostly shapes break into swirls from which the vampire Bela Kun fled Hungary for Lenin's lair, vampires now battling for pack supremacy, Stalin's OGPU slashing all challengers' necks and draining their blood into buckets, Stalin feasting on rivals and adversaries and supplicants alike, his NKVD herding tens of millions into gulag concentration camps, exterminating seven million Ukrainians . . .

Henry's head was throbbing, he heard his veins throbbing, he heard the throbbing applause of Western artists and intellectuals cheering Stalin's mask of utopian ideals, applauding even as Stalin continued corralling kulaks and serfs, bourgeoisie and proletarians, aristocrats and Bolsheviks, applauding even when the mask slipped and failed to conceal his blood red face, applauding not because they could not see the fangs but because they did not want to see the fangs, applauding while Stalin exterminated twenty million and more of his nation . . .

Train shuddering, Henry fell back against his seat, banging his head, silver sparklets shattering, vampire shapeshifters ever mutating, sprouting wings, metamorphosing into bats and wolves, a coil of vampire virus mutating into a breed of Munich werewolves, socialist breeds now competing for territorial dominance, bombing and preying, Hitler's National Socialist werewolves decimating or transmuting all other vampire breeds, howling triumphantly under their own blood red flag . . .

Henry held his ears against the howling train, saw throbbing phantom images of Europe's two largest vampire packs embracing as blood brothers, sharing Poland in 1939, sharing Rumania in 1940, sharing envy and hate and blood thirst and utopian ideals. Henry shouted to Anya, maybe she heard but all he heard were the howling and shrieking of predators and prey as dwindling hunting territory drove the two great vampire packs into mortal combat . . .

Eardrums pounding, Henry saw spectral boots sloshing through the bloody mud of Europe, trudging in unison to the clattering of the train, he opened wide his eyes but still only saw phantoms in the dark, young Ceausescu entering Stalin's lair to learn the way of the vampire, returning to Bucharest in 1950, the virus mutating new strains in Asia and Africa and the Americas, the vampire Mao eating greater numbers than Hitler or Stalin, slurping rivers of blood even as Western students and artists and intellectuals erected altars unto him, yearning to feel the bite of Mao and Che and Castro, businessmen eager to sell rope to the vampire nations so nosferatu may more easily bind its victims . . .

Metallic clanging and clattering, flashing lights, Henry saw ghostly stripes stretching taffylike and realized he was watching passing signal lights outside the train window . . .

His vision clarified in an instant.

Henry could see again. Everything bright and clear and sharp.

Metallic clanging and stomping intensified, a clamor without origin. But Henry didn't notice it. He was staring at Anya.

Anya looked different.

Strange and bizarre and . . . different.

NINETEEN

Henry stared at Anya, stunned by her appearance. She had changed into something magical. At least she appeared changed through the prism of his heightened vampire vision.

Cold electrical shivers swept through Henry as the blood rush subsided, seemingly cleansing his eyes and ears, giving him a stark clarity of sight and sound. Everything the same, but different. Edges sharper. Surfaces shimmering. And although the silver gun was nowhere in sight, the compartment was amply illuminated, its solitary light bulb now flickering brightly.

Sounds were heightened and clarified. Train wheels screeching against tracks, nuts and bolts and screws straining and creaking within decrepit cars, horn blaring. And an intensifying metallic stomping.

Yet Henry remained mesmerized by Anya. Her skin radiated a milky golden aura, an ethereal silvery gold sheen. Her golden brown hair brightened to golden honey, with every strand distinct and glowing. When she faced him, Henry heard her hair rustling thickly, heard each strand distinct from the metallic stomping.

"You see again?" Anya asked, the edges of her Russian accent softened, her previously deep silky voice now less deep, but more silky. A voice muffled with honey.

Henry blinked forcefully. "I see something."

Anya frowned. "You see clearly?"

"Yeah, I guess. I saw . . . " Henry espied white phantoms whirling outside the window, then realized they were not ghosts but snow flurries sprinkling the dark scorched earth. "I had a dream."

Anya nodded. "Ceausescu's memories."

"Is that what I saw?" Henry strained to recall, the ghosts still visible but fading. At the edge memory. "I saw back centuries."

"You saw much," Anya smiled. "Always remember it."

"Ceausescu can't be that old."

"You saw his shared racial memories. The collective unconscious of the vampire race, their entire socialist holocaust. I expect you saw Stalin's holocaust? The holocaust the West first ignored, then denied, then forgot. At times even supported."

"I saw blood. Too much blood." Henry glanced about the compartment. "This how Ceausescu sees?"

"No. If vampire blood were cocaine, you only took one hit, whereas Ceausescu's system is nothing but. His sight is perhaps sharper, perhaps more distorted. Most likely both."

Henry examined his own hands. Nothing. If he had an aura, it was too faint to discern in this light.

"I don't see myself glowing," he said.

"Did you expect to?"

"You're glowing."

Smiling, Anya shrugged.

Henry heard a door open somewhere, a heightened sound of wind and clattering wheels. Then it deadened and the stomping resumed, louder than before.

"You hear what I hear?" asked Henry.

"I assume so." Glancing at the door, Anya slipped a hand under her cape. "Or something similar. Every blood recipient responds differently, according to their own unique biochemical makeup and history."

"It's too damn loud. How do I turn it off?"

"No, you want to hear that. Securitate bootsteps."

"Fucking great. They're coming closer?"

Anya nodded.

Henry realized that if he heard them, maybe they heard him. Sitting motionless, he whispered, "Sure taking them long to get here."

"Perhaps you first heard them since they were several cars away."

"Where are they now?"

The door rattled loudly.

"Outside," said Anya.

She had locked the door. Henry expected the DSS to break it down but instead they started knocking, then barking commands.

With both hands under her cape, Anya whispered, "Open it. But remember, you are a Securitate general. Behave as such."

Henry wobbled upon standing as the last rush of vampire blood subsided. He pulled low his cap and ascertained his greatcoat was fully buttoned. "Wait you capitalist imbeciles!" Henry shouted in his vampire surliest as he unlocked the door.

And nearly fainted upon seeing them. For although Henry knew his eyesight was newly sensitized, he was unprepared for what he saw standing outside.

A vampire in a black leather trench coat and fedora loomed over Henry, red star glinting in his lapel, gloved hand resting on his holstered pistol. His taut skin starkly revealed the contours of his skull, while throbbing blood vessels protruded from his face, petering out into an abstract of varicose veins. His face appeared to have shrunk onto his skull, disinterring the still pulsing blood vessels to the surface. Likewise, pulsating capillaries webbed his bulging yellow eyeballs.

Henry was staring at a fanged skull splattered with bloodily squirming spaghetti.

Two soldiers in olive green tunics stood behind the black leather vampire, their own skull faces a nightmare of protruding purple veins and throbbing blood clots.

"The General will forgive my intrusion," hissed the leather vampire, "but I only recently learned this compartment was occupied by our unexpected, but most highly esteemed guest."

Struggling to regain his voice, Henry shouted, "Well you know it now! And now you can leave!"

"At once. As soon as I see the Comrade General's papers. I must examine them at this checkpoint."

"What checkpoint you imperialist idiot? This train hasn't stopped!"

"A routine formality whenever we cross district lines."

Henry grimaced against the vampire's gangrenous breath. Why was he hissing? Was it meant to convey a threat? Or was hissing, like glowering, another common vampire mannerism? His expression was impossible to read. How do you read a blood-splattered skull with throbbing eyeballs?

"You idiot exploiter of the working masses," Henry stammered, "that don't apply to generals of my rank! Didn't you read Securitate Memo #1789? Don't bug the generals! That's straight from Ceausescu. Great guy. And by the way, you didn't say 'long life to the President.' I was waiting for you, and you didn't say it. Don't worry. I'm not gonna take down names. This is a first offense. But I better not catch you forgetting next time. Now get out of here. I'm on a secret mission. Highly classified stuff. Real top secret. Stuff only us Securitate generals can know about. Sorry I can't say more, but you understand. And don't mention me to anyone. You don't want to get in any more trouble. Long life to the General Secretary. Bye now."

Henry tried to shut the door but the vampire blocked the way.

The vampire examined the insignia and purple trim on Henry's oversized brown greatcoat. He peered under Henry's visor to scrutinize his face. Henry wondered what he looked like to this vampire. Pale cheeks? Rosy cheeks? Tasty cheeks?

"The esteemed Colonel General will please excuse me for saying so," the vampire hissed, "but he appears in admirably good health."

"I am, you capitalist moron. I drink good blood."

The soldiers raised their rifles but did not aim. The leather vampire gripped his pistol but kept it holstered. Henry wondered if he'd said something wrong. And where was Anya? What was she doing? He dare not turn around to check. Then he realized the vampires couldn't see her either. They were in the corridor and Henry was blocking the doorway.

Still scrutinizing Henry, the leather vampire hissed, "Very good health. And very young."

"Get out of my face!" Henry shouted. "You've obviously never seen a DSS Colonel General before."

"Ah but I have," the vampire replied. "I am a DSS Major."

Henry forced a sardonic laugh. "I don't know what piss poor branch of Securitate you work in, but it's obviously not the MI Troops. Seems you're just a gumshoe chaperoning toy soldiers. A flatfoot checking tickets. Hey, that's okay. Don't get me wrong. I'm not putting you down. We need guys like you. But we do things a little different in my elite branch of Securitate. Us MI Troops, we're about young people with young ideas. Young officers. We're kinda the MTV of Securitate. Don't feel bad about it. Not everyone makes the cut."

Henry tried to close the door again but the Major held it open merely by standing in the way.

"The General will excuse my ignorance," the Major hissed. "It is true I have not served with Ministry Troops. But I have never seen any officer, in any DSS *directorate,* so in need of a haircut."

Henry forced another laugh. "Yeah well, next time you're in Bucharest, drop in on Nicu. Tell him I sent you. Nicu Ceausescu? Name ring a bell? Close personal friend of mine. Same hair. We played in the same college band. That's why Nicu told his old man, hey, make Henry a general. He's a cool dude. We need young generals in Securitate. Shake up the old boy's network."

Eyeball capillaries throbbing ever more vigorously, the Major hissed, "You are Colonel General *Henry . . . ?*"

"Nickname! I'm Colonel General Iulian Vlad, head of Securitate Troops. But my friends call me Henry. Don't worry if you don't get it. It's an inside joke."

Henry tried to close the door again.

"I have heard of the esteemed Colonel General Vlad," hissed the Major. "But I was under the impression Ministry Troops were commanded by Major General Grigore Ghita."

Was that true? Or was it a test? Henry tried desperately to recall whether anyone had actually said that Vlad commanded the

MI Troops. Vlad had shown up with the Troops, but so had Postelnicu. Big deal. Might not mean shit. *And where was Anya?*

"Pretty sad I have to teach you this," said Henry, "but Colonel General outranks Major General."

"Very true," replied the vampire.

"Duh. Maybe you should go back to Securitate school? Try and catch some remedial lessons."

"The General will please forgive my ignorance for expecting someone older."

"No problem. I get it a lot. Long life to the President."

The Major held the door, hindering any attempts to shut it. "The Comrade General is most understanding. Now I need only examine his papers and I will intrude upon him no longer."

"Man, you don't listen! I got top secret stuff going on in here!" Glowering menacingly, Henry fumbled pointlessly with his pockets. "I'll check if I got something I'm allowed to show you, but you're pissing me off big time."

"Iulian!" Anya called from behind Henry. "Please hurry. I am lonely in here."

The Major brushed past Henry and entered the compartment. The two soldiers followed. Henry began to protest. But then he saw Anya and became speechless. The vampires only gawked and ogled.

Anya lay seductively across the bench. Her cape and greatcoat and jacket were open on one side, sweater pulled past her shoulder, blouse unbuttoned. Exposing her delicate long neck. The neck of a young supermodel, pristine and unblemished.

Anya's other side remained fully clad, still covered with her cape.

Pointing to Anya, Henry said, "Ah ... my ah ... my top secret thing."

Henry wondered if the vampires saw the golden sheen upon Anya's silky white flesh. Whatever they saw, they liked it. The Major's eyeballs inflated and swelled from their sockets, jutting farther out, capillaries pumping spasmodically. His facial blood vessels dilated, pulse quickening. His black lips stretched open, fangs lengthening, even widening, enlarging to the point that closing his mouth became impossible.

The soldiers stared and salivated at Anya, vainly struggling to shut their mouths. Although low in the vampire hierarchy, they were young and virile, their dirty broken fangs ballooning to monster proportions, gashing their own lips, blood and spit drooling down their massive bone-hard shafts.

Seeing Anya, Henry felt both longing and embarrassment. Her provocative pose and bared flesh reminded him of her femininity. Yet he knew her pose was insincere, compelled by circumstance and executed with cold professionalism. He felt embarrassed for her, degraded watching her, ashamed both for himself and for her.

"Watch who you're drooling at, Major," Henry grumbled. "That young lady belongs to a Securitate general."

"Mmmmm, Iulian, who is your sexy friend?" asked Anya, stroking her unscarred neck while eying the Major's fangs. "He is so big! I hope he is hungry! I am so frustrated to be so full of virgin blood! Will no one take the first bite?"

The Major spun upon Henry, eyeballs begging permission while viscous gray saliva oozed down colossal tusks resembling pointy sausages more than bones.

Henry wanted to kill the Major but had no idea how. And Anya seemed to want the creature to approach her.

The soldiers were bleeding onto their shabby green uniforms, their immense tusks so chipped and broken they were biting their own cheeks raw. Then Henry realized they were chewing themselves raw on purpose, ogling Anya while sucking their own blood, maybe fantasizing their blood was hers.

"Like what you see, boys?" Henry asked the soldiers, wanting to kill them next. "Better cut down or you'll go blind."

They made no reply. Their tusks rendered them unable to eat or talk. They could only bite and drink blood. Henry felt like a pimp talking to them.

The Major crept toward Anya even as he awaited Henry's okay, his facial blood vessels engorged and near exploding their load. Would he even obey Henry's refusal?

Anya beckoned the creature closer.

Henry waved his permission.

The Major fell upon Anya.

Anya threw off her cape, revealing the silver gun, slamming it against his swollen blood vessels, burning and bursting them open.

He fell back screaming, face spouting and spraying blood from assorted pinpricks and punctures and geysers.

Anya snatched the pistol from his holster and blasted several bullets into his heart, blood erupting through his chest and back. She fired twice more, both soldiers' heads exploding like red coconuts.

Henry held his ears against the gunfire echoing in the small compartment, drowning out the clattering wheels. He squinted at the carnage about his feet, everything bathe in the gun's silver radiance. Bright, but not blindingly so. Not as bright as during his initial blood rush. Nor as bright as the silver cross.

Anya tossed the pistol aside and began buttoning up.

When the ringing in his ears subsided, Henry said, "I should have done that. Gone for his gun."

Done buttoning her blouse's ruffled high-collar, Anya began wrapping her silk scarf around her neck. "It makes no difference."

"Yeah it does. Sorry you had to go through that."

She smiled. "No, I enjoy it."

"You did?"

"Yes. That is why I only shoot him in the heart."

Henry glanced at the Major's chest, gushing blood like a broken fire hydrant, his blood pooling with that from the soldiers' volcanically spouting neck stumps. Henry saw his greatcoat was dragging the ground and soaking up blood like a sponge. He waded away, unsticking his sneakers from the floor.

The Major grabbed Henry's greatcoat.

"What the fuck!" screamed Henry, yanking his coat.

The vampire wouldn't let go, pulling Henry closer, squirming spastically on the floor, black blood gurgling from his mouth.

Adjusting her burgundy sweater, Anya plucked her blouse's ruffles past its sleeves and collar. "Unless silver, a bullet in the heart is insufficient. Remember the vampire in the tunnels?"

"Yeah I remember, now do something!" Henry tried kicking the Major but the greatcoat blocked his feet.

"Have you any silver bullets?" asked Anya.

"No, of course not!"

"Silver arrows?"

"No! You know I don't!"

Anya finished tucking her blouse into her skirt, then began buttoning her tweed jacket. "Well what do you suggest?"

"I don't know!"

"Really, Henry. You should have some idea. This is for your benefit. What if we become separated? How will you cope?"

The Major clutched Henry's greatcoat while groping under its hem. Henry stomped at the Major's hand, edging back, dragging the spastically-bleeding Major through widening blood puddles.

"What does it want?" screamed Henry.

"Instinctively, it seeks blood to replenish its diminishing supply." Anya patted down her coat. "Please do not struggle so much, Henry. You gave me a new stain."

"I'll buy you a new coat! Get him off!"

"It is not a matter of the coat, but of preserving our own civilized dignity among barbarians. We who enter the jungle must endeavor the jungle does not enter us." After brushing her coat off, Anya inspected her hands. "I wish this compartment had running water."

"Get him off me!"

"I should not have to remind you, Henry, that another effective alternative is decapitation."

Snatching pistol, Anya blasted a rapid succession of shots into the Major's skull, disintegrating it in a bloody splash of brain and bone fragments, then splintering the fragments like a skeet shooter.

Clicking the pistol uselessly several times, she tossed it aside.

Henry held his ears until the ringing subsided again, then shook his greatcoat free of skull fragments.

Anya finished adjusting her cape, pinning its collar with her silver clasp. "Come. We soon depart."

"Our stop's coming up?"

Anya took the holy water gun, then dropped it. "Henry, the gun."

Henry took the gun, silver scorching his palms. He tossed it from hand to hand, then dropped it. "I don't think I can. What about the Major's pistol?"

"Empty." Anya frisked the Major. "And no magazines. Not even a spare bullet."

Henry picked up a soldier's rifle.

"Not loaded," said Anya.

"He acted like it was."

Taking the rifle from him, Anya checked its magazine. "I told you. Conscripted labor carries no bullets." She tossed the rifle aside.

"Great. Leaves us with nothing."

Anya removed the Major's gloves, peeling them off his hands along with a bloody mass of veins. She shook them clean as best she could. "I think these will fit you."

"Too big. I usually take small to medium—"

"Put them on and get the gun!" Anya snapped. "Now!"

Henry did so, cringing from the glove's cold sticky wetness, holding the holy water gun as lightly as possible. He followed Anya into the corridor, silver gun illuminating their path.

Henry smelled smoke. No, it was steam. The silver gun was cooking the blood on his gloves, steaming its exterior, broiling its interior. Warming Henry's hands.

A group of army officers exited a compartment ahead. One of them pointed at Henry. Vlad's uniform may have passed muster, but not the blood soaked into it. And the silver gun was a giveaway.

Anya grabbed Henry's arm and ran. The officers pursued, ordering them to halt. Several drew pistols. None fired.

Still running, Henry aimed the gun at the officers, his hands slipping within the bloody gloves, the gun sliding against the wet gloves. He pulled the trigger.

The gun coughed a puff of mist then slipped from his hands.

Anya pulled Henry into the vestibule, its doorway open, wind blasting snow into Henry's face.

He barely had time to examine the powdery terrain clattering by to assure a soft landing. Anya ordered him to jump while pushing him and he was out the doorway.

TWENTY

Henry struck hard ground, knees collapsing, tripping over his greatcoat, rolling down an embankment, tumbling against rocks and gravel, cushioned by his coat and recent snow.

The train was still clattering past when he clambered to his hands and knees, struggling within and stepping on his coat, hands gripping earth, fresh scabs stinging from frigid snow. He arose just as the last car disappeared behind a veil of flurries.

A dark form approached him, silver glinting upon her neck.

"You dropped my gun," Anya shouted. She didn't sound angry. She was shouting to be heard over the wind.

Henry examined his hands. The gloves had fallen off somewhere between the train corridor and the embankment bottom. Bloody scabs on his palms shimmered in the night, a brilliant ruby red. Must be his vampire vision.

"Told you they were too big for me," shouted Henry.

Anya took his hand in hers, examining them further.

"Gloves were slippery," Henry continued. "Real slippery. Both sides. Especially with the silver steaming up all that blood."

"I am not blaming you."

Henry tried to discern from her tone whether she really did or didn't. "I tried to shoot them," he added.

"That was unnecessary. I told you they carried no bullets."

"Well, you ran."

"Yes, I ran. Our departure point had arrived and I was uninterested in confrontation." Anya released his hand. "The Major's blood may have entered your system. Do you perceive a difference?"

"The skull creature's blood? Fucking great."

"Do you perceive a difference?"

Henry glanced about. Overcast sky, no moon, no stars, no street lamps. He should see nothing, just complete blackness. And yet he saw. He saw a netherworld of hues ranging from rich blacks to murky grays. And his own glittering blood. Was this how bats and owls saw the night?

Shrouded by snow flurries, Anya's aura was barely discernible. Her silver clasp shone far brighter. Henry examined his hands again. He saw blood, but no aura. Others may see one on him, he couldn't.

"I dunno," Henry answered. "I have some kind of night vision, but what does that mean? Could be Ceausescu's blood. Could be the waiter's blood. Who knows?"

Anya nodded. "No immediate perceptual difference. Ceausescu's blood likely overpowered the Major's. Even so, it may provide you an additional boost." She turned and strode away.

Henry took it as a cue to follow. Pocketing his hands, he raised the coat's hem off the ground, careful not to trip.

"We now rely on bureaucratic incompetence," Anya continued. "The army officers will confiscate my gun. How soon before they report it to Securitate? Immediately? Or will they jealously guard their find and report through their own military channels? Which DSS district will first learn of it? How soon before news reaches a DSS officer who realizes we were the passengers? How soon before they realize our departure point is within walking distance of Snagov?"

"We're not at Snagov?" asked Henry.

"Walking distance."

"How far is walking distance?"

"Perhaps an hour."

Groaning, Henry wanted to complain that he couldn't easily keep up with Anya, not with his coat dragging the ground, but he didn't want her to consider him a whiner. Especially after she'd gone to the trouble of securing the coat for him.

They marched in silence, Henry's downcast eyes watching his precarious steps. His brown coat appeared black in the moonless night, a black shovel sweeping aside the soft snow powder, bloodstains scintillating within its coarse wet wool. His feet felt cold and wet. His coat and sneakers both trailed blood. A bloodhound could easily find and track Henry. Did vampires use bloodhounds? Werewolves used German shepherds, so Henry supposed Rumanian vampires probably used something.

They had left the railroad tracks behind and were trudging through dense forest, which Henry knew to be the Vlasie forest. Knew it effortlessly and instantly from Ceausescu's blood memory, and felt creepy in knowing it. Glancing about the dark trees and murky gray snow, Henry knew the forest's name, knew Snagov was in the vicinity, but had no idea where he was in relation to the lake. Presumably, Ceausescu himself would be lost if plopped down in here.

Anya's gray cape appeared black before him. Henry was only able to follow her because of the silvery golden sheen in her hair, and because he heard her crisp bootsteps in the powdery snow. Her boots crunched whereas his sneakers squished and squeaked.

How do boots make crisp crunching noises in powdery snow? Must be his vampire hearing. And if he heard her bootsteps so distinctly, what would Snagov's MI Troops hear? What would they see? The woods provided some cover, but although the trees were densely packed, their branches were barren.

In time the wind and snow subsided. They exited the forest onto a highway devoid of cars, its snowy blanket unmarred by tire tracks. They trudged along its shoulder until they came to a sign: **Snagov 2 km.**

"We're here," said Henry.

"We are near," said Anya.

Henry began walking in the direction the sign pointed. Not that there was any reason to hurry. They were cold and tired and unarmed, and Ceausescu was surrounded by MI Troops. Only blind momentum, and equally blind faith in Anya, propelled him forward.

Anya gripped his coat and tugged him back.

"No," she said. "It does not seem right."

"None of it seems right. You wanna turn back?"

"The sign points one way, but my sense of direction points another. And my blood. My blood tells me the sign is wrong."

"Whose blood? Ceausescu's? His blood tells me nothing about this sign." Henry pushed the sign. Metal sign, sturdy wooden posts. "Feels okay. Wind hasn't blown it off."

Anya linked arms with him, drew him close and leaned into his ear. "Close your eyes."

Henry did so.

"Remember the DSS map of Rumania?" she asked. "The MI Troop insignia at Baneasa?"

"Yeah. I guess."

"Do you see it now?"

Henry sighed. It was too cold for this. "I can try."

"Do so." She waited. "You should now better understand the meaning of the map. You have Ceausescu's blood in your veins. Locate the railroad tracks exiting from the north of Bucharest. Locate Snagov to the east of those tracks. We exited the train roughly parallel to Snagov. Find our departure point. Estimate as best you can. Move east until you hit a highway that runs between the tracks and the lake."

Henry concentrated, so cold and weary and hungry that he anticipated trouble recalling the map. Yet with fresh vampire memories in his veins, he envisioned the map quickly and clearly, its secret red insignias strewn amidst Rumania's black railroads and highways. Henry saw it clearer than before, and understood it better.

"You see it?" asked Anya.

Henry nodded.

"You see our location?"

"I can guess our location."

"Do so. Then without opening your eyes, point to Snagov."

Henry did so.

"Open your eyes," said Anya.

He did so. His arm was pointing away from the sign.

Anya was smiling. "Disinformation. Not unexpected. Misleading traffic signs are routinely placed around military and security installations. Another legacy of Prague Spring and Ceausescu's fear of Soviet invasion."

They left the highway and continued trudging toward Snagov through the forest. Engulfed by its dense darkness, Henry heard more than he saw. Wind blowing snow from branches, whistling while reshaping the powdery mounds on the ground. Their greatcoats plowing through snow and swoshing and sweeping it aside. Boots crunching crisply. Sneakers squishing wetly. Growling in the distance.

Growling.

Deep and guttural growling. A bear or a wolf. Maybe even a vampire. Damn shapeshifters mutating into ever new monstrosities. If a spaghetti blood-splattered skull, why not a growling spaghetti blood-splattered skull?

Anya marched on stoically, without hesitation.

Assuming that she heard it too, and thought nothing of it, Henry said nothing. But what if she didn't hear it? Everyone responded differently to vampire blood. Maybe his ears were extra sensitive to growling. Hypersensitive, even. In which case, the creatures might be a safe distance off . . .

Howling.

Great. Now he heard howling. So they were wolves, not bears. Or maybe shapeshifters. Vampires transmogrified into werewolves. Flying MI Troop werewolves. Hell, who knew what strange beasts guarded Ceausescu out here? Children of the night with their damn fucking music.

And still, Anya said nothing

A pale white tendril flickered past distant trees. A fleeting luminosity, suddenly there, then gone. Same pallid color as the mist Henry had seen near the Orthodox dome at the moonscape. But also the same color as the phantoms in Henry's blood rush on the train. Was vampire blood like LSD, so that he was cursed to experience flashbacks for the rest of his life?

Henry wondered if he should mention it to Anya. Damn frustrating, not being able to trust his own senses. Might have been a blood memory flashback, or something unearthly but real seen by his heightened vision, or a delusion that he would have imagined in any event.

Anya halted and held Henry back.

She stood motionless, scanning the forest, eyes flashing catlike, wolflike. Henry shuddered despite his faith in her. But maybe his eyes too flashed spookily. Was that how he looked to others? Retinas like a cat? How else could he see the full spectrum of black, from charcoal to jet? But shades of black were all he saw amidst the trees. No more pale lights. Had Anya seen it? He should have said something when he had the chance. Too late now. She clearly wanted silence.

Anya pointed into the night.

Henry followed her finger. At first he saw only black against black. But in staring, in straining to see, he aroused a rancid blood and gangrene taste in his mouth. Staring had unconsciously and reflexively stimulated his vampire vision, much as staring might unconsciously and reflexively stimulate his eyes to focus.

Shades of black clarified. Black outlines delineating against black backgrounds. Straight lines within rough lines.

Amidst the craggy black outlines of trees and branches lurked the smooth black lines of tanks and guns and helmets.

TWENTY-ONE

The tanks lurked in the distance, silent and still. Henry thought he saw soldiers moving about, looking in his direction. He crouched instinctively, his line of sight obscured by intervening trees. All he saw were bits and pieces of guns and turrets.

Anya remained standing, her aura faint but noticeable. Too faint to illuminate anything outside itself, but bright enough to contrast against the black forest. Why didn't she at least tuck her glowing hair under her cape, or pile it under her hat?

Henry rose. Not wanting to even whisper, he nudged her and shrugged, awaiting instructions.

Anya continued onward, away from the troops. Henry followed cautiously, every step amplified in his ears. After some fifteen minutes they exited the forest and stood before an empty field.

A bright full moon shown through a break in the clouds, enabling Henry to see colors again. The field glistened snowy white and crystalline blue. Although the flurries had stopped, a sharp wind whistled across the field, spraying snow and piling up large sparkling mounds in some areas while uncovering the ground elsewhere. The exposed areas were smooth and icy blue.

Three towers arose from a wooded hill in the middle of the field. Henry pointed to them. "Ceausescu's home?"

Anya shook her head. "A monastery. Or rather, a church. Most of the monastery is long since destroyed. Centuries ago, a fortress occupied that entire island."

"Island? Then that's no field?"

"I told you the lake froze in winter." Anya smiled, pleased at his surprise. "In winter, the occupants would fire cannons to break the ice and drown approaching enemies." She began walking toward the distant church towers. "Come. We may find weapons. A cross. Holy water. Holy ice."

As the shoreline was invisible beneath the white powder, Henry stepped lightly, realizing that at some point they would no longer be threading snow-covered ground, but snow-covered ice.

"Surprised Ceausescu hasn't torn it down," he said.

"Dracula lies buried in that church. Or so they say." Anya grabbed her hat against a sudden gust. "They never found a body. An empty crypt, yes. Perhaps the body was long ago stolen."

"Who'd steal . . . ?" Until tonight, Henry would have regarded exploring Dracula's crypt an adventure. But then, until tonight, he hadn't believed in vampires. "Maybe, if Ceausescu's afraid of Dracula, maybe we should look for crosses somewhere else?"

"Ceausescu does not fear Dracula."

"So then—" Henry trudged over a snow mound, exhausted despite his nap on the train. "So then, how come Ceausescu's afraid of demolishing the church? Assuming it was Dracula's final resting place."

"Not afraid. Ceausescu regards Dracula a Rumanian national hero. So he preserves Dracula's fortress monastery, church and all. He erects statues to Dracula. Issues stamps commemorating Dracula. Ironic, yes? A socialist honoring an aristocrat? Of course, Dracula sites also attract Western tourists. Real vampires prefer dollars even to blood."

"Stanescu was gonna show me all the Dracula spots. Maybe even that island." Scanning the lake for cracks, Henry thread ever more carefully. All he saw was unbroken snow. No way to spot a crack until you were in the water. "I only came to this piss poor country to scout locations for a vampire film."

Anya plodded forcefully, apparently unconcerned about falling through ice. "Dracula was no vampire, just a Machiavellian prince who killed thousands. It is utopians and idealists who kill millions. Make a horror film about them."

"Maybe I will," Henry grunted. "When we get back, I might

get another project going. Get you a part. Help you break in as an actress."

"Why would I wish to be an actress?"

"All models wanna be actresses."

She laughed. "That is worse than modeling. Not only must I look stupid, I must act stupid. Already, I am sick of fending off ugly hairy men who claim to be producers and promise to make me a star. Now you say I should work for them? I would rather shut up and look silly and go home to my music."

Henry considered it. He wasn't hairy, so she couldn't mean him. "Maybe I'll help you break in composing movie music?"

"I have no interest composing show tunes and jingles."

Henry sighed. Seemed all he could do for Anya was follow her and fight her enemies. But he wanted to do more for her, something personal. He also wanted to do less, avoid tonight's fight and flee with her now. He watched his greatcoat sweeping aside snow, blood glistening redly in its wool. He smelt blood. Felt icy gusts cutting his face, whipping his coat, carrying the blood scent . . .

Vampires had a keen sense of smell!

Henry glanced about. Despite his heightened vision, he saw nothing lurking in the woods, no one along the shoreline. Snow blew across the lake, crystalline flakes spiraling within tiny tornadoes, sparkling in the moonlight, some powdery whirlwinds even glowing.

All around was white. Henry was struck by how ridiculously exposed they were. Two dark figures crossing a pristine white surface. Anya's hands and face and hair glowing golden-silver.

And *something* was watching them.

"We should of taken another route," said Henry. "Found another church. Or done without weapons."

"We not only seek weapons. We are bypassing Ceausescu's security. Circling his troops so to attack his estate from the lake. Until then, we are hidden behind the island."

"We're not hidden. You look like a glow worm."

"And you."

Henry checked his hands. "I don't see it."

"I have been drinking vampire blood longer. Yes, your aura is fainter. But I see it."

"Fucking great. And how long have Ceausescu's MI Troops been drinking blood?"

"Longer than I."

"You must look like a Roman candle to them."

She laughed. "They will see our auras, yes. But that is our camouflage."

"Camouflage? Maybe in a neon factory."

Anya's laughter filled the crisp air, stark and loud, carried by wind into the woods.

Shushing and waving her to be quiet, Henry whispered, "They can see us. Now they'll hear you."

"Who?"

"Who?! DSS. Militia. Troops in the tanks. You tell me."

Anya glanced about the lake. "I see no tanks. All I see are ghosts."

"Ghosts?"

Anya pointed to several of the snowy spirals, the ones that glowed. "Perhaps you do not see them."

"I see them," said Henry. "I thought that was snow."

"No, they are ghosts." She pointed elsewhere. "That is snow."

"Yeah, I see. The ghosts glow."

He watched the pale wispy tendrils. Some tendrils a few feet high, whirling briefly then fading out. Others glowing brighter, denser, extending diaphanous appendages that jelled into arms and legs before dissolving into the swirling snow.

"You saw a ghost at the hospital," said Anya. "Unless it was blood memory."

"Ghosts, I think." Henry flinched at his memory of the legless girl and the spectral quacks sawing away her limbs. "I definitely saw one on the moonscape. And one in the woods."

"Do you understand what you saw?"

Henry didn't think now was the time to hold a conference on metaphysics, exposed and aglow on an empty frozen lake. He knew something was watching them. Maybe the ghosts. Maybe something else. "I know about ghosts," he replied. "Let's go."

But Anya stood her ground, apparently determined he get it right. "A ghost is the restless spirit of one who died violently or unjustly. Ghosts usually haunt their places of death. But if an area is heavily soaked in innocent blood, it creates a vortex, pulling ghosts from afar, siphoning them from their original haunts."

All across the lake, snowflake clouds gusted through the ectoplasmic spirits, sometimes sparkling within their spectral light, sometimes gusting so densely the snowflakes altogether smothered their ghostly glow. Shrill winds deepened into wails, seemingly giving voice to their occupants. For these ghosts did indeed travel the wind, camouflaged by snow. Phantoms and flurries creating a trick picture: find the hidden ghosts in the snowy tableau. Whose voice: wind or ghost?

"Spectral vortexes resemble black holes," Anya continued. "The more ghosts they capture, the stronger their pull. Dracula created the Snagov vortex with his island torture chamber. Ever since, it has been gaining in strength and population."

"I see them," said Henry. "I don't *think* I hear them."

"You are fortunate," Anya smiled. "Their voices are rarely pleasant."

Henry edged forward, hoping Anya would follow. The glowing wintry whirlwinds were pretty to behold until you knew what they were. Then they seemed creepy.

Anya resumed the lead. "During the last century, the island served as a prison. Fifty-nine prisoners were crossing a pontoon bridge when it sank under the weight of their chains. The single largest increase in the lake's ghost population until socialism." She pointed to the mainland. "A cross right about there marks the spot where bridge met shore."

"A cross?"

"Too heavy for our purposes." Anya glanced at him over her

billowing cape. "Socialism has created more ghosts throughout the world than all other belief systems and social paradigms combined. Over a hundred million. More than religion. More than feudalism."

Scanning the lake with new awareness, Henry spotted dozens of ghosts, impossible to count with any precision. Many ghosts were obscured by snow, many glowed too faintly, many kept fading in and out. How to distinguish new ghosts from those previously faded but now returning?

Anya continued, "Hitler and Stalin each contributed several hundred thousand ghosts to Rumania. Ceausescu and Gheorghiu-Dej together, perhaps another two hundred thousand."

"I see plenty of ghosts," said Henry, "but not thousands."

"I do not say a half million ghosts haunt Snagov. Certainly Jilava has its share. And Aiud. But thousands are here. Tens of thousands. Not all are manifest at any one moment. And of those present, not all are visible to our senses. More ghosts haunt Snagov than you or I see. Perhaps even now, we walk through them."

Henry shuddered. "Thanks for the image."

Anya smiled. "We have no reason to fear ghosts. Their only weapon is guilt, and we are innocent of vampirism. Perhaps even Dracula's ghost is here now with us, looking on with favor. He should. My family provided the tsar with officers since the days of Ivan the Great. I am the aristocrat, not Ceausescu."

"You ain't Rumanian."

"Neither was Dracula. Rumania never existed until 1859. Dracula was a Wallachian prince, and Transylvanian-born. For that matter, Ceausescu is perhaps not Rumanian, but *arnaut.*"

"Another kind of vampire?" asked Henry.

"No, although local peasants may disagree. The *arnauts* are Moslem Albanians, imported by the Turks in the 1700s to supervise their serfs. Rumanian peasants referred to their *arnaut* overseers as *ceaus,* it being a rank in the Ottoman army. Naturally, Ceausescu's family would have Rumanianized their name after independence. Not that it matters, except to him."

"Why would he care?"

"As his socialist economy decays, Ceausescu has increasingly turned to strident Rumanian nationalism to legitimize his dictatorship. Which requires *him* to be pure-blooded Rumanian. And for whatever reason, he had all archival records pertaining to his family origins destroyed."

Ahead was a line of trees, which Henry supposed edged the island shore. They approached a gap in the trees, which might have faced a dock, or might not. Impossible to tell under the smooth snow. Beyond the gap arose a hill. Atop the hill stood the church towers.

"I suppose it'd be ironic," said Henry, "if the most beloved son of the Rumanian people wasn't even Rumanian."

"But not unusual. Stalin was Georgian, not Russian. Hitler was Austrian, not German, and possibly even partly Jewish. And Napoleon was Corsican, not French, not really. An interesting phenomena, nativist leaders not native to their soil. Perhaps compensating for some insecurity."

As before, Henry was unable to discern the shoreline beneath the snow. But when they began passing trees it was obvious they were on the island. "I may not be guilty of vampirism, but I'm still glad to leave those ghosts behind."

"You shall see more ghosts before dawn," said Anya. "Thousands. If we are lucky, tens of thousands."

TWENTY-TWO

Henry clambered over the snow piled before the church's wooden door. No doorknob. Just a black iron ring frozen in place. He unstuck the ring, then pulled and tugged with both hands.

Door didn't budge.

Anya stood watching and waiting.

Henry painfully unstuck his fingers from the ring. The door might be locked. But there was no keyhole. Might be bolted from inside. Or the hinges were frozen. Or snow was impeding it. He had no idea which, but he wanted to open it himself. Embarrassing, having a woman watch you struggling with an unlocked door.

It better be locked.

Henry was clearing away snow from the doorway with his wet sneakers when Anya stepped forward and gripped the ring.

"Try again," she said.

Together they budged the door, tugging it open in fits and starts until a gap widened far enough for them to slip into the church.

Inside was black, the stone walls slit open by only a few narrow stained glass windows, spaced at distant and irregular intervals. Probably dim even at noon, at night this place was darker than the Vlasie. What minuscule moonlight penetrated was likely imperceptible to normal eyes; Henry saw only the murkiest shades of charcoal against black.

Anya strode to the stone altar, her aura brighter against this absolute darkness, bouncing and flowing with the swish of her hair. Brighter and less golden, more silvery.

Henry pulled the door shut, wondering if there was someone on the island who might otherwise notice. As the door sealed in the dark, his hands came aglow. A silvery gray shimmering, faint but detectable. Anya had claimed to see his aura, but only in this extreme dark could he see it. She said their auras were camouflage. But if he couldn't see his skin "camouflaged" outdoors, would the vampires?

Anya was searching the altar, her luminous hands seemingly disembodied and floating in the dark. The Orthodox cross on her clasp glinted at her neck, a silver star in the church's night.

Henry approached and waited.

"Nothing," Anya's voice echoed in the dark. "We attack as we are."

"Without weapons?" Startled his own echo, Henry whispered, "Wooden stakes? Plenty of wood on the island."

"We have no time. Once our presence on the train is reported, Securitate will expect us. An attack will become difficult."

Henry remembered the tanks. "It ain't easy now."

"So we move quickly. While we have the surprise."

"We can't kill Ceausescu with nothing!"

"I can break his neck. With only my bare hands and feet. And enjoy it all the more." Anya wasn't shouting, yet her echo was uncomfortably loud. "You saw me do so at the Palace."

"You can't karate kick a tank battalion. They'll blast us before we ever get close."

"And with stakes?"

Henry sighed. "Good point." He scrutinized the surrounding shades of black, desperate for . . . something. Yet it was ridiculous expecting to find anything in here. Don't have to be an intelligence expert to know there'd be no loose weapons lying around next door to Ceausescu's dacha. Securitate would have seen to that.

Henry blinked. What looked like a cross, a big one, protruded from behind a silk banner in a recess behind the altar. How could Anya have missed it?

Because his vision differed from hers.

Darting behind the altar, Henry pulled aside the banner and snatched. It was a cross. Its cold heavy metal filled him with confidence. Swinging it several times, testing his wrist action, he imagined burying its arm into Ceausescu's brain.

Henry trembled, once again both afraid and excited. This was life on the edge, always pumped, high on adrenalin, danger as his middle name. Soon he would be an anti-Communist assassin, a professional in wet work. Just like Anya. Well, it wasn't such a big step. He'd already terminated one vampire with extreme prejudice, helping Anya bring her silver cross to that MI Trooper's neck. Like setting a match to a propane tank. Braining Ceausescu would be no different.

Henry raised the cross, awaiting Anya's approval.

Anya gripped the cross. "What do you feel?"

"Cold hard steel."

"Cold. Yes. Very cold."

Henry grimaced, immediately chagrined. No way this cross could burn vampire flesh. No way it could blind. May as well bash Ceausescu with a stone. He should have seen it himself.

"My mistake," Henry mumbled. "It's gotta be silver."

"No. Silver helps. But more importantly, it must be hallowed." Anya took the cross from him, slammed it upon the altar several times, then flung it aside. Metallic clattering echoed against stone. "The Orthodox establishment long ago sold out to vampirism. This church is dead and everything in it."

"Great. We came for nothing."

"Not for nothing. We found no weapons. We may yet find allies." Scanning the floor, Anya chose a spot near the altar. She removed her clasp. "Give me your hand."

Henry placed his hand in hers.

Her clasp's pin glistened.

Anticipating her next move, Henry drew back reflexively, but Anya's grip was too strong. She raked the pin across his palm, a brilliant red fountain erupting—!

Screams reverberating against stone, Henry doubled over and clasped his hand, suddenly heavy and throbbing and burning after being sliced in half, his knuckles and four fingers lopped off.

He stared at his good hand gripping the severed one, afraid to unclasp, afraid to see the stump. Afraid to stop screaming.

Slowly, he became aware of Anya tapping his forehead.

"Do not be a baby," she shouted. "It is only a scratch."

"A scratch?!"

"Watch." Anya raked the pin across her own palm, tearing open a dazzling red hairline scratch. Burning bright as a stop light, but a scratch nonetheless.

Henry looked at his own clasped hands. No blood. His fingers were still attached. He unclasped them. His palm appeared soaked in blood, glowing redly in the night. But upon examination he saw no serious wound, just smeared blood. And a slender scratch bleeding brightly across his palm.

"Hurts like hell," he muttered.

"You did not hear me scream."

"No," Henry pouted, suddenly ashamed. "But you expected it."

"You should know by now how sensitive vampire blood is to silver. I expect you to know such things." She sighed. "Perhaps I should have prepared you. I apologize."

"It's all right. No problem."

"Are you certain? We must not be at odds. We have serious work tonight."

"Yeah, don't worry about it." Then Henry realized how much more painful the scratch must have been for her. She hadn't even flinched. "You're right. I was a baby. It's good you did that. I'm glad you did it."

"Are you?"

"Sure." Henry tried to block out the pain. His hand still ached, though not so much now that he knew he still had one. "I don't know why you did it, but you know what you're doing."

Smiling, Anya took his cheek and kissed it. After which, she could have driven a silver stake through his heart with his blessing. For a second kiss, he'd gladly hold the stake while she raised the hammer.

"Next time I shall warn you," Anya promised.
"Great. Look forward to it."
She held out her hand. "I warn you."
"What?"
"Your other hand." Was she suppressing a smile?

Hoping it was a joke, Henry complied. And when she actually raked his flesh, he yelped but did not scream. Then Anya scraped her other hand. Now all hands were bleeding bright.

She repinned her cape. "Now to conjure an army."

Henry nursed his freshly bleeding hand. "Army? What kind of army?"

"Ghosts, I hope."

He looked at her. "You hope?"

"I have never conjured before. I hope to avoid demons."

"Yeah. Try and avoid those." He examined both hands. "I never heard of blood being used for a seance."

"Not a seance. A conjuration. I do not wish to communicate with the dead, but to command them."

Glancing down, Henry saw they were standing on a large stone slab, the size and shape of a coffin lid. "Shouldn't we be inside a pentagram? For protection?"

"We cannot stay in one spot and lead an army." Anya raised her palms to him. "I expect the ghosts will appreciate their assigned tasks. That will be our protection."

Henry locked fingers with her, palms stinging as their wounds met, blood mingling. A warm rush permeated his hands, spreading up his arms into his chest and neck and head. The pain in his hands subsided, numbed by . . . Anya's blood?

"Clear your mind," said Anya. "Say nothing."

Henry complied.

Anya called upon the spirits of the lake, imploring them to arise and manifest. Having always spoken English to Henry, now she spoke Russian, yet he understood, she spoke what he knew to be a medieval incantation. Then he saw her lips were still. He was hearing her thoughts flow into him with her blood. Not her whole consciousness, just her immediate thoughts, maybe because the cuts on their hands only bled a trickle . . .

A pale light dawned, slow and uneven. At first a dim glow against a wall, then a luminous mist under the roof. Some ectoplasmic jelly forms congealed in corners and kept to themselves, silent and still. Other ghosts circled Henry and Anya, fusing themselves into a bright shrieking whirlwind, their glare and clamor increasing with their numbers . . .

No, not *their* clamor, but that of some otherworldly force or wind expelling them into this mortal dimension, the ghosts merely borrowing the windstorm to voice their rage. Henry saw misshapen faces twisting in the maelstrom, ectoplasmic eyes and noses spun into taffy contortions, a vortex of spinning howling torment . . .

Socialism had claimed a hundred million plus victims. So said Anya. How many here at the lake? Surely she didn't expect to conjure them all? Glancing about, Henry wondered if maybe he and Anya didn't already have enough allies . . .

The floor trembled, the stone slab under their feet rattling and rumbling. Henry felt Anya tighten her grip, her blood thoughts commanding him to stay put.

The slab shuddered. The white whirlwind quickened into a luminous tornado funnel, flashing and roaring, shiny and shrill. Yet its ghost glow illuminated nothing apart from itself. The coffin-shaped slab remained enshrouded in charcoal darkness.

Henry felt it rise, lifting him and Anya a teetering inch, then drop.

We have enough allies, thought Henry, let's leave.

Anya replied, many are required to attack a vampire lair.

You'll never control them all.

My will is theirs, they shall obey willingly, for Ceausescu is their enemy.

And Henry knew it was true.

The slab rose slowly, shuddering, dropping suddenly and unevenly, falling outside its slot. Dust rose from around its edges. Steadying his feet, Henry felt Anya's fingernails cut his flesh.

They're rising from under us, thought Henry.

Mere energy residue, Anya replied, the grave beneath us was found empty.

Whose grave?

Dracula was said to be buried beneath this slab—

Oh great!

—but it was found empty in the 1930s.

The slab rumbled under them.

Let's leave! thought Henry.

Dark energy residue, thought Anya, reacting to our light energy, but if Dracula's ghost does manifest then so much the worse for Ceausescu, for all I conjure must obey me.

The ghosts may want to, Henry replied, but Dracula's got nothing against Ceausescu, and maybe something against us . . .

As the whirlwind's flickering shades of white intensified, the slab erupted and shattered, plunging Henry and Anya into the grave below.

TWENTY-THREE

The whirlwind dissipated the instant their hands unlocked. Henry tumbled through the rubble, Anya collapsed and let go his hands, and the whirlwind was gone.

But not the ghosts.

The tap was shut, the funnel closed, the supernatural wind silenced. But the ghosts already manifest remained. Hundreds. Maybe thousands.

Anya estimated ten to twelve thousand.

Henry had no idea how she figured that, but the lake was aglow with ghosts. Phantoms floating above lit the sky. Spirits gliding across the lake set the snow aglitter. Spooks drifting deep within the frozen waters illuminated its icy crust. A lake overcrowded with overlapping ghosts, sliding into each other and intensifying their numinous glow.

Looking through the translucent rows of marching ectoplasm, Henry saw hundreds of specters staring back at him. A mosaic of somber faces and hollow eyes and bitter scowls. Every mouth was still, every lip sealed. Yet the wind, this time a natural wind, resonated a mournful wail, occasionally rising in pitch to scattered shrieks.

Beside Henry, three ghosts walked inside one another, more or less. Two wore prison garb, the other a business suit. They might have been executed by Stalin in 1940, or by Hitler after that, or by Stalin again after that, or by Gheorghiu-Dej or Ceausescu. A uniformed ghost marched beside Anya, its boots shuffling beneath the lake's icy crust.

Henry shivered within his greatcoat, struggling to keep from tripping over its hem. Creepy, wading in this ocean of ectoplasmic misery.

"These guys don't talk much," Henry shouted over the wind.

"They know their instructions," Anya replied. "Apart from that, we do not interest them."

"Some of them are looking pretty mean."

"You too would feel mean if you spent your youth in a slave labor camp. Or had all you owned confiscated because others were envious. Or were executed for owning more than your neighbor."

Henry nodded. "Still, you'd think they'd appreciate what we're doing for them."

"I expect they resent what we have already done."

"What have we done?" asked Henry.

"Western support for Karl Marx's great experiment."

"You mean MFN?"

"And much else." Anya stumbled over a snow pile, but managed to stay upright. She had been limping, almost imperceptibly, ever since crawling out of the empty grave under the broken slab. Henry guessed she was tiring. He was near exhaustion and he'd napped on the train. She hadn't.

"Auster mentioned MFN," said Henry. "He didn't get into specifics."

"Most Favored Nation trade status. Under MFN, Western banks and corporations can loan money or sell on credit to Rumania, and if Ceausescu defaults, the US government pays if off."

"You mean this whole country's US taxpayer subsidized?"

"As are all MFN nations, and the banks and companies trading with them. Businesses can lend or sell recklessly to deadbeat nations, because MFN guarantees to pay the bills." Anya's silky voice was hoarsening. "Other MFN benefits include lower tariffs and access to sensitive technology."

"High tech?" Henry's own throat was turning sore from cold. "We're selling high tech weapons to the Commies?"

"Or technology that can be converted to military use."

"That doesn't make sense. Even if CEOs wanna make a buck, the Commies will kill them if they take over."

"Yes, but Wall Street does not think long term. *Après nous, le*

Déluge. And selling weapons to an enemy means selling more weapons to the Pentagon. Besides which, socialist governments mainly kill their own people, not Western businessmen." Coughing, Anya limped over another snow mound. "Lenin said capitalists would bid to sell the rope to hang themselves with, and he was right. Wall Street loves MFN."

"You're coming down with something," said Henry. "Sorry I mentioned MFN. Save your voice."

"No, you need to know these things. And remember it when I'm gone."

Henry felt sickened inside. "Don't talk like that."

"Like what?"

"Like you expect to die."

"I am ready to die. I do not expect it."

"See that you don't. You promised to get me out of this hellhole. You owe me not to die."

Anya smiled, lips scarred with cold blisters. "We discussed this outside Ceausescu's house. And we survived."

"We were better armed. We attacked an empty house. And we still got captured." Henry immediately regretted his words. Bad for morale. "Don't worry. I won't forget anything you said."

Anya paused to face him, allowing rows of ghosts to glide silently past. Henry cringed as they floated through his body; talk about an invasion of privacy. Why didn't they stop when Anya stopped? A herd of sheep, following the shepherd but at their own pace.

Anya hugged him gently, wind tossing her glowing hair about his face. "We are nearly there," she rasped into his ear. "I no longer need you. Return to the church. Dawn is an hour off. If I do not join you by noon, I am dead. You must escape as best you can."

"I'm not asking to drop out."

"Two deaths achieve nothing. One survivor may yet bear witness."

"You won't die," Henry insisted. "Anyway, they didn't believe Reagan when he called it an evil empire. Why believe me? I'm going with you."

Anya considered it. "You remember what he looks like?"

"I remember his picture. I remember everything."

She took his arm. "Well then, comrade . . ."

They commenced walking with the ghosts.

Dark trees lined the approaching lakeshore. Henry thought he saw lights ahead. Hard to tell through the ectoplasm's hazy glow. Like trying to discern specific stars through a gas nebula cloud.

Closer in, Henry saw troops and tanks onshore, guns facing the lake. Dark uniforms, heavily padded, brown rather than green . . .

Machine gun bursts cracked the night.

Henry halted and hunched. Useless gesture. Absolutely nothing to hide behind on this frozen lake.

Anya gripped his arm and pulled him along. "Idiot vampires!" she shouted. "Bullets do not tear ectoplasm."

Advancing into gunfire, Henry wanted to pull Anya to safety and retreat, wanted to shield her and lead the attack, wanted to run but refused to abandon her.

"You cannot kill the dead," Anya continued shouting. "Even the undead know it. Yet still they shoot."

Bullets struck the lake a hundred yards ahead, splintering ice and spraying snow.

Realization dawned on Henry. "They're not firing at us?"

"Their aim is not so poor."

"At the ghosts?"

"At our camouflage."

Machine gun muzzles flashed along the shoreline. Snow and ice sputtered across the lake.

"Camouflage?" Henry examined his hands. If they were glowing, he didn't see it. "Looks nice and solid and dark to me."

"I see your aura," said Anya. "So shall Securitate. More so. Auras appear brighter to them. Ectoplasm too."

An explosion flashed and thundered onshore. A white geyser

erupted forty yards their right, showering them with frigid water. Ice wobbled underfoot.

Tank guns.

"What do I do, wave my glowing hands?" shouted Henry. "We don't look like ghosts, not unless we strip naked."

"The vampires are afraid and disoriented." Anya pulled him along. "Even if they see our dark clothes through the ectoplasm, they'll see bright faces, think ghost, and glance on."

Another tank fired, blasting ice thirty yards to their left, water spouting then cascading onto them amidst a drizzle of ice fragments. Unperturbed ghosts continued gliding over the newly exposed lake water.

Henry felt the ice crack and shift under his feet. "They'll know we're not ghosts when we drown."

Anya gripped him and yanked. "Hurry!"

They stumbled forward, shattered ice sinking under their feet, its solidity breaking into floating stepping stones as tank shells fractured the frozen lake crust, drenching them with water and snow and slush. Ghosts streamed past them, unimpeded by the bombardment. Yet although slowed by the fragmenting ice, Henry advanced without hesitation, eyes averted, drawn along by Anya, alive and determined so long as he felt her hand in his . . .

Silence.

All guns quiet.

They halted, motionless.

A sudden stillness, new sounds emerging slowly. Ice cracking and breaking. Water lapping against floes. A shrill wind rustling nearby trees.

Someone shouting.

Anya tugged and they continued onward, Henry struggling to step quietly, the silent ghosts doing nothing to camouflage water sloshing underfoot. Then as they neared shore the ice firmed and their steps softened.

A long dock stretched forward, gleaming marble legs rooted in ice.

The guy had a marble dock!

Dark brown MI Troops stood amidst the ghosts gliding onshore and fanning out. An officer was berating the Troops for wasting bullets, for firing at nothing.

Stepping ashore, or where he supposed the shoreline lay under the snow, Henry drew Anya close and whispered, "Seems the head guy can't see ghosts."

"He sees," Anya replied. "But the Party denies the existence of ghosts. Ideologically, everyone is happy in Rumania. Everyone is healthy and well fed. He sees, but knows he must not."

Henry stiffened as they passed the helmeted troops, but their yellow eyes were averted. Squeezing Anya's hand, Henry whispered, "They're ignoring us."

She squeezed back. "Trotsky coined the phrase 'politically correct.' It means to speak and believe as you are supposed to, regardless of your conscience, regardless of reality. Almost all these ghosts are victims of socialism. These ghosts are politically incorrect. It is forbidden to see or believe in them."

Although pointedly ignoring the ghosts, the troopers dodged and cringed to avoid touching them, wincing whenever some ghost floated through. And the ghosts were increasingly difficult to avoid.

Vision blurred as the ectoplasmic fog rolled in, the ghosts crowding ashore and into each other. For every ten ghosts that dispersed into the nearby buildings, twenty more arrived from the lake, blanketing the shore under a glowing pea soup. One almost didn't need an aura for camouflage. Everything was obscured.

Henry breathed easier after passing the shoreline defense, but still stiffened whenever a dark form scurried past. Uniformed or plainclothes, security was omnipresent.

"Some of these armored SWAT boys are blue, not brown," Henry whispered.

"FOI Militia," Anya replied. "Forces for Internal Order."

"His elite MI boys not enough? Suppose we should feel flattered."

"They are not for us. The FOI are likely watching the MI, in case of insurrection. And visa versa."

The ground felt different. Glancing down, Henry saw a stone path under his feet, shoveled clean of snow. Brightly lit buildings shone through the ectoplasmic mist.

Anya began pointing. "I think that houses the bowling alley. There the wine cellar. Movie theater. Gazebo. Volleyball court."

"Nice setup. Where does the big guy sleep?"

"Various of these buildings house his extended family, staff, servants, and security. His will be the most ostentatious. Elena would tolerate no less."

Henry couldn't discern fine architectural details through the ectoplasm, but the brightest and warmest lights shone from a large modern mansion atop a hill, dazzling even through the glowing mist. Stone steps wound their way up the hill to the rear of the mansion.

Her limp overpowered by eager anticipation, Anya hurried up the steps. They were confronted by a heavy oaken door. And no vampires. Just ghosts floating through the wall, into the mansion.

Anya gripped the doorknob.

What if someone saw them enter? Ghosts don't use doors.

Anya opened the door and entered.

Too late to worry about a silent alarm. Henry followed Anya into Ceausescu's lair.

TWENTY-FOUR

They entered a kaleidoscopic fog of rainbow sparklets, the ectoplasm of a thousand ghosts diffracting all light, creating a prismatic blur through which Henry saw an opulent living room, dazzlingly lit. Colorful stars twinkled upon every light bulb, rainbow spikes radiating from golden wall fixtures, porcelain lamps, crystal chandeliers.

Henry blinked instinctively, as though having just exited a swimming pool. Naturally, the sparklets remained. How would a vampire see him? Like a glowing face floating murkily within a starry mist?

A vampire in a waiter's jacket entered from the hallway with a golden tray. He saw the open door and stopped.

Anya nudged Henry back.

Ghosts continued seeping through both solid walls and open doorway.

The waiter scurried to the door, averting his eyes from the ghosts' accusatory stares. Setting aside his tray, he grabbed the doorknob . . .

Then he noticed Anya and Henry.

Henry saw a holster under the waiter's jacket. The guy was plainclothes DSS, as at the Palace. His face a bloodily pulsing spaghetti plate, as on the train.

The waiter glanced from Anya to Henry, staring them in the eyes, his dark purple lips scowling distaste. Then he observed the ghost beside Henry. A pretty coed in a 1950s skirt suit, defiant and translucent. Whereas Henry was opaque.

The waiter scrutinized Henry.

"Aren't you brilliant!" shouted a female vampire entering from the hall. "Why not open the door wider so the entire cemetery can enter, you damned shit!"

"I was just now closing it, Comrade Elena," the waiter replied.

Henry nearly barfed at the sight of Nicu's mother.

Elena Ceausescu was a dumpy sixtysomething. Blood vessels undulated just under the surface of her plump red face. Orange hair pulled into a fright wig bun. Wide gaps between her stubby yellow fangs. Pot belly and long pendulous breasts sagging under a gray velvet dressing gown, half unbuttoned to expose more than any mortal man would care to see. Fat peasant ankles and big bony feet stuffed into fluffy pink slippers.

Elena waddled over to the waiter. "He was just now closing it! Aren't you nice!" She grabbed his tie, yanking vigorously. "Why open the door at all, you peasant, you *mascalzone!*"

"I didn't, Comrade Elena," the waiter exclaimed, "the ghosts must have—"

"Miserable scum! When you're talking to me, keep your mouth shut!" Shoving him aside, Elena waved at the spectral assembly. "Ghosts! What ghosts? You mean these miserable sheep herders? They can't even open their pants, how do you expect them to open a door? What an idiot you are! Dead fascists polluting the home of the Rumanian President and what are you doing about it? Nothing! You worm!"

"I will immediately notify Major General Velicu—"

"Velicu! Why not the maid? Or the stable boy?" Elena was pounding the waiter's chest with a stubby finger. "Vlad should be here to mop up this mess, not his damn underlings! He's the damn shit who let the spies escape! If the miserable scum can't keep two assassins under his big nose from waltzing off, let him scrub ghosts out of toilets for a living!" Elena threw her arms in disgust. "Get me Nuta, not his damn shop clerk! I want Nuta! And Ghita!"

"At once, Comrade Elena!" Snatching his tray, the waiter glanced at Henry, then at Elena. As Elena seemed unperturbed about Henry, the waiter scurried from the room.

"His wife," Anya whispered to Henry, "can lead us to Ceausescu."

Henry nodded, hoping Anya would say no more . . .

Too late.

Elena glanced in their direction, squinting through the glowing ectoplasmic mist. Henry worried she might approach and touch their corporeal bodies. But then Anya raised a glowing hand toward Elena and the vampire quickly edged away.

Seemed Elena was more afraid than she'd let on to the waiter. Or at least less comfortable.

Ghosts encircled Elena, crowding around and into her, entering her flesh. Pretending not to notice, she paced with folded arms, examining the colorfully embroidered Persian rugs to avoid eye contact. A peasant ghost in lederhosen, sporting a handlebar mustache and a gaping hole in his skull, leaned into Elena's ear. He screamed until his jaw dropped off.

Henry heard nothing but Elena flinched.

"She hears them," Henry whispered to Anya.

Anya nodded.

Elena opened a gold bonbonnière and selected a dark chocolate. But she had no more than bitten into it when a ghost passed his gangrenous stump through Elena's mouth. Elena immediately spat out the partially masticated bonbon.

Two vampires hurried into the room, uniforms bedecked with braids and medals and red stars. One wore brown, the other blue. They ran to Elena, eyes averted from the ghosts pawing at them, flinching their way through the spectral gauntlet.

"Here come the two fiddlers!" Elena exclaimed. "What a pair of idiots!"

Anya leaned toward Henry. "Major General Grigore Ghita, head of MI Troops. Major General Constantin Nuta, head of FOI."

Smiling nervously, Ghita bowed low. "Bajenaru reports you wish to see us, esteemed Comrade Elena."

"How sweet! Why would he say that?"

Ghita and Nuta glanced nervously at the ghosts, then at each other. Neither wanted to reply first.

Elena snorted. "Tell me Comrade Fatso, do your idiot troops always shoot their tanks at empty air?"

"Oh yes of course, the tanks!" Ghita exclaimed. "Yes, the troops were in error, there was nothing there. You will not be disturbed again, most esteemed Comrade Elena."

"Nothing there!" Elena yanked and shook Ghita's lapels. "Do you have cataracts! Look around, you miserable shepherd! Filthy ghosts everywhere!"

"Oh the ghosts!" Nuta exclaimed. "Yes, I see the ghosts!"

"Yes I see the ghosts too!" said Ghita.

"Oh-ho, so *now* the two geniuses see ghosts!" Elena began rattling Ghita like a rag doll, the general dare not resisting. "I want these dead shits thrown out! They do not exist! I want them exorcised, do you idiots understand, exorcised!"

"At once, Comrade Elena!" exclaimed Nuta. "I will direct the Patriarch to send a priest."

Releasing Ghita, Elena turned on Nuta. "I don't want a filthy priest! I am a scientist, not a witch doctor! I am a Marxist! I want a Party exorcist!"

Sweat glistened upon Nuta's bloodily throbbing face. "Not to worry, most highly esteemed Comrade Elena. All our Orthodox exorcists are authorized by the Department of Cults."

"Bunch of idiots! If our Orthodox church had any power why is Rumania still plagued with ghost infestations! It gets worse, not better!" Elena swatted at a spectral Orthodox priest yelling into her face, to no effect. "Get Bobu! The fat scum claims to be a good atheist. He claims not to believe in ghosts. Let him prove it! Let him exorcise these shits!"

"At once!" Nuta replied.

"Marvelous!" exclaimed Ghita. "You are certainly right, Comrade Elena!"

"I am certainly right! I am certainly right!" mimicked Elena. "Who are you to decide if Rumania's leading scientist is right or wrong? Maybe you think you were born a military genius, not created by the Comrade and me!"

As new ghosts continued crowding into the room, Elena became ever louder, ever more hysterical, straining to ignore the maggot-ridden wraiths floating through her. Ghita and Nuta stared fixedly at Elena, desperate not to flinch as ghosts gouged open their own skulls and torsos to extract bullets, heads rupturing in a replay of old executions, necks opening along piano wire scars, ectoplasmic worms digesting spectral flesh in quick motion.

It seemed to Henry as if the vampires were screaming ever louder, whether screaming abuse or adulation, largely to drown out the spectral cacophony. Vampires whipping themselves into hysteria to numb their consciousness, if not their consciences. Shouting pointlessly and at great length, afraid to stop and hear and see the ghosts . . .

"You were nothing but a miserable shit until the Party gave you an education!" Elena shouted at Ghita. "Nothing but a damned incompetent who only came to Snagov for a free trip! Ten minutes ago you were shooting at ghosts, at empty air, and now you think you are an expert on exorcising them!"

"Not at all, most esteemed Comrade Elena!" hollered Ghita, barking like a recruit addressing a drill sergeant.

"Comrade Elena!" Nuta interjected, "with your permission, I shall leave to immediately arrange for Bobu's investiture—"

"What investiture?" Elena shouted.

"His investiture as Party exorcist, as directed by you, with the approval of the Political Executive Committee of the Rumanian Communist Party, as directed by the Rumanian Constitution—"

"Listen to him!" screamed Elena, hammering Nuta's chest. "Approval by the Political Executive Committee of the Rumanian Communist Party! Have you forgotten who the Party is?"

"No, esteemed Comrade Elena!" Nuta shouted, throbbing eyeballs confused and uncertain.

"The Party is the Comrade and me! The Political Executive Committee is the Comrade and me! Who do you think those lazy idiot fiddlers are to give approval?! Yesterday we made you a general, tomorrow we can make you a damned shit! Believe me!"

"I believe you, Comrade Elena! I mean, most highly esteemed Comrade Elena, the most highly illustrious and beloved daughter of the Rumanian people—"

"Don't you make fun of me, you miserable scum!" Elena began slapping Nuta. "I'll make you curse your mother for bringing you into this world if you can't learn who your betters are!"

Watching Nuta cringe under Elena's blows, Henry noted that vampire masters not only demanded obsequious praise, but expected it to sound sincere.

"Yes, esteemed—" Nuta began, "Yes, Comrade Elena!"

"I'll tell you who the Political Executive Committee is, *Monsieur!*" Elena screamed. "It's a bunch of miserable peasants who yesterday were shit and today have limousines. The Comrade and I wiped their asses and gave them pants and put them there. When we don't need them anymore, they'll be shit again. Do you understand?"

"Yes of course, Comrade Elena!"

"What would you be if we fired you today? A miserable shit again! That house you enjoy with your fat wife isn't yours. It belongs to the Party! So does your car and everything you have. That's Communism, *Monsieur!* In Communism no one has anything for himself. You are only rewarded as long as you are useful to the Party. Do you understand?"

"Yes, esteemed—"

"Get out!" Elena screamed.

Nuta ran off, not even trying to maneuver his way around the ghosts. They were packed too tight anyway.

"Get Bobu!" Elena shouted after him. "I want these dead shits exorcised tonight!" She turned to Ghita. "You too, you miserable goat herder!"

Ghita was already running when Elena added, "And train your idiot troops not to waste the working class's precious bullets on dead fascists! Superstitious peasants!"

The generals gone, Elena began flailing at ghosts, grimacing and cursing.

Approaching Elena, Anya shouted, "Foolish woman! Bobu cannot harm us! Only the President himself, Nicolae Ceausescu, can exorcise us from this house!"

Henry easily heard Anya. But could Elena hear anything over all those screaming spirits? Didn't seem like she could.

Nevertheless, when Elena exited the room, Anya followed. And Henry followed Anya. Down the hallway. Two thousand ghosts flowing with them, streaming into and through them.

Henry glanced at his arms, permeated by spirits. Didn't hurt. Didn't feel a thing.

What did Elena feel? Ectoplasm was said to be clammy. Cold and wet. Did Elena feel the ectoplasm in her skin? Did it chill her bones, grip her heart, pierce her brain?

Then Henry did begin to feel something. As ghosts continued compressing upon them, seeping in from walls and floor and ceiling, Henry began to ache. Not physically, but emotionally. Even spiritually. For while the ghosts inflicted no physical pain, Henry felt himself absorbed into a despairing black hole. Like he was wading through a foggy bog of vengeful hate and suicidal despair. Not that the ghosts were draining him, as a vampire might. Rather, they were saturating him with their own misery.

Anya continued badgering Elena, trailing and goading Elena, feigning fear that Elena might call upon her husband Nicolae to exorcise the house.

Elena quickened her waddle, meaty arms futilely swatting the ghosts under her skin. What bothered her most, their clamminess or their suffocating gloom? And how bad was it for her? For despite Western support for the socialist bloc nations, these ghosts' animus was directed not at Henry or Anya, but at the vampires themselves. Vampires had drained all hope, happiness, and life from these ghosts' former mortal selves, leaving their psychic shells empty of everything but lingering hostility.

No wonder Elena babbled so loudly, so incessantly. One must find some way to steel oneself against this spectral onslaught. How did a Lenin or Hitler or Stalin steel themselves against such psychic misery? A steeling beyond that of mortals?

And then from somewhere in his blood memory, Henry recalled that Stalin was an assumed name. Stalin meant *steel*.

He should ask Anya about it.

Henry glanced up.

Anya was gone.

He'd been traveling the luminous blur, contemplating ghosts, feeling their misery, and only now realized that Elena had hurried ahead. No doubt Anya followed, still badgering Elena and neglecting to check if Henry was keeping up.

His fault, not Anya's.

Still, she might have checked.

Henry scanned the hallways, searching for . . . something. A clue. Really, just wandering aimlessly, examining the gleaming oaken beams, the glistening marble tables—

Gleaming oak. Glistening marble.

Everything clear!

Where was the ectoplasm?

Henry spun about. No ghosts. Thousands before, now none. They must have flowed after Elena. Leaving Henry without camouflage.

Henry scurried down redly carpeted hallways, desperate to step quietly, sneakers squeaking wetly. Find the ectoplasm and Anya and safety. Until then he was naked and exposed. A young American in a soiled and blood-stained DSS general's greatcoat. And no, he did not look like a vampire. The DSS major on the train would have figured that out, had Anya's virgin neck not distracted him . . .

Ectoplasm down the hall!

And the luminous fog was thickening!

Yet hadn't Elena taken a different path?

No matter. Henry ran toward the ectoplasm. An open door, a brightly lit room. He entered and saw a small man sitting alone.

Nicolae Ceausescu.

TWENTY-FIVE

Nicolae Ceausescu only vaguely resembled his portraits and paintings and mosaics and embroidered rugs. Unlike the virile visionary with jet black hair, Ceausescu was a frail dwarfish vampire of about seventy. Gray hair. Ashen red skin. Spruce white turtleneck offset by rumpled gray pants.

Ceausescu sat deep within the pillowy cushions of a blue velvet sofa. Before him was a marble coffee table laden with onions, tomatoes, and feta cheese. Around him spun a whirlwind of shrieking spirits, an ectoplasmic twister pulling ghosts through the walls and into its vortex. Ceausescu sat motionless in the eye of the twister, perhaps petrified into inaction. Except for his head, which jerked erratically, seemingly following this or that spinning phantom.

Was Ceausescu afraid? Henry couldn't read his expression, not through the blur of three thousand ghosts.

Oddly, although ghosts glutted the room, their gaping mouths elongating and twisting taffylike before evanescing back into the funnel . . . the ambient sound was so muffled, so deathly still.

What did Ceausescu hear?

Then Henry noticed something odder still.

Despite the sepulchral silence, he couldn't hear or understand Ceausescu's mutterings. The vampire was moving his mouth, yet only sporadically emitting noises. Was he conjuring demons in some occult language? Or summoning Securitate? And if Henry heard nothing, would any guards outside?

Henry crept toward Ceausescu, more from curiosity than any clear plan. Here sat the target of their crusade, exposed and unprotected, and there was nothing Henry could do about it. He carried no weapons, he knew no martial arts. Maybe he should go find

Anya. But that would require leaving the ectoplasm's safe cover. And would Ceausescu still be here when they returned?

Henry halted at the coffee table, mere feet from the Supreme Commander of all Rumanian vampires. Ceausescu was still twitching his head spasmodically. Henry had assumed the vampire was following the ghosts, but now that theory seemed less tenable.

At intermittent moments, Ceausescu gazed glassy-eyed into empty space, expression blank, oblivious to the world. Then he would appear to hear something to his right, or something might catch his eye on the left. His head would jerk that way, beady eyes darting toward some specific point in space. Then he either scrutinized whatever was there, analyzing it in minute detail, or his expression would go blank again, as if tuning out whatever he saw.

Whether Ceausescu was sincerely trying to see, or intentionally ignoring reality, was impossible to say. Henry had no idea.

Ceausescu jerked his head toward Henry, squinting.

Henry stared back.

Tiny worn capillaries pulsated upon Ceausescu's eyeballs, sallow eyeballs almost wholly lost within his skull. As before, Henry struggled to read the expression of a bloodily throbbing eyeball. Yet despite the difficulty, he somehow felt assured that Ceausescu did not actually see him. Or if Ceausescu did see, that he did not actually believe in Henry. Perhaps here was a vampire who truly did not believe in ghosts—at least not in ghosts of his making. For despite his initially intense gaze, Ceausescu soon zoned out, leaving Henry with the sense that Ceausescu was staring through him, looking past him, not seeing him at all.

Ceausescu jerked his head elsewhere, now watching empty space, his attention riveted by a blank spot on the wall, his concentration unperturbed by spectral screams.

No point staying here all night. Somehow, Henry had to deliver Ceausescu to Anya.

Where was Anya? Probably with Elena.

Henry tried an experiment. He cupped his hands and yelled, "Booooo!"

Ceausescu gave no indication he heard anything.

Although Ceausescu was either deaf or catatonic, Henry shouted, "Hope he don't go for Elena! That old bag can exorcise us just by showing up!"

Ceausescu sat motionless for several moments. Then he muttered something unintelligible. He twisted his head askew to examine a blank spot on the ceiling. He mouthed something rapidly but silently.

Then Ceausescu moved.

He snatched a large tomato and bit into it, spattering his white turtleneck red. Ghosts passed their maggot-strewn hands through his mouth, to no avail. Ceausescu chomped and chewed, oblivious to the ghosts, red juice dribbling down his chin.

A waiter appeared at the doorway. Bajenaru.

"Comrade General Secretary," exclaimed Bajenaru, "the Political Executive Committee is in session and awaits your presence."

Without a word, Ceausescu rose and exited. Bajenaru followed Ceausescu down the hall. The ghosts followed the vampires. Henry followed everyone.

And through the blur, Henry saw another oddity.

Still jerking his head erratically, Ceausescu was now also flailing his arms disjointedly while his legs strode purposefully forward. As before, Henry would have guessed that Ceausescu was watching and pummeling the ghosts. Yet once again the theory was untenable. For Ceausescu's attention was directed neither to the ghosts, nor to where his legs led, nor to what his arms assailed. Instead he sauntered with a haphazard incoordination, seemingly uninterested either in his surroundings or with what his various limbs were up to.

Henry knew the abnormal was normal in vampire society, but he wondered whether Ceausescu's gait was a normal abnormality or an abnormal abnormality. Bajenaru strode "normally," yet behaved as though Ceausescu's silly walk was normal too.

They entered a large conference room.

The vampires of the Political Executive Committee of the Rumanian Communist Party rose upon seeing Ceausescu. Henry recognized several from Nicu's party. Stefan Andrei was here. And Gheorghe Oprea. But not Nicu. Perhaps the young lad was still recuperating from Anya's silver pistol. Vlad wasn't here, but his boss Tudor Postelnicu was. Henry also recognized some new faces, Ceausescu's blood memories still coursing through his veins.

"Long life to the President!" exclaimed a tall vampire in gold-rimmed glasses. Oprea. His previously puffy cherry-red face was now a throbbing spaghetti plate of misshapen blood vessels pumping black pustules to the point of eruption.

Ceausescu made no reply, gave no recognition. He strode to the head of the table, sat down, and gazed into space.

Exchanging glances, the vampires began lowering themselves into their chairs. None wanted to sit first. Finally, all vampires sank down collectively. And then said nothing.

Ghosts swirled about and through everyone, mouthing shrieks, their ranks swelling. Whatever the reason, Henry thought he heard them now, faintly, a shrill whine undercutting the muffled silence. In which case they sounded that much louder to the vampires, who strained not to flinch as ghosts hollered into their ears, not to wince as spirits penetrated their bloodily pulsating bodies.

Ceausescu gazed into space. A mini-vortex had engulfed him, an offshoot of the ectoplasmic whirlwind saturating the room. He showed no fear, no awareness. Behind him hung his portrait, the virile visionary exuding wisdom, fortitude, benevolence. Across the room hung a golden PCR seal: hammer and cycle framed by wheat. Tricolor national flags and red PCR flags draped the dark paneled walls.

Plainclothes DSS guarded every corner, holsters bulging under their jackets. Of the vampires sitting at the table, most wore expensive suits, some wore uniforms. None wanted to speak first. All waited for Ceausescu to open the session.

Ceausescu bent down and tied a shoelace.

Blood memory informed Henry that the Political Executive Committee was Rumania's version of the Soviet Politburo, the name chosen by Ceausescu to impart a Western sheen to Rumanian communism. Henry also knew that not every vampire seated here was a PEC member. And that not all PEC members were present. And that none of it mattered. Ceausescu was present and that made it a quorum.

Ceausescu snatched pen and pad and began scribbling.

The vampires of the Political Executive Committee glanced at the ghosts and at each other. Oprea squinted behind his glasses, but dare not shut his eyeballs. Black hair dye streaked the face of another vampire, the cheap greasy oil trickling down from under his hat and staining the collar of his green uniform. Henry knew him to be General Vasile Milea, Minister of National Defense.

A dozen other red spaghetti faces glistened sweat. But perspiring most profusely was Lina Ciobanu, Chairman of the General Union of Trade Unions, a squat creature with hair fiercely yanked back into a tight bun, an enormous jutting chest the only indication of her sex. She sat at rigid attention clutching a sheaf of papers, marring it with wrinkles and sweat, whimpering through quivering purple lips as wraiths saturated her body.

Ciobanu was a leaky dam set to burst.

The DSS guards also saw the spirits, their pulsating eyeballs following the ghosts swirling about the room, but most anxiously watching those encircling their leader.

Ceausescu scribbled furiously, apparently seeing nothing. Or maybe he saw the ghosts, but decided they did not exist. Until he gave a clear indication of the Party line, no vampire wanted to be first to admit to seeing ghosts.

Henry realized this might be his last best chance for assassination. But how? Stab Ceausescu with a pen?

With no clear plan, Henry entered the mini-twister encircling Ceausescu. The room became hazy and blurred. Ceausescu clarified. At least Henry would see what the vampire was writing . . .

The DSS guards saw Henry approach Ceausescu. They glanced at each other, then at Ceausescu. They shifted nervously but said nothing, afraid to act until Ceausescu indicated that he too saw Henry.

Ceausescu remained engrossed in his work, oblivious to Henry, oblivious to the ghosts, oblivious to the PEC.

Henry glanced at Ceausescu's work.

Doodles.

Ceausescu was doodling, covering his pad with black geometric shapes. Tonight his Presidential Palace had been invaded, his son injured, himself and his wife nearly assassinated at home, and now here he was amidst hostile spirits while chairing a session of the highest political body in his government . . .

And he was doodling.

Ghosts continued entering the room, permeating the vampires ever more densely, swirling ever faster, glowing ever brighter. Henry squinted against their blue-white radiance, ears aching from their sharp wailing, bones chilled and skin horripilated from the ectoplasm saturating his body.

Bright and loud and cold for *him*.

How much worse for the vampires?

The vampires sat stiffly, tense. Sweating despite the cold ectoplasm. And all the while Ceausescu doodled.

Ciobanu was first to break.

She jumped to her feet, reading her speech, shouting without pause, "With deep esteem and high value, with love and happiness, we welcome the most beloved son of our people, Comrade Nicolae Ceausescu, fiery revolutionary and patriot, experienced nationalist, who has done and is doing everything for his people for the cause of peace and socialism, to you, brilliant personality of the modern world, indefatigable militant, we owe the full manifestation of our motherland's independence and sovereignty—"

A blue-white nova exploded in Ciobanu's face. She screamed and dropped her speech, scattering papers upon the table. Ghost filaments flared and dissipated like the dying sparks of a spent firework.

Henry wondered if the ghosts who had detonated themselves in Ciobanu's face had committed a sort of suicide. More likely they had merely expended their immediate energy, and were perhaps even now reconstituting their ectoplasmic manifestations.

Ceausescu grimaced, his constipated face indicating what a painful burden it was for him to listen to Ciobanu. He uttered something unintelligible, then said no more.

Ciobanu scrambled to collect her speech but made no progress, frazzled by both Ceausescu's sour countenance and by a second swarm of ghosts.

But she had broken the ice.

Rising hesitantly, General Milea bowed and stated, "Comrade Supreme Commander, we are here to discuss tonight's KGB attack upon The House of the Republic, and the measures since taken by the military and the security forces to protect the most beloved son and daughter of the Rumanian people from future assassination attempts by the forces of fascism and reactionism. Towards this end we have formulated a plan—"

Ceausescu interrupted Milea by sputtering a stream of gibberish. Milea leaned forward, straining to understand, desperate to learn what was expected of him. He was probably greatly relieved when Ceausescu unexpectedly became articulate.

"Did you shits screw up again?!" Ceausescu shouted.

Milea bowed low, as though accepting a compliment. "If I may display . . . ?" Opening a leather satchel, he removed and spread some papers on the table. "We have positioned Patriotic Guards along the highway, backed by Militia—"

Ceausescu stammered some invectives, then more gibberish, then finally shouted, "Securitate along fence and t-t-tanks driving snow mobiles from the lake."

Milea froze. It seemed unclear whether Ceausescu was asking a question, making a comment, or giving an order.

Ceausescu pounded the table. "Ministry T-T-Troops have dialectical materialism, the cocaine of the working class! Sniff it once or t-t-t-twice, it may not change your life, but use it d-d-daily, it makes you into an addict, a New Communist Man! That's qualitative t-t-transformation!"

Milea gaped at the other vampires, begging to be relieved by another speaker. None uttered a word.

Oprea finally contributed, "The President is so profound!"

Grimacing at Oprea, Ceausescu rotated his head disjointedly while stammering unintelligibles. Every vampire leaned forward, straining to understand. Ceausescu stammered incoherently, then demanded, "You think of a b-b-better plan?"

The vampires exchanged glances, uncertain who Ceausescu was addressing. Before anyone replied, Ceausescu shouted, "B-b-bears in Bessarabia fucking Hungarians in Transylvania," then muttered some gibberish, finally snapping at Milea, "Is the plan good?"

Milea bowed low. "Yes, esteemed Comrade General Secretary. Everything is perfect."

"If it's p-p-p-perfect, then why didn't you do it?! What's the matter?! You need my advice?!"

Milea bowed again. "Yes, most esteemed Comrade President. We need your guidance. We cannot do it by ourselves."

Ceausescu muttered and spat incoherently. He finally shouted, "Then do it, yeah, do it! It is a good plan."

Henry sensed relief surge through the vampires, their fears subsiding, if only marginally. These vampires were choking on fear. Fear of Ceausescu, fear of ghosts, fear of each other. Fear suppressed and controlled with lies and self-deceit, but never overcome or eliminated.

Everyone in the room sensed something wrong with Ceausescu, but none knew what. Henry knew, or thought he had seen enough pieces to guess the full picture.

Ceausescu was the most progressive vampire in the room, the natural and inevitable creation of socialism, New Socialist Man fully evolved and erect, the late stage of a progressive disease. Anya had said that vampires could not bear their own reality, thus they shunned mirrors. But unlike Milea or Oprea, still mired in

Orwellian doublethink, Ceausescu had progressed in his self-deceit. He lived in a world entirely of his own making, his Marxist contradictions never challenged, his delusions ever-reinforced by sycophants. Ceausescu believed his lies fully and sincerely, blinding himself to any opposing facts. The louder and brighter his spectral victims, the deeper Ceausescu retreated into his delusions, simultaneously retreating from all reality. And as everyone here was likewise infected with progressive socialism, none perceived Ceausescu's degeneration as abnormal. Frightening perhaps, but fear was a norm in vampire society.

Ceausescu was a confident psychotic ruling a pack of insecure neurotics. His ideals were unencumbered by reality. Ghosts did not exist and so he did not see them. He knew 2+2 to be whatever Marxism required at any given moment. He saw and heard and lived the utopia that all other vampires affirmed. How could they see Ceausescu as anything other than normal?

Ceausescu pointed to a thuggish vampire in brown uniform. "You! What do you think?"

Henry recognized the vampire as Colonel General Constantin Olteanu, nicknamed General Cognac. Olteanu lurched to his feet, having already numbed some of his reality.

Ceausescu slammed the table. "That you know it all?!"

Olteanu tensed. Henry guessed his dilemma. How to respond? Claim to be a "know it all" or admit ignorance? It wasn't even clear what Olteanu would be admitting ignorance to.

Milea crouched without sitting, uncertain whether his presentation was finished after barely beginning.

Ceausescu muttered some gibberish, then let Olteanu off the hook by shouting, "You shits all agree to it?"

There could be only one right answer. The vampires about the table exchanged glances, then nodded hesitantly.

Ceausescu wagged his finger, hand trembling. "I am not s-s-surprised the bear wants to kill me! I am not some melon-headed Gorbachev who b-b-befouls the basic tenets of Communism! He knows mine is the only Communist state where p-p-private property is not only illegal, but something to be ashamed of! Isn't that so, Andrei?"

If Andrei recognized Henry standing beside Ceausescu, he gave no indication. Henry himself barely recognized the Secretary for Economic Affairs through the blurry mini-twister.

"Absolutely, esteemed Comrade President!" Andrei exclaimed.

"I do not t-t-tolerate chaos or provoke counterrevolution! Nowhere in the entire Warsaw Pact is the p-p-p-population better monitored than in Rumania! What other nation has one s-s-security officer for every fifteen people?! Tell me, Postelnicu!"

"No other nation!" replied the Minister State Secretary for DSS.

"I have been a Communist since I was f-f-fifteen! Communism is everything to me! I never did, I never shall make ideological compromises! When it comes to Marxism, I do not go halfway!"

"The General Secretary is so inspiring!" Oprea marveled.

"Gorbachev knows it and wants to kill me!" Ceausescu banged the table with both fists. "He will not s-s-s-succeed! Marxism does not, cannot, tolerate ideological compromise! Deviationists must be expelled, excreted, shit full force from the body like a disease, a virus that the healthy Marxist body must vomit into the dustbin of history or else it dies in its own diarrhea!"

"What a sensitive remark!" Oprea added.

"Comrades, I believe the KGB knows this!" shouted Ceausescu, newly energized, his stutter vanishing. "Mark my words, it is a matter of time! Gorbachev's own KGB will do him in! Their survival depends on it! They know this! History is with us! The workers are with us!"

Hundreds of ghosts thundered protest in a massive blue-white explosion, irradiating the room in cold sunlight, blasting frigid winds, Henry shuddering under their shrieking radiance, his eardrums aching, eyes burning, bones freezing . . .

How much louder and brighter and colder for the vampires? Ceausescu seemed to notice nothing. But what of the rest?

Whether to bolster his nerves or simply stay warm, Oprea

began pounding the table, chanting, "Ceausescu and the people! Ceausescu and the people! Ceausescu and the people!"

The other vampires joined in.

Ceausescu rose to his feet, waving his squat arms in broad sweeps. "We are now building a beautiful new life for the Rumanian people! Every year marks a new milestone in our Communist history! Let us make 1986 another cornerstone! Let us again be unique in the Warsaw Pact! Let us again be first in the entire world!"

Vampires pounding the table, faces giddy with fear, roaring approval and chanting, "Ceausescu and the people! Ceausescu and the people! Ceausescu and the people!"

"With our Securitate microphones in every home, we shall be the only country on earth to know what every one of its citizens is thinking! Yesterday we gave our people a new more scientific diet. Tomorrow we give them the gift of a new more scientific form of government!" Glazed eyes blind to the ghosts, Ceausescu envisioned only his utopia. "Why is American imperialism so unpopular? Because it does not know what its people think! It is not scientific! What our Securitate is doing is the real science of government! It is a true public opinion survey! Our Communist system is the most scientific ever put at the service of mankind!"

Postelnicu hollered over the chorus, both hands slamming the table, hoarsely screaming, "Ceausescu and the people! Ceausescu and the people! Ceausescu and the people!"

Ceausescu waved both arms for silence, to no avail. "It is unfortunate we cannot tell our workers how the Communist Party is looking out for them! Wouldn't the farmers go out and plow more fields if they could be certain the Party was watching over their children every single moment? Wouldn't the miners dig more coal if they were assured the Party knew what their wives were doing every minute? They would, comrades, they would!"

The room was trembling, the numinous whirlwind whipping the walls, flapping the flags, Ceausescu's portrait and the PCR seal vibrating against the dark paneling. Henry didn't know whether the ghosts' outrage had escalated to the point of moving matter, or whether the walls were shuddering from the vampires beating their fists raw upon the table.

Ceausescu jerked his arms spasmodically, maybe for silence, maybe to further inspire his audience. "But we cannot talk about our system today! The Western press would accuse us of being a police state! That is imperialist propaganda! We do not have a police state, we will never have a police state! We are a proletarian dictatorship preserving our ideological purity! Communism is the only real democracy and history will attest to that for generations to come!"

Although standing beside Ceausescu, Henry barely heard the speech over the intensifying spectral screams and the vampires' pounding and chanting of, "Ceausescu and the people! Ceausescu and the people! Ceausescu and the people!"

Pummeling the air with both fists, Ceausescu stretched to his full 5'5" height. "But someday we shall talk of our deeds! The day our proletarian world revolution defeats the capitalist hydra! The day our red flag flies everywhere on Earth!"

All vampires arose, applauding or pounding the table, their shouting and chanting barely audible over ten thousand shrieking ghosts.

The double doors at the end of the room slammed open. Elena entered with a stupid smile plastered on her face, trailed by her own ectoplasmic retinue.

Anya nowhere in sight.

Upon seeing the pandemonium Elena dropped her smile, waving the ministers and generals to shush. "What the hell is going on here?! You fiddlers think the Comrade hasn't anything better to do than listen to your drivel! And where is that imbecile Bobu? Fucking his fat whore wife in Bucharest no doubt, when he should be here doing the work of the people!" She smiled again, focusing on Ceausescu, trying to defocus the ghosts engulfing her and him. "And you, Nic! I've been looking everywhere for you!"

Cowed, the vampires of the Political Executive Committee of the Rumanian Communist Party became silent and still. Ceausescu resumed muttering unintelligibles, blankly watching the approaching Elena.

The whirlwind surrounding the vampires flashed and screamed. The mist engulfing Elena flashed and shrieked. The mini-twister around Henry and Ceausescu flashed and thundered.

Elena waddled toward Ceausescu, her coquettish simper baring stubby yellow fangs. "I need you, Nic. Come to bed."

Anya darted from behind Elena and ran past her, eyes fixated on Nicolae Ceausescu . . .

TWENTY-SIX

Three ghost clouds. The dense twister encircling Ceausescu and Henry. The fog trailing Elena. The whirlwind saturating the room, harassing the vampires.

Three overlapping ectoplasmic clouds separating Henry and Anya, obscuring Anya, such that Henry was never certain of what he saw next.

Henry saw the Countess Anya Amasovich emerge from the fog engulfing Elena. He recognized Anya's blurry silhouette, dark cape and fur hat, shimmering silvery golden hair. He saw her running toward the twister engulfing him and Ceausescu . . .

The DSS guards saw Anya too, and ignored her, she was just another glowing phantom . . .

White flash.

The blue-white flash of a ghost flaring off the twister, spun from its funnel, shot from its vortex, fired at Anya . . .

Exploding in her face, brighter than any ghost Henry had seen, blasting into a thousand fiery filaments . . .

Anya fell back, against Elena and the vampires, a domino fall of tumbling bodies . . .

A guard squinted through the blurry shrieking whirlwind, squinting at Anya, squinting and shouting, "That is a ghost?"

Another guard inched toward Anya. "I think maybe . . . ?"

Henry ducked under the table, crawling toward Anya, greatcoat hindering his legs, dragging himself by his hands, rolling from under the table, grabbing Anya . . .

"The esteemed Mr. Willoughby!" Andrei exclaimed, muffled by ghostly screams so the guards did not hear, yet still they crept closer . . .

Anya was groaning, eyes fixed on Henry but seeing nothing, semiconscious, perhaps only temporarily blinded . . .

Henry slammed an elbow into Andrei's fangs, heard a crack and a whimper, scooped up Anya and fled the room.

The last Henry saw of Nicolae Ceausescu, the vampire was still muttering gibberish and gesticulating erratically, maybe masterminding the recapture of the KGB assassins, maybe expounding his vision in blissful ignorance of all that had just occurred. Either way, no one followed. Which was good, because the air was clearer in the hallways. A slight ghost mist, but not nearly so dense as in the conference room.

Knowing nothing of the mansion's layout, Henry followed the mist "upstream," running against its flow, endeavoring to find an exit while staying within the ectoplasmic camouflage. Down a red carpeted hallway toward a heavy oaken door, plainclothes DSS standing guard . . .

Henry slowed as he approached, Anya heavy in his arms.

The guard gazed past them, tensely ignoring the ghosts permeating his flesh, glassy eyes blind to reality. He never even noticed it when Henry opened the door rather than seep through.

Outside again.

Frigid wind rustling trees. Snow swept from a stone pathway. A violet sky, traced with an approaching pink dawn.

No lake.

Lake must be behind the mansion. This was the front. No matter. Although most of the ghosts had arrived from the lake, they'd been here too, some still floating in from the Vlasie. FOI Militia and MI Troops stood guard, dazed and drowsy, eyes glazed with utopian dreams in an attempt to avoid seeing their victims.

Henry hurried down the path, off the path and into the snow, trying to remain within ghost clouds, darting between their misty patches. Damn few ghosts floating in Henry's direction, most of them gliding toward the mansion, hindering his attempts to remain under constant cover. Very annoying.

Henry carried Anya past tanks and troops, into the forest, snow crunching underfoot. The mansion's warm glow dimmed behind them. Ectoplasm thinner out here. Troops maybe more alert. But not so many. And the lightening violet sky made them easier to spot, easier to avoid.

Anya stirred, moaning.

Henry knelt, exhausted, resting her in the snow, holding her close.

She jolted awake. "Ceausescu?!"

"Can you see?" asked Henry.

She nodded, swallowing. She licked her chapped and bloodied lips. "What of Ceausescu?"

"Alive."

Anya sighed. "We must return."

"And do what? We have no weapons and you're in no shape to do anything."

"Tomorrow then."

"And where will he be tomorrow? We gotta escape. Now."

She didn't reply.

Henry let her rest a few minutes, listening for approaching bootsteps. He heard only wind. The violet sky was turning blue. Dawn in a half hour. Maybe sooner.

Henry nudged her softly. "Can you walk?"

"Certainly I can walk." Anya arose swooning, but remained on her feet. "What happened?"

"I'm not sure. I think you were attacked by a ghost." He took her arm, tugging her away from the mansion. "Your turn to make good. You promised to help me escape."

Anya offered token resistance but proceeded with him.

"Sure surprised me," Henry croaked, his throat sore. "Those ghosts seemed to have it in for Ceausescu. Hated him. Hated all the vampires. Makes no sense to attack you."

"Not every ghost was a victim of socialism. The overwhelming majority, yes. But vampires too have friends and admirers. Especially in the West."

"I don't think this ghost was a Western Commie."

"You recognized who attacked me?"

Henry nodded. "I think so."

"I saw only a flash. Who do you think you saw?"

"Dracula."

Anya halted. "Impossible."

"Why impossible?"

"I am an aristocrat. From a very old family. Prince Dracula would not aid a vampire over me."

Henry shrugged. "You didn't put him on a postage stamp."

"You are certain it was him?"

"I know what the guy looks like. Long hair, big eyes, bushy mustache. Pointy hat with lots of jewels."

Anya pocketed her hands, puzzling over it. "Perhaps because I am Russian. Dracula did renounce his Orthodoxy for the Roman church."

Henry nodded, not wanting to offend the Countess Amasovich, but wondering if maybe princes didn't just naturally empathize with vampires rather than vampire hunters. But he said nothing. No point in upsetting her.

And no point standing in the cold, especially with daylight approaching. Henry placed an arm around her. "Don't worry about it. Dracula likes Ceausescu better than us. Who knows why?"

They continued onward.

Anya took his cold hand from her waist and moved it into her pocket, rubbing his fingers warm. "So then we failed. Ceausescu lives. We are betrayed by my own kind."

"I don't think so. You started something back there. You unleashed something powerful."

"The ghosts? They were always there."

"Yeah, but you stirred them up, set them free. Or put the idea of freedom into their heads. Whatever you set loose, I'm not sure the vampires know how to contain it."

Anya halted and glanced back. Ceausescu's mansion was a blurry glow in the distance, its warm light smothered in pale ectoplasm.

"You think he will not survive the haunting?" Anya asked.

"Vampires do not believe in sin. They have no conscience, no shame, no guilt."

"Yeah they do. They just hide from it. You told me that. That's why we scare them. We remind them of what they are."

She smiled. "Do we?"

"Maybe not Ceausescu. Guy seemed pretty far gone. But you sicced so many ghosts on them, now every socialist hack in the government will have to go insane just to get through the day, just to avoid seeing his victims. Maybe everybody in Rumania will go mad trying to survive. And if they don't, well, how long can lunatics govern normal folk?"

Anya kissed his cheek. "You sound like a veteran vampire hunter."

Henry felt warm despite the cold.

"Perhaps you are right," Anya continued. "The Chinese say, if you wish to destroy a man, let him live. And the maps in your head are valuable. Well worth smuggling out."

"Great. Let's go."

"Even so, I preferred to kill him. East European vampirism was ready to fall years ago. But the West keeps propping it up. Stalin died in his sleep."

Henry squeezed her hand, still in her pocket. "Don't worry about it. You pushed these guys to the edge. You did your part. All Rumania needs now, maybe the whole socialist bloc, is a good push. Maybe Reagan will do it."

Anya smirked. "Only if he ignores the Ivy League foreign policy 'experts' at State. And the pundits in the news media. The West's 'best and brightest,' its artists and intellectuals, have long believed vampirism to be a noble experiment. Especially when experimented on others."

"Don't worry, the Gipper's no Ivy League intellectual. He's too smart to be an intellectual."

"I hope so. As Orwell said, some ideas are so stupid, only an intellectual can believe it."

Henry scanned the bluing sky, saw a patch of pink horizon

through the trees. Must be nearly seven. "You said you could get us out of this country. You had a plan."

"I claimed no plan. I improvise. I am good at it."

"Okay. So improvise."

Anya pulled him along, resuming the lead. "We are in a resort area. For *nomenclatura* only. But I know of a tourist hotel a few short miles from here. If your legs can hold."

"They can hold, but I'm not sure it's worth the trip. I've seen socialist hotels."

Laughing, Anya pulled him close. "Do not worry, comrade. I carry plenty of dollars."

AFTERWORD

Throughout the 1980s, President Reagan worked to stem low interest loans and technology transfers to Warsaw Pact nations, and induced Saudi Arabia to increase its oil production, thus driving down the price of Soviet and Rumanian crude. All this further aggravated Rumania's domestic economic woes.

On December 16, 1989, a small protest demonstration in Timisoara, Transylvania, escalated over the coming days into large anti-Ceausescu rallies in Bucharest, eventuating in the arrest and execution of Nicolae and Elena Ceausescu on Christmas Day 1989. Nicolae Ceausescu is the only Communist dictator to be violently overthrown during the 1989-91 fall of East European Communism.

Vasile Milea reportedly refused Ceausescu's instructions to order the army to shoot demonstrators, instead ordering them to fire on demonstrators' legs (neither order was carried out). He died immediately thereafter on December 22. Reports vary as to whether Milea was executed or committed suicide.

Iulian Vlad (by then chief of DSS) was arrested on charges of "complicity to genocide" on December 28 for his role in killing demonstrators. On July 22, 1991 he was found guilty of the lesser charge of "favoring genocide" and sentenced to nine years imprisonment. He was paroled on December 30, 1993.

Tudor Postelnicu (by then Minister of Interior) was found guilty of "genocide" on February 2, 1990 for his role in killing demonstrators. He was sentenced to life imprisonment. He was later released, but was re-sentenced to eighteen years on December 10, 1997.

Emil Bobu (then Prime Minister) also received a life sentence for "complicity in genocide." He was released on June 18, 1993 for reasons of "age and health." He was 65 years old.

Lina Ciobanu was sentenced to fourteen years on April 20, 1992 for her role in suppressing demonstrators. She suffered a paralyzing stroke two days later. She received a presidential pardon in November 1996.

Stefan Andrei's sentence was suspended "for health reasons" in November 1992. He received his presidential pardon in March 1994.

Nicu Ceausescu (by then First Secretary for the county of Sibiu) was charged with "genocide." Charges were later reduced to "aggravated murder," then to "illegal possession of weapons." He was released in 1993 "for health reasons." On August 8, 1996, *Ziua* reported a rumor that Nicu was preparing to open a nightclub. He died the following month, on September 25, of cirrhosis of the liver in a Vienna hospital while on the waiting list for a new liver. He was 45 years old.

Whether the '89 revolution was spontaneous, or a coup d'état engineered at least to some extent by the Securitate, or a bit of both, remains a matter of controversy to this day. So too the extent to which Gorbachev aided the coup, if any.

After the revolution Rumania instituted a program of privatization, transferring much state property into the hands of former members of the Rumanian Communist Party and the Securitate.

Printed in the United Kingdom
by Lightning Source UK Ltd.
93279